Burn Out

Sharon McCone Mysteries
By Marcia Muller

THE EVER-RUNNING MAN
VANISHING POINT
THE DANGEROUS HOUR
DEAD MIDNIGHT
LISTEN TO THE SILENCE
A WALK THROUGH THE FIRE
WHILE OTHER PEOPLE SLEEP
BOTH ENDS OF THE NIGHT
THE BROKEN PROMISE LAND
A WILD AND LONELY PLACE
TILL THE BUTCHERS CUT HIM DOWN
WOLF IN THE SHADOWS
PENNIES ON A DEAD WOMAN'S EYES
WHERE ECHOES LIVE
TROPHIES AND DEAD THINGS
THE SHAPE OF DREAD
THERE'S SOMETHING IN A SUNDAY
EYE OF THE STORM
THERE'S NOTHING TO BE AFRAID OF
DOUBLE (With Bill Pronzini)
LEAVE A MESSAGE FOR WILLIE
GAMES TO KEEP THE DARK AWAY
THE CHESHIRE CAT'S EYE
ASK THE CARDS A QUESTION
EDWIN OF THE IRON SHOES

Nonseries
CAPE PERDIDO
CYANIDE WELLS
POINT DECEPTION

Burn Out

Marcia Muller

NEW YORK BOSTON

Grand Central Publishing
Hachette Book Group
237 Park Avenue
New York, NY 10017

Visit our Web site at www.HachetteBookGroup.com.

Printed in the United States of America

First Edition: October 2008
10 9 8 7 6 5 4 3 2 1

Grand Central Publishing is a division of Hachette Book Group, Inc.
The Grand Central Publishing name and logo is a trademark of Hachette Book Group, Inc.

Library of Congress Cataloging-in-Publication Data
Muller, Marcia.
Burn out / Marcia Muller. — 1st ed.
p. cm.
Summary: "Here is Marcia Muller's stalwart heroine Sharon McCone as you've never seen her before, in a new novel set in California's high desert country"—Provided by the publisher.
ISBN-13: 978-0-446-58107-3
1. McCone, Sharon (Fictitious character)—Fiction. 2. Women private investigators—California—Fiction. I. Title.
PS3563.U397B87 2008
813'.54—dc22 2008004500

For Melissa Meith and Mike White:
Friends through both the good times and the bad.

Thanks to:
Marcie Galick, good friend to horses—and to me.
Bill, my first editor and best friend.
Les Pockell—your suggestions were right on.
Celia Johnson—yours, too.

Burn Out

Tuesday

✦

OCTOBER 23

I sat on the bluff's edge, facing southeast, where a newly risen full moon cast a shimmery path over the waters of Tufa Lake. To my right, the towering peaks of Yosemite had disappeared into purple darkness. Here in the high desert the evening cooled quickly this time of year, but I'd prepared for it, appropriating a shearling jacket several sizes too big for me from the closet at the ranch house. As I'd appropriated it every night since I'd come up here from the city ten days ago.

Behind me, my husband Hy's twenty-year-old horse, Lear Jet—an ironic name for the red dun gelding, which had never willingly picked up the pace in its life—whickered. I hadn't ridden a horse in more than a decade. Pretty much disliked the creatures, in fact. Lear Jet was big—about fifteen hands and twelve hundred pounds—with a white star on his forehead and a white snip on his nose. He didn't like me any more than I liked him. Every chance he got he'd lean hard on me, try to stomp my feet, bare his yellow teeth and snort.

I wasn't riding the creature for pleasure but in response to a challenge from Hy's ranch manager, Ramon Perez, who lived on the property and tended Lear Jet and the small herd of sheep Hy kept.

I sat watching the water as the moon rose higher. No longer visible by night or day were the brownish-white towers of calcified vegetation—tufa—that gave the lake its name. Years ago, the siphoning off of feeder streams for drought-stricken southern California had caused the lake's level gradually to sink and reveal the underwater towers; the brine shrimp that inhabited it and the waterfowl that fed on them had seemed doomed. But they were saved by the efforts of a coalition of conservationists, headed by Hy, and now the streams flowed freely, the lake teemed with life.

I wished I were so alive, but all I felt was burned out and hollow inside.

Last February I'd escaped death by mere seconds when a building where Hy and I had been temporarily living blew up—one of a series of bombings directed at the security company in which he was a partner. I'd solved the case of the Ever-Running Man, as the bomber had been called, but the fear and nightmares lingered; the grinding day-to-day effort of managing a growing investigative agency had sucked my spirit dry. Throughout spring and summer depression dragged me down. I'd tried coping with it myself, eventually resorted to antidepressants, and, when the pills hadn't worked, consulted a therapist. Therapy didn't work, either; I'm a private person, and I found myself lying to the doctor whenever she probed too close to the root causes of my condition.

Severe depression is like being at the bottom of a deep, dark pit: you want to put your feet and your hands against the walls and, squirming like an overturned spider, crawl up into the sunlight. Only when you try you find you can't move your limbs. I dreamed of being in that pit night after night. Finally, at Hy's urging, I'd come to the ranch for a change of pace—rather than the more familiar environs at Touchstone, our place on the Mendocino Coast. I'd planned to rest, regain my perspective, and rethink my future.

Well, everything but the rest part had so far eluded me. *That* I managed just fine, sometimes sleeping twelve to fourteen hours at a stretch. It wasn't good, and I knew it.

I also knew the choice of this spot on the bluff that I returned to night after night wasn't good, but here I sat again. It was the place Hy had come the night his first wife, Julie Spaulding, died of a long, debilitating illness. He'd told me how the sunset had flared above the Sierras, then died on the water. . . .

You're not coming here tomorrow, McCone. It just depresses you more. Get on with figuring out your life.

Behind me, Lear Jet snorted impatiently. He wanted his alfalfa.

"Okay, you smelly old thing," I called and got to my feet. "I'm coming."

The horse, of course, was obstinate. He turned his back on me and tried to pull the reins loose from where I'd tied them to a tree root. I took the reins myself, but when I tried to mount him he sidestepped. I hung on, got my left foot in the stirrup, and threw my right leg over his back. Before I could locate the other stirrup, he began walking; I clung to the pommel until my foot was secure. Then he stopped.

I clicked my heels authoritatively against his sides.

He snorted and put his head down.

"Look, you miserable bag of bones, I'm not in the mood for your antics!" I clicked my heels harder.

Lear Jet took off at a sudden wild run across the mesa.

I lost both stirrups, yanking hard on the reins. "Slow down, dammit!"

And he did—jerking to a dead stop. I flew from the saddle over his lowered head and landed on my butt in an area of soft dried grass.

As the horse turned away and trotted toward the stables, I could have sworn I heard him snicker.

I wasn't hurt, although I'd probably be sore in the morning, but I stayed where I was for a while, lying on my back, my knees bent upward, cursing Lear Jet and watching the emerging stars.

What *else* could go wrong today? That morning I'd nicked myself with a kitchen knife; been snappish for no reason with my office manager, Ted Smalley, who was holding down the fort back in the city; been even more snappish when my sister Charlene, who lived in the LA area, called to see how I was doing.

That afternoon Citibank's fraud division called to tell me someone was using my MasterCard to make Internet purchases; they'd frozen the account and a new card would have to be issued. I should have been grateful to them for spotting the problem within hours, but instead I grumbled at the representative about the inconvenience of having to change the number on all my automatic payments. Then I called my nephew and agency computer expert, Mick Savage, and asked him to find out who'd made the charges; he could work faster than Citibank, who were bound to have more important cases on their hands than mine. When he said he was swamped, and why not let the bank handle it, I yelled at him and hung up. Then I slept the rest of the afternoon.

Now I'd been thrown by a horrible, hateful horse.

Well, at least you're not having a bad hair day, my inner voice said.

"Shut up," I said. "It's not funny."

Now I was losing my sense of humor! I'd always depended on it to get me through the rough patches, but it was fading along with everything else.

I got up, brushing dried grass from my pants and hair, and started toward the house. The moon and starlight showed me the way, and eventually I found a familiar well-traveled path.

A bobbing light was coming toward me, I saw then. "Sharon?" Ramon Perez's voice called.

"I'm here."

"Lear came back to the stable without you. I thought I'd better mount a search."

"The son of a bitch threw me."

"Are you all right?" I'd come into the circle of Ramon's flashlight, and he frowned as he looked me up and down.

"I'll live."

Ramon Perez was a Northern Paiute, a tribe closely associated and often confused with my own forebears, the Shoshone. A stocky, weathered man in his late forties who spoke little but always had gentle hands for animals and a kind smile for humans. He'd opened up some to me since I told him I'd discovered I was adopted and a full-blooded Indian; since then we'd spent a good bit of time discussing his and my tribes' commonalities and differences.

Which was what had started this horse thing.

We'd been sitting on bales of hay in the stable two nights ago when Ramon said, "You really should learn to ride."

"Why would I want to do that?"

"Your people are good with horses. They acquired them, I

think from the Apaches, in the seventeen-hundreds. Earlier than my people."

"Well then, I'm a piss-poor Shoshone. I took riding lessons in my mid-twenties and did okay, but I quit because I discovered I hate the critters."

Ramon shook his head. "You just don't understand them, is all. What you need to do is show them that you're in control, and that you respect them. Then comes the love."

I eyed him skeptically.

"Take Lear out tomorrow morning."

I shrugged.

"Dare you."

"Oh, Ramon, come on. . . ."

"Double-dare you."

Ah, the games of our childhood . . .

"Double-dog-dare you."

"You're on."

The next morning I'd shown up at nine for my ride. Lear raised his lip in a sneer while Ramon helped me adjust the saddle, bridle, and stirrups, but otherwise he'd walked peaceably enough around the nearby meadow. When I unsaddled him he twitched his tail impatiently.

"Ride him tonight," Ramon suggested. "Let him get used to you. I've seen you walking on the mesa; let him take you there."

I sighed, "Okay. But isn't it dangerous to ride at twilight?"

He laughed. "Horse knows every inch of this ranch. He'll get you there and back just fine. Bring him a piece of carrot as a reward."

Lear had given me a disdainful look and tried to nip my fingers when he took the carrot, but otherwise the ride had gone well. And then tonight . . .

I took Ramon's arm as we started walking back toward the cluster of ranch buildings. "Lear's not getting the carrot I brought for him."

"No, he shouldn't. He knows he acted out."

"And I'm not riding him again."

Ramon was silent for a moment, and then he said softly, "We'll see."

Ten minutes later I let myself into the house through the door to the mudroom, hung the jacket on a peg, and went into the kitchen. It felt like stepping back into the fifties: black-and-white linoleum floor, yellow Formica countertops, old fridge and stove, porcelain sink, enameled cabinets with scalloped bottoms. A chrome-and-Formica table—yellow, with chairs upholstered in red vinyl—stood in a breakfast nook. I liked the kitchen and the fact that neither Hy nor Julie had attempted to remodel it. It spoke to me of continuity and an acceptance of the past.

And now if I can only learn to accept certain things in my past . . .

No philosophizing, I told myself. I was hungry.

I went to the fridge and peered inside. Bag of salad greens—wilted. Tomato—wrinkling. No eggs—I'd fried the last one for my lunchtime sandwich. Milk, but when I picked up the carton and sniffed it, it smelled bad. Ditto the sandwich meat. I'd used the last edible pieces of bread for lunch; the rest of it had turned hard as stone. And in the ice-clogged freezer—they didn't self-defrost when this one was made, and I hadn't bothered to do anything about it—I spotted a submerged package of lima beans that had perhaps been there since 2002.

This was what else could go wrong today.

Good God, what was wrong with me? Why hadn't I noticed this lack of food earlier? I hadn't come here to starve myself!

I investigated the pantry. Badly stocked, unless I wanted anchovies and garbanzo beans for dinner. No more wine, either.

That did it. In a minute I was back in the shearling jacket and out the door to Hy's Land Rover.

The town of Vernon, on the shore of Tufa Lake, had changed little over the years since I'd first come there. The red-and-gold neon sign atop Zelda's—a rustic tavern and restaurant where you could dance on the weekends to country-and-western bands—flashed far out at the end of the long point extending into the lake. The liquor store had a new name, and one of the off-brand gas stations was now a Union 76, but otherwise the small businesses in the strip malls along the main street remained: an insurance broker, real-estate agents, a pizza parlor, a bank, the post office, a haircutting salon, a florist, two bars, and various other establishments that provided the necessities of everyday life. The shabby motel on the lakeshore showed a NO VACANCY sign, which never would have been the case in the old days; but the marginally better and more scenic Willow Grove Lodge was closed and up for sale, following the death of its owner, Rose Whittington. I'd stayed there on my first visits to Vernon, and remembered Mrs. Whittington as a pleasant innkeeper with a passion for gardening and trucker movies.

As always, the Food Mart was doing a turn-away business.

I pulled into the lot, parked the Land Rover, and started for the supermarket. Its windows were brightly lighted, and through them I saw busy checkers, stacks of specials, and shoppers pushing carts along the aisles. The lot and the building's plain white facade were well lighted too, but there was a pocket of darkness beyond where a soft-drink machine and some newspaper vending racks stood. With a city dweller's conditioning, I glanced over there.

A young woman—a girl, really, she couldn't have been more than fourteen or fifteen—stood alone; from the way her gaze darted around the parking lot, I assumed she was waiting for a ride. She wore a thin cotton blouse and jeans and hugged herself against the cold. Her hunched posture reminded me of the victims of sexual and domestic violence to whom I'd taught a self-defense course at San Francisco City College last year. When she swung her head around, her long black hair flared out in the chill breeze; her features, I saw, were Indian. Probably Paiute.

The girl projected such an air of loneliness that I paused. The lights of a car pulling into the lot and waiting for a space focused on her, and she blinked at the glare, then looked away in my direction. Her eyes locked on mine, and I was close enough, the lights bright enough that I saw something besides loneliness: fear.

I wondered if I should go over to her, ask if she was all right. But then she began scanning the other side of the lot. I watched her for a few more seconds before I went inside. As I passed along the aisles, buying enough food to last a week, the Indian girl's image stayed with me. When I left the store I looked for her, but she was gone.

Wednesday

✦

OCTOBER 24

to

Monday

✦

OCTOBER 29

For the greater part of the week after my outing to the Food Mart, I stayed on the ranch—reading, watching old movies on TV, sleeping, and steadfastly avoiding any thought of the future. And every evening, in spite of my vow, I returned to the same place on the bluff to watch the moon rise.

I didn't ride Lear Jet again, but after a day I did go to the stables at the time that Ramon returned from exercising him. I'd watch while he groomed and fed the horse, sitting on a bale of hay in amicable silence.

Ramon, I knew, had made overtures to Hy about buying the ranch, but out of sentiment Hy didn't want to sell. He'd grown up there, and it had been willed to him by his mother and stepfather. He'd returned there after a tumultuous stint as a charter pilot in southeast Asia. He'd lived there with Julie and eventually watched her waste away. He'd grieved there, and recovered there. And we'd first slept together there. While we didn't visit often now, the moments we shared in the high desert were precious. Ramon had understood: sentiment ran thick in his veins too.

Sometimes when he was done with the horse, he'd join me

and talk about our heritages. "You know, our tribes generally had good relationships," he said one afternoon. "Maybe that's why we get along so well, huh?"

"Maybe it's got more to do with the fact we're both quiet."

"Well, that *is* a virtue." He took out a cigarette, lit it, and doused the match thoroughly. With Ramon, I never worried about accidental fires; he was too mindful a man.

"Sara, God love her, she chatters," he added. Sara was his wife of thirty-some years. "Of course, when I married a Mexican, I knew she would. And chattering's not such a bad thing; how else would I know what's going on in the world? Now, that man of yours doesn't talk much."

"He's getting better at conversation."

"Since he met you. When I first came to work here for him, about a year after his first wife died, he barely spoke at all. A more depressed man I'd never met."

We sat in silence for a while, Ramon smoking his cigarette, then grinding it out on the floor and putting the butt in his shirt pocket.

"You're damn depressed yourself," he said.

I shrugged.

"You want to talk about it?"

"... I don't think so. Not now, anyway."

"You change your mind, I'm here."

The next day I brought Ramon a book on Shoshone tribal customs that my birth father, Elwood Farmer, had given me. Lear Jet glowered at me from his stall. Did he think I should've brought *him* something? No way, not after he'd thrown me.

Throughout the week I had contact with the outside world, of course. Daily calls came from my operative Patrick Neilan, to whom I'd turned over administrative matters at the agency, as well as my office manager, Ted Smalley.

Just general reports: everything's okay here, we wrapped up the so-and-so case, three new jobs came in today. It was all I cared to know about a business I'd nurtured lovingly for years. And that unnerved me.

Mick had relented and located the person who'd been using my credit card: a deliveryman employed by a Chinese restaurant in our neighborhood who frequently delivered takeout to us. Citibank and the police were dealing with him.

There was also a daily call from Hy, who was restructuring the corporate security firm—formerly RKI, now Ripinsky International—of which he'd become sole owner after the death of one partner and the decampment of another. He'd moved their world headquarters to San Francisco, turned over marginal accounts to other firms, and closed unnecessary branch offices, and was busy creating a corporate culture that—unlike the old RKI's—was free of corruption. His calls further depressed me, although I did my best to hide it. I'd never heard Hy so vibrant and optimistic, but could only briefly get caught up in his enthusiasm. His feelings about his work were so opposite to how I felt about mine that once the calls were over, I wanted to crawl into bed and bury my head under the pillows.

Which I did most nights, falling into a restless sleep that was repeatedly visited by the dream of the pit, as well as an odd new one: an Indian girl standing in the cold shadows outside a large white building. She looked at me in the glare of passing headlights, eyes afraid, and then the earth at her feet cracked open and swallowed her up.

Tuesday

✦

OCTOBER 30

I awoke with the dreams heavy upon me, like a hangover. My hands shook as I fixed coffee and my head throbbed dully, even though I'd had nothing alcoholic to drink the night before.

I took my coffee to the living room and curled up under a woven throw in one of the deeply cushioned chairs by the stone fireplace. Unlike the kitchen, this room was pure Hy: Indian rugs on the pegged-pine floor, antique rifles over the fireplace, and in the bookcases flanking it to either side, his collection of Western novels from the thirties and forties and nonfiction accounts of the Old West. Over the time I'd been staying here, I'd read some of the novels, paged through a few of the nonfiction volumes. But this morning my mind was not on history—at least not anything going back more than five months.

This stay in the high desert wasn't working out as I'd thought it would. I'd managed to fill up empty hours with useless activity, while avoiding the larger issues: Did I really want to go on sitting behind a desk hour after hour, reviewing client reports, okaying invoices and expense logs, interviewing new clients, assigning jobs, and mediating employee disputes? Did I really want to continue taking on the larger, more complex cases that required me to be on the move a lot and that—too often in the past year—had ended in danger and near death?

Over the course of my career I'd been stabbed, nearly drowned, beaten up, falsely imprisoned, held at gunpoint, and once, ignominiously, shot in the ass. I'd killed two people and nearly succumbed to violent urges against others. Last winter I'd come close to being killed in the explosion. Enough, already.

But taking on a strictly administrative role wasn't an option for me; I'd go crazy confined to my desk. How could I continue activities that had lost their appeal, where I was just going through the motions?

The agency was profitable and well respected. I could sell it for big bucks to another firm looking to grow, negotiate a deal where my present employees would remain on staff. Take the money and . . . then what?

I wasn't cut out for everyday leisure. I didn't play golf or tennis or bridge, take classes, have hobbies, or enjoy most of the activities retired people do.

Retired people.

My God, I was in my early forties! Given the life expectancy of my birth family—relatives on both sides had lived into their nineties—that was a lot of time to fill up. And that's all I'd be doing—just filling it up.

Okay, begin a second career. Lots of people did that. But what? My college degree was in sociology, and that hadn't gotten me anywhere even when my diploma was freshly minted. Consult? That would only put me back in the thick of things. Write a book on investigative techniques, as I'd recently been asked to? No. I'd rather become a neurosurgeon, train as a master chef, or apply to NASA and fly to Mars. None of which was going to happen either.

Investigation was what I knew how to do—and do well—but I didn't want to work at it any more. At least not now. Maybe not ever.

Hy had suggested I come in as a partner with him, but that wouldn't work. We'd take our business home with us, and ultimately it would consume our marriage. Besides, an executive position in corporate security wasn't to my liking; it didn't provide much involvement with the clients, one aspect that I used to enjoy.

I went to get some more coffee. My headache had faded, and my hands were steady. Back in my chair by the fireplace, I told myself that at least I'd seriously considered the issues I was facing, even if it hadn't solved anything.

Didn't have to be done quickly anyway. The business was in good hands, and I had all the time in the world. A solution would come to me eventually. In the meantime, why not fill up the rest of today with pleasurable activity?

I would have liked to go flying, but Hy had needed our Cessna 270B, so he'd dropped me off at Tufa Tower Airport and flown back to the Bay Area. The airport had a couple of clunker planes I could rent for a nominal fee, but Hy had told me they were untrustworthy, and from a cursory inspection I'd concluded he was correct.

Maybe a picnic. Pack a good book, pick up a sandwich from the Food Mart deli, and go—where? Well, the old Willow Grove Lodge had nice grounds and a dock overlooking the lake. It was closed and isolated. The only people likely to show up there would be real-estate agents with prospective buyers, and I doubted that would happen. If it did, I'd concoct some story to explain my presence and leave.

The main lodge and six cabins that were scattered over several cottonwood- and willow-shaded acres looked shabby. True, the cabins had never been in great condition, but their nineteen-fifties-vintage furnishings, smoke-stained woodstoves, primitive kitchens, and underlying odor of dry rot reminded me of the resorts where my financially strapped family had stayed on summer vacations during my childhood. And even after the death of her husband, Rose Whittington had worked hard to keep the place up. Now the cabins' green trim was blistered and faded, dark brown wood splintered and cracked, composition roofs sagging. Graffiti decorated their walls. Rose's garden had long gone to the weeds. A developer's dream: bulldoze it and put up condos or a luxury hotel. The hell with the love and care that the Whittingtons had put into this place over their fifty-year marriage, let alone the happy memories of all the people who'd stayed here.

Of course, it was hard to argue with a would-be buyer's logic; these buildings were not salvageable. I only hoped that whoever bought the acreage would leave the trees.

I parked behind the lodge where the Land Rover couldn't be seen from the highway, carried my deli lunch down the rocky slope to the rickety dock, and spread an old blanket on its planks. Sat down, feeling the pale autumn sunshine on my face. The lake rippled on the stones below, and in the distance I could see plovers doing touch-and-goes on the massive central island. The lake is a major stop on the Pacific Flyway, along which approximately a hundred thousand migratory birds travel, and over the years I've seen most every kind there. If the lake had not been saved through the efforts of dedicated environmentalists like Hy, the birds would have had a long journey to their next stop.

A natural wonder restored, a man-made resort dying.

Suddenly I didn't feel as sad about the Willow Grove Lodge's demise. Long after whatever replaced it was gone, the lake would endure.

The book I'd brought along wasn't very engaging—a long-winded narrative about a former alcoholic holed up in the woods to contemplate what he claimed wasn't a midlife crisis, but that damned well sounded like one, as I should know. After I finished my lunch, I dozed off while reading and woke to a chill wind gusting off the lake. The shadows of the trees had moved over me.

I sat up, disoriented. In my peripheral vision, something moved through the dark grove to the right. I turned my head, narrowed my eyes. Nothing there. Then I saw it again—a figure that darted from trunk to trunk, creating a ripple effect.

An animal? A person? Either way, I was the interloper here. Time to get going.

I folded the blanket, grabbed the book and the sack of leavings from my picnic. At the Land Rover I looked back at the grove. No more motion, but a prickly sensation arose at the base of my spine, spread up to the back of my neck. Something colder than the wind washed over me.

My old woolen peacoat was in the Land Rover and before I drove out I put it on. As I stopped at the top of the drive, I saw the yellow-leafed aspens in the declivities of the hills to the far side of the highway swaying softly in the breeze; the late afternoon sunlight made them gleam like a river of molten gold.

There had been gold in these hills long ago and some poor

veins remained. Normally the beauty of this view would have entranced me, but now its glow was dimmed by the aura of what I'd felt at the lodge. I thought of the ravages that cyanide—which the big mining companies had used to extract gold from the waste dumps and tailings of played-out claims—had wreaked upon the land.

The thought took me back to the case I'd been working here when I met Hy, investigating a conglomerate that planned to start up a large-scale and environmentally unsound mining operation above a semi-ghost town called Promiseville. I remembered us fleeing hand in hand from a dynamite blast that took out a part of a mountain. And Hy saying, as we lay on the ground gasping and panting from our flight, ". . . You've got even more of a death wish than I do."

Not any more.

I waited for a logging truck to pass, then turned left toward town. The highway topped a rise, then began a gradual descent into Vernon. Halfway down I saw an old brown pickup truck, its paint spotted gray like a piebald horse. It was pulled onto the opposite shoulder and, as I approached, its passenger-side door flew open and the figure of a woman hurtled out into the ditch. The truck's driver—bearded, with a knit cap pulled low on his brow—got out and stood on the edge of the ditch, yelling down at her.

Reflexively I U-turned across the highway and pulled onto the shoulder. As I jumped out of the Rover the man turned, his features mostly obscured by his hat and turned-up collar.

"Just a family fight, lady," he said in a rough voice. "No need to get involved."

"The hell you say!" I started forward just as the woman clawed her way up the incline. It was the Indian girl whose face had been haunting my dreams. Now her long hair was tangled, and she looked dazed.

The man made a menacing gesture toward me. I braced for an attack, feet spread wide, arms flexed. He stood still, studying me, then muttered something that sounded like "Ah, fuck it!" He whirled and got into the pickup, revved its engine, and sped off, spraying gravel.

I went over and helped the girl to her feet. I couldn't tell if she recognized me or not; her expression was blank.

"Are you all right?" I asked.

". . . Yes, I'm okay. No big deal." She brushed at her clothing, smoothed down her hair. She was dressed more warmly than she had been the last time I saw her, in a quilted jacket, jeans, and hiking boots.

"What happened here?"

She shrugged. "I said it was no big deal."

"Do you need a ride someplace? I can—"

"Look," she said, "it's none of your business. Okay? I take care of myself, nobody else does." Then she turned and began walking the way the truck had gone.

I watched until she disappeared over the rise, berating myself for trying to intervene in a private matter. It was as if I had a compulsion to get involved in things that didn't concern me—just as I'd often involved myself too deeply in cases I'd handled. Dammit, why couldn't I leave people alone? That was what I wanted to do, wasn't it? It was what I'd been telling myself.

I got back into the Land Rover. A fight with a relative or her boyfriend, I thought. They live someplace up the highway and by the time she gets there he'll be sorry.

But the way she shot out of that truck, it looked like he pushed her. He's an abuser and all abusers feel sorry—until they do it again.

As she said, it was none of my business. She didn't want my help.

I could ask around in Vernon. . . .

No, I couldn't. Or, more correctly, wouldn't. That kind of uninvited snooping had no place in the new life I was hoping to create.

I stopped by the Food Mart because I was getting low on milk. And only for that reason.

But as the tired-looking woman at the checkstand was ringing up my purchases—I can never go into a grocery store and buy just one item—I said, "There was an Indian girl waiting for a ride outside here last Tuesday night. I wonder if you know her?" I described her and what she was wearing.

The checker nodded and began bagging my groceries. "That's Amy Perez. She stocks shelves here a couple days a week. What d'you want with her?"

Don't go on with this, McCone. Don't.

"She . . . dropped something, and I'd like to return it." God, the lies that rippled off my tongue after so many years in my business! It had gotten to the point that I didn't need to think them up ahead of time.

"You can give it to me, I'll see she gets it."

"Actually, I'd like to return it in person. It's a bracelet, and I want to ask her where she got it, so I can buy one for myself."

The checker shrugged. "Well, I don't know where she's living these days. She moves around a lot, you know what I mean?"

I asked, "Is she any relation to Ramon Perez up at the Ripinsky place?"

"A niece maybe, I'm not sure. There're Perezes all over Mono County, some related, some not. But, yeah, I think Ramon's her uncle."

I thanked her, paid, and left.

It wouldn't hurt, I thought, to ask Ramon about Amy, tell him what I had witnessed that afternoon. If she was in trouble, maybe her uncle could help.

"Yeah, Amy's my niece." Ramon was sitting on the bale of hay inside the stable door.

Lear Jet was already in his stall. I glared at him, and he glared back.

I said, "Tell me about her."

His gaze shifted to the darkness gathering in the empty stalls beyond Lear Jet's. "My sister-in-law's youngest. She was such a beautiful little girl, and she loved her Uncle Ramon."

"And now?"

"She's still beautiful. You saw that."

"And she still loves you?"

He sighed heavily. "Who knows? Who knows anything these days?"

I couldn't debate the latter question. "She's in trouble, Ramon." I told him what I'd seen that afternoon, and Amy's reaction to my offer of help. "The clerk at Food Mart said she 'moves around a lot.'"

"One boyfriend, another boyfriend, sometimes she crashes at my sister-in-law's house."

"How old is she?"

"Eighteen in three months. She looks a lot younger."

"Still underage, then. Can't her mother rein her in?"

He looked at me, eyes sad. "Look, Sharon, it's not that simple. Her mother has her own problems."

"There's no father in the picture?"

"My son-of-a-bitch brother Jimmy took off when Amy was a year old. Miri—that's his wife—did her best by all five kids, but it wasn't good enough. Her older girl left town nine years ago, before she finished high school. We don't know where she is. Last I heard was a postcard from Las Vegas, and that was over a year ago. The two older boys're in prison. The younger boy was killed in a car wreck—his fault, he'd been drinking."

"And now Miri's in danger of losing Amy, too."

He looked down at where his thick-fingered hands were spread on his denim-covered thighs. "I don't think she'd even notice if Amy was gone."

"Drugs? Booze? Men?"

"You got it. When Vic—the youngest boy—died, Miri totally fell apart."

"What about the kids' Uncle Ramon? Where do you fit into the picture?"

"I don't. Miri and I had a big fight, four, maybe five years ago. The times I came around to apologize, she ran me off with a shotgun."

"D'you think Amy might listen to you, let you help her?"

"Like I said, I don't know how she feels about me these days." He paused, and in the silence Lear Jet whickered. "You say this guy pushed her out of a pickup?"

"Yes. Brown, probably a Ford, with a lot of Bondo on it."

"You see him?"

"Yes. He has a dark brown beard; I couldn't really tell about his features. After he threw Amy out of the truck he went to the edge of the shoulder and was shouting at her. When I intervened, he thought about attacking me, then took off."

"Boz Sheppard. That asshole. If she's hooked up with him, it's statutory rape."

"How old is this Boz?"

"Late twenties, maybe thirty. Hard to tell. Too damn old to be messing with a young girl like Amy."

"Who is he?"

"Local lowlife—not that we haven't got plenty of them. Claims to be a carpenter, but he's usually so stoned he couldn't drive a nail in straight if his life depended on it."

"He from around here?"

"No. Showed up in Vernon one day, took a trailer at that crappy park up the highway. Does odd jobs, but I hear mostly he deals drugs. Rumor is he's got a record."

If he did, I could get Derek Ford, Mick's assistant at the agency, to access it. "Definitely not good company for your niece," I said.

"Yeah. Which way you say she was going when she walked off?"

"North from town."

"Toward that trailer park." Ramon stood. "Think I'll take a run out there, pay a visit. Want to ride along?"

"Ramon, it's a family matter—"

"One that could use a woman's touch."

Well, why not? I had nothing else to do that evening.

The park extended from the edge of the highway to the hillside—two dozen or so old-model trailers up on cement blocks. No amenities such as a rec center, plantings, or even paved parking areas. No trees. Only a sagging barbed-wire fence between it and the outside world.

Personally, I'd rather have lived in a cave.

Ramon stopped the truck in front of a one-windowed shack with a sign saying OFFICE. Got out, but came right back. "Nobody there."

I looked around, pointed out a woman walking a dog. Ramon nodded and approached her. When he slid into the truck he said, "Last trailer, last row in back. From the look the lady gave me, I'd say Boz's dealing, all right."

We drove back there in silence, gravel crunching under the truck's wheels. The rows were dimly lighted—minimum county requirement—and most of the trailers were dark. Boz Sheppard's was by far the worst of them all—ancient, small, humpbacked, its formerly white paint peeling off to reveal gunmetal gray and rust. There was a glow in its rear window.

Ramon took a deep breath. "I don't know what to say to her."

"Tell her you love her and want to help."

"What if she doesn't think she needs it?"

I pictured the look of defiance in Amy's eyes before she'd turned her back on me that afternoon. Underneath there had been fear—and not of me.

"She does, whether she knows it or not," I said. "This Boz—he'll try to intervene. We should separate them."

"How?"

"Leave that to me." I didn't have a plan, but once we confronted Boz, my instincts would tell me what to do.

We got out of the truck and went up to the door. Ramon knocked.

No answer.

He knocked again, rattling the flimsy door in its frame.

Nothing.

"See if it's unlocked," I said.

"That's not legal—"

"You have probable cause to be concerned for your niece."

"Damn right I do!" He turned the knob and pushed the door inward so hard it smacked into the wall behind it. Moved up the two low steps and inside.

A growl. At first I thought it came from a watchdog, then realized that Ramon himself had made the sound. I pushed around him. And stopped.

The room was tidy, the pullout bed made up into a couch. A woman lay collapsed beside it, her arms outflung on the bloodstained carpet, long dark hair covering most of her face. Freshly spilled blood. It pooled beneath her, and the front of her black silk dress was torn and scorched where a bullet—or bullets—had entered. The scent of cordite was strong on the air.

Before I could stop him, Ramon went to the woman and brushed her hair from her face. Gasped and recoiled.

I went over and pulled on his arm. "Go outside. This is a crime scene. We can't disturb anything more than we already have."

He hesitated, then went, shaking his head.

I looked down at the woman's face. Not Amy, but someone older who closely resembled her. The dress looked expensive, her costume jewelry gaudy. One red spike-heeled shoe had come off her foot and lay on the carpet. I glanced at the breakfast bar on the counter: a half-full shaker of martinis and two glasses, one lying on its side, broken, liquid pooling beside it.

I backed up, left the trailer without touching anything. Ramon was leaning against his truck, trying to light a cigarette with shaking hands.

"You know her?" I asked.

He nodded.

"Who is she?"

He took a deep drag on the cigarette and exhaled. "Hayley."

"And Hayley is . . . ?"

"Amy's older sister. The one I told you sent me a postcard from Las Vegas."

How the hell did I get myself into this? I came up here to make plans to leave this kind of thing behind me—the stench of death, the flashing lights, the paramedics, the radios and official voices droning on and on and on . . .

I should've told Ramon to bring Sara along with him if he felt the situation required a woman's touch. I should've stayed home, waited for the agency calls, phoned Hy. I should've jumped into the Rover and gotten the hell out of Mono County.

Well, you're involved now, McCone, whether you like it or not. At least you're an outsider, an observer with professional judgment, rather than a torn-up family member like Ramon. . . .

He was in one of the sheriff's department cars now, giving his statement to a deputy, but before they'd arrived he'd been crying in my arms. Later he'd be embarrassed by that, I knew, but at the time he'd needed comfort. I'd never mention his tears, and neither would he, but eventually they'd either put up a wall or forge a stronger bond between us.

Another deputy approached me. "Ms. McCone, I'm Deputy Drew Warnell. Can we talk?"

He was young, so smooth-faced that I'd bet he didn't shave but every other day, and he turned his hat in his hands as he spoke, his dark hair falling in a thick shock over his forehead. I suggested we go sit in Ramon's truck.

When we were settled, Deputy Warnell took out a notepad. "I understand you were with Mr. Perez when he discovered the deceased?"

I explained how I'd encountered Amy under disturbing circumstances that afternoon and told Ramon about them. "The man who rented the trailer, Boz Sheppard, was the one who threw her out of his truck. Ramon decided to come here and talk with him. He asked me to come along."

"Why?"

"He said the situation needed a woman's touch."

"It wasn't because you're a private investigator?"

"No, I came as a friend."

"So Mr. Perez entered the trailer and found the victim?"

"Yes."

"Why didn't you take steps to ensure that he didn't disturb the crime scene?"

"Because he moved too fast. I'd only seen the body seconds before he touched it. I did get him outside as quickly as I could."

"Mr. Perez has identified the young woman as his other niece, Hayley Perez, last known address Las Vegas."

"Yes."

"Did you know Hayley Perez?"

"I don't know any of the family, except for Ramon and his wife, Sara. He's foreman at my husband's and my ranch."

"The Ripinsky place?"

"Yes."

For a moment his official facade slipped and Drew Warnell seemed even younger. "I used to ride horses up there. My mom and dad were friends of Hy's and Julie's."

"There's only one horse left now—Lear Jet."

He shook his head. "Must've come after my time. And I

don't think Mr. Perez was working there then." He paused, seeming at a loss for further questions.

I asked, "D'you have any idea how long Hayley Perez has been dead?"

"Not long. The ME said within the last hour."

Shortly before Ramon and I had arrived, then. "Shot at close range. How many times?"

"Once, straight into her heart—" He broke off, then said, "Ms. McCone, I'm sorry, but I shouldn't be giving you these details."

"And I shouldn't've asked—professional habit."

"You work for what agency?"

"I own McCone Investigations, in San Francisco."

Something flickered in his eyes as he put it together. There had been huge publicity earlier in the year on the serial bomber case.

"Sorry," he said. "I must be slow tonight. I didn't make the connection until just now."

"No worries."

"I should've—"

I held up my hand to forestall yet another apology. "As I indicated earlier, I'm not here in a professional capacity. I see your colleague's done with Ramon, and I really should be getting back to him. If you need to ask any further questions, you can reach me at the ranch."

Ramon wasn't fit to drive yet, so I took the wheel of his truck. As I turned onto the highway, he said, "I told the cops I'd break the news to Miri."

"Where does she live?"

"You don't want to go with me."

"Remember what you said before? A woman's touch?"

He was silent for a moment. Then he said, "Make a right turn on the first street this side of the Food Mart."

After I'd driven into town and turned off, he said, "This won't be pretty."

"It never is."

But the small gray clapboard house in the middle of the block was dark, and no one answered when Ramon knocked.

He said, "Miri's probably at one of the bars or the motel—or passed out inside."

"You have a key?"

"Nope." He tried the knob, but unlike at the trailer where we'd found his niece's body, the door was locked. "I better check the bars. Something like this, news gets around fast. A deputy goes off duty, he starts talking. That's no way for Miri to find out."

"Okay, where do we start?"

He looked away from me. "Not we—me. I'm okay now. You take the truck back to the ranch, get some rest. It's almost midnight."

I felt a flash of relief, but still felt compelled to say, "I don't mind—"

"Sharon, I appreciate all you've done tonight. But Miri—I've got to handle her myself."

"How'll you get home?"

"I'll call Sara when I'm done, ask her to come and get me."

"Okay, then. Good luck with Miri."

Wednesday

✦

OCTOBER 31

The phone was ringing when I let myself into the ranch house. As I went to pick up, I noticed the time on the old-fashioned kitchen clock: 12:23.

"Happy Halloween, McCone." Hy.

"And the same to you." I'd completely forgotten what the date was.

"Where've you been all this time? I've left messages on the machine, and on your cell."

"Sorry I haven't checked either. Where I've been is an awfully sad story."

His voice sharpened when he asked, "What's wrong?"

I went over the events of the evening.

"Jesus," he said when I'd finished. "Poor Ramon. How're you?"

"I'm handling it."

"And?"

"That's all. I was there for Ramon when he needed me. Now the county sheriff can deal with it."

". . . Right."

"What does that mean?"

"Nothing, really."

"You think this is going to suck me in, don't you? You think that next thing I'll be prowling around, trying to find out who killed that woman."

"Not necessarily."

"Well, good, because it's not going to happen. That part of my life is over. *Over.*"

"I hear you. Have you made any decisions yet? About your future?"

"No, not yet."

We went on to discuss his day, our cats, and his coming up here on the weekend. After we ended the conversation, I took a hot shower and crawled into bed.

All I wanted was to blot out the events of a long, horrible day. Maybe if I could do that, even for a few hours, I'd be able to distance myself from Ramon's trouble.

Maybe.

Distance—sure.

At around ten-thirty that morning I was washing out my coffee cup at the kitchen sink when Sara Perez's SUV drove in and parked next to Ramon's truck. She got out, looked inside the truck. Then she spotted me through the window, waved, and moved toward the house.

Sara was a short, heavy woman with gray hair in a long braid that hung nearly to her waist. In spite of her girth, she moved gracefully. A native of Oaxaca, Mexico, she was a midwife and concocter of herbal medicines, assisting at births and dispensing natural panaceas in remote towns all over the county, as well as a writer of children's books aimed at the state's soon-to-be-dominant Latino population.

When I met her at the mudroom door, I saw that her eyes

were worried, her full lips cracked and raw as if she'd been nibbling at them.

"Ramon didn't come home last night," she said. "I heard about Hayley. The radio said he found her body and that you were with him."

Damn! Why did they have to give out that information? No privacy—

I motioned her in from the cold. "Ramon asked me to drop him off in town, and that he'd call you for a ride home. He had to break the news to Miri."

"He go to her house?"

"Yes, he had me drive him there, but—"

"She was off someplace, or passed out drunk."

"That's what he thought."

"Well, I've tried calling Miri's. No answer there."

"Last I saw him, he was going to look for her in the bars."

"May I use your phone?"

"Sure." I motioned toward it, went to pour her a cup of coffee.

"Bob?" she said into the phone. "Sara. Did my man come in there last night looking for his miserable sister? . . . Yeah . . . Right, about what time? . . . Thanks, Bob, I appreciate it."

To me she said, "He went to Zelda's, Miri hadn't been in." Sara dialed again and left a message on a machine. Made another call. "Jenny, it's Sara. Did Ramon . . . ? Right. She wasn't . . . I see . . . Will you call me if . . . Thanks."

She turned to me, took the cup of coffee I held out. "Those're the only bars in Vernon," she said, "and the one where I got the machine has eighty-sixed Miri so many times she'd never go there. Ramon was at the other two a little after midnight, asking for her. She hadn't been in."

"Maybe he went back to Miri's and found her there."

"And now nobody's answering the phone?"

"That *is* strange. You should go down there."

Sara shook her head, her braid switching from side to side. "I can't. The last time I tried to reach out to Miri, she threatened me with her shotgun, said she'd kill me if I ever came near the place again. Now, with Hayley dead, she'll be ready to take on the world. Will you go for me?"

No, a thousand times no.

Sara's dark eyes pleaded with me.

Please don't suck me into this. . . .

"I don't have anybody else to ask," she said. "None of our other friends want anything to do with Miri."

She looked so alone. If I could bring Ramon back to her . . .

"I'll go," I said, "and call to tell you what I find out."

Before I left the ranch house, Ted phoned. After he gave me his daily report he asked, "Any idea when you're coming back to the city?"

"No. Why?"

"We miss you. The place isn't the same without you."

And I wasn't the same without it. But I wasn't the same when I was there, either.

"Shar?"

"I'm here."

"Look, we're doing what we can to hold this agency together, but we need you."

"The agency seems to be doing fine without me."

Long pause. "You sound so . . . cold."

I supposed I did. A frozen shell around my emotions was

the best way to distance myself from the people I'd known and cared for all these years.

"I'm sorry, Ted. I'm . . . preoccupied this morning, that's all."

"Shar, this is me you're talking to. Ted, from the old days at All Souls."

The poverty law cooperative where we used to work, he as secretary and me as staff investigator. When I'd first met him he'd been sitting with his bare feet propped on his desk, working a *New York Times* crossword puzzle in ink. Those had been good years: filled with camaraderie, poker and Monopoly games in the off hours, and long soul-baring discussions late into the night as we sat around the big oak table in the kitchen of All Souls' Bernal Heights Victorian. Since the co-op had been dissolved and I'd formed my own agency—taking Ted and Mick with me—the camaraderie had continued and enlarged to embrace new people. But these days we were so caught up with a huge caseload and an upscale image—to say nothing of large earning power—that much of the excitement and closeness had bled away.

I said, "I know who I'm talking to, Ted."

"Then really talk. Tell me what's going on with you. Maybe I can help."

Tears stung my eyes, as they had all too often over the past months.

"I can't do that now," I said. "There's someplace I have to be."

Hy's comment about it being Halloween had made me wonder how the locals celebrated. As I drove into town I noticed jack-o'-lanterns on nearly every doorstep. Several bales of hay had been trucked into the Food Mart's parking lot, and beside them stood a scarecrow. Big deal in a small town. The decorations must've been there days before, but I hadn't been attuned to the holiday.

As I hadn't been attuned to so many things.

I turned onto Miri Perez's street and drove along, bouncing in and out of potholes, to her small gray house. The yard was fenced with chain link, its browned grass littered with takeout containers, soda and beer bottles; an old rusted bicycle that was missing its front wheel lay on its side under a juniper bush. No vehicles out front or in the driveway. As I went up the walk to the concrete stoop, I heard nothing.

I knocked on the door, waited. Knocked again, called out to Mrs. Perez and Ramon. No response.

The windows to either side of the door had their blinds drawn. I went along the driveway, noting that the windows there were too high to see through without a ladder. The backyard was the same as the front: browned grass, dead plants, more litter. A decrepit swing set sat near the rear fence.

The windows here were also covered by blinds. Another concrete stoop led to a back door. I climbed it, looked through the single pane. Straight ahead were an old refrigerator and a counter, to the right an archway.

I reached for the doorknob, pulled my hand away.

Don't do it, McCone.

But Ramon and Miri have gone missing, and Sara asked me—

Don't do it!

Holding fast to my new resolve, I didn't.

It was noon, time for the watering holes to open their doors. I decided to stop in at the bar on whose answering machine Sara had left a message. Hobo's was your typical tavern, the kind I'd visited over and over in the course of my investigations. At night it would be dimly lighted and its scars wouldn't show; by day the shabby booths and chairs and tables and banged-up walls were more obvious. Three old men hunched at the long bar, staring up at a TV that was broadcasting a replay of last weekend's Forty-Niners game. The bartender—white-haired, with a thick beard and a large gut—was setting out bowls of popcorn.

As I took a stool at the bar, I thought of all the hours I'd wasted seeking information in such establishments.

"Help you, ma'am?"

"Maybe. Sara Perez sent me."

"Oh, yeah, I haven't got around to returning her call." The man picked up a rag and began wiping the surface in front of me.

He added, "Reason I've been putting it off is that I had an ugly scene with Miri Perez in here last night, and then this morning I heard the news about Hayley from one of my delivery drivers."

"Did you know her?"

"Hayley? Not really. She was just one of the kids who would come in to drag their drunken parents home. She ran away before she even finished high school."

"What kind of ugly scene did you have with Miri?"

He frowned at me. "You a friend of the Perez family?"

"Ramon's the manager on my husband's and my ranch."

"You're Hy Ripinsky's wife."

"Right."

"Well, then." He leaned forward on the bar, lowering his voice and glancing at the patrons. They were absorbed in watching a 'Niners pass completion. "Miri came in last night about nine-thirty. I'd permanently eighty-sixed her a year ago, on account of she's a problem drunk. But she was sober and behaving herself so I let her stay. My mistake."

"What happened?"

"She was alone when she came in, but Miri's never alone for long. Not because she's particularly attractive—not any more, anyway—but because she has this reputation." He stopped, probably abashed at having said that much to a friend of Ramon and Sara.

"I know about Miri's problems," I said. "Go on."

"Well, there was a bunch of guys down from Bridgeport. Not bad guys, but they get kinda rowdy when the wives aren't around. One of them started buying Miri shots and she got rowdy too. Started making nasty remarks to the people at the next table, lobbed some popcorn at them, then threw a drink in one woman's face. Was cussing me out and swinging at me when I cut her off. I had to escort her out. The guy went with her."

"What time was this?"

"After eleven, but not much. Ramon came in looking for Miri around midnight."

"You know the name of the guy she left with?"

"His friends called him Dino. Like Dean Martin, the singer."

"What about his friends? You have a full name for any of them?"

"Only Cullen Bradley. Owns a hardware store in Bridgeport."

"Any idea where this Dino and Miri might've been heading?"

"Her place? The motel? That's the usual deal with Miri. No, wait a minute." He touched his fingers to his brow. "Before I escorted them out the guy said something to her about the Outhouse."

"The *what*?"

He smiled. "It's a tavern, up the highway about fifteen miles. Used to be a gas station. They've got the best fried chicken in the county."

Somehow I doubted Dino and Miri were headed there for the food. "Did you mention this to Ramon?"

"Yeah, I did. He wasn't happy about it."

"You say this place is fifteen miles up the highway?"

"Give or take."

"Ramon couldn't have followed them—he didn't have a vehicle."

"Miri did. I saw her old van in the lot when I showed them the door. But they didn't take it; they got into a red Jeep Cherokee. And the van was gone when I closed up."

"You notice the license plate number of the Cherokee?"

"My eyesight hasn't been that good since 1992."

"So you think Ramon might've taken the van?"

"Maybe."

"It's unlikely he had a key; he and Miri haven't been on speaking terms for years."

"Ramon wouldn't've needed a key. Not old Magic Fingers."

"What does that mean?"

"Ramon's been hot-wiring cars since he was a kid. Made the mistake of getting caught after he was eighteen, did a stretch in prison for it."

As I drove up the highway toward the Outhouse, I thought about the assumptions we make about people and how sometimes they're totally wrong. Hardworking, upwardly mobile

Ramon Perez—a car thief? An ex-con? Did Hy know about his past? Most likely: Vernon was a small town, and Hy had grown up there.

Why hadn't he mentioned it to me? Probably because Ramon had turned his life around and his misdeeds weren't relevant any more. Hy was big on giving people second chances; God knew he'd received more than his fair share of them.

It was a beautiful day, and I tried to enjoy the drive. The lake spread below me as I negotiated the road's switchbacks, its placid surface reflecting the clear blue of the sky. In the distance I could glimpse the dark, glassy mound of Obsidian Dome, one of the many distinctive formations created by the volcanic activity that shaped this land. In 1982 the U.S. Geological Survey issued a hazard warning that an eruption the size of the 1980 Mount Saint Helens disaster could occur here at any time. The warning is in effect to this day.

After I reached the ten-mile mark, the road—still climbing—veered to the east and cut between rocky slopes to which scrub pine clung. Five miles more, and the Outhouse appeared on my left. It was a typical old-fashioned gas station with a roof over the pumps, but the main structure had been considerably enlarged; the pumps were antiques—Socony before it became Mobil Oil—and lighted beer signs hung in the front windows. I parked in the gravel lot and went inside.

In spite of being far from any town, the place was doing a good business: most of the tables and booths were taken. I found one of the last empty seats at the bar. The air was heavy with the smell of frying; my stomach rumbled in response. The best fried chicken in the county, huh? I hadn't had really good fried chicken in ages.

The bartender was working hard; I waited, looking around at the decor: old automobile license plates from various states; signed celebrity photos from the forties and fifties; mildly amusing signs such as IN GOD WE TRUST. ALL OTHERS MUST PAY CASH; mounted animal heads wearing party hats. I'd been in other supposedly vintage places and knew decorations of this kind could be purchased new as a package from restaurant-equipment firms, but the Outhouse's seemed to be the real thing.

When the bartender finally got to me, I ordered a Sierra Nevada and a basket of chicken and fries. The beer came quickly, the chicken much later. "Sorry about the wait," he said as he set it down.

"No problem. You're busy."

"Swamped and shorthanded." Someone down the bar called out to him, and he hurried away.

I ate slowly. The chicken was some of the best I'd ever tasted. The seats around me gradually emptied, as did the booths and tables. I was toying with a french fry when the last customer left.

The bartender—a youngish guy with long hair pulled back in a ponytail—went to the door and turned the sign to CLOSED. Came back around the bar to me and said, "Anything else, ma'am?" Clearly he hoped I'd say no.

"Some information, if you don't mind. You hear about Hayley Perez being killed last night?"

"Yeah." He shook his head. "Tough break, but Hayley always lived dangerously. One wild child."

"You knew her well?"

"No. We went to high school together, but she was older and we didn't run with the same crowd."

"Who did she run with?"

"The wrong people. Druggies, dropouts, you know."

"Any names?"

"Why the interest?"

"I'm a friend of the family. I'm helping them get a list together for the memorial service."

That satisfied him. "Well, let's see. She was tight with a girl named Loni . . . something, but I haven't seen her around in a long time. Her boyfriend was Tom Mathers; he's married now, runs a wilderness supply and guide service. And then there was Rich Three Wings; they had a thing going too, was what broke Hayley and Tom up. You can forget about him, he'd never come to a service."

"Why not?"

"Because him and Hayley left town together and he came back alone three years later. Wouldn't ever talk about what happened. Now he lives alone in a cabin on Elk Lake. I hear he's got a girlfriend who lives in Vernon, spends weekends at the lake with him."

"You know her name?"

He shook his head.

"I take it Three Wings is Indian."

"Paiute." He studied my features. "You're . . . ?"

"Shoshone."

"Well then, maybe you can get through to Rich. You people have a way of communicating, even if you're from different tribes."

You people.

I'd been hearing that all my life, even back before I found out I was adopted, when I'd thought I was seven-eighths Scotch-Irish and my looks a throwback to my Shoshone great-grandmother. I counted to ten—well, seven, actually—

and said, "I understand Hayley's mother may have come in here last night. Were you working then?"

"Yeah. I'm doing a triple shift. Like I said, we're short-handed."

"And Miri . . . ?"

"She didn't come in. I'd've noticed, because she's on our watch list. Terrible, mean drunk."

"What about her brother-in-law, Ramon?"

"He was here. Asked me about her."

"When was this?"

"Around one. I told him I'd call if she turned up, and then he left."

"He say where he was going?"

"Nope. He seemed kind of . . . I don't know. Angry, but keeping a lid on it. Now I understand. If my niece had been murdered, I don't know what I'd do."

I paid for my lunch, including a substantial tip, and left.

Bridgeport, the county seat and the town where the man who had left Hobo's with Miri lived, was some thirty miles northwest on Highway 395. I knew of a cutoff that would take me there from this road. It was early yet, and I didn't feel like going back to the ranch—there would surely be a call from Ted pleading for me to open up to him—so I decided to drive up north and see if I could find the hardware store owner, Cullen Bradley.

Bridgeport is a charming town, with its stately eighteen-eighties courthouse, old homes, and steepled churches. Once known as Big Meadows because of the vast grazing land around it, it's also an outdoor person's paradise, surrounded by pristine lakes and streams for fishing or boating. Its greatest claim to fame is that it was used as the location for many of the scenes in the classic 1947 film noir *Out of the Past.* Hy disputes that; he says its claim to fame is being the only place that a drunken young man succeeded in lassoing and pulling down a street lamp from the bed of a moving pickup. The young man, of course, was Hy—whose reward for his feat was having to perform community service and pay for a new light pole. Every now and then when we're there we visit it, and he says someday he's going to mount a plaque on it.

I found Bradley's Hardware on a side street two blocks from the courthouse. It had a graveled parking lot in back; I pulled in, left the Land Rover there, and entered through the rear door. I love hardware stores and this smelled like a good one: not the sanitized, filtered odor of a Home Depot, but a mixture of wood and metal and paint and other unidentifiable but appropriate items. The bare floors were warped, the shelves sagging under their wares. I had to weave my way through a warren of aisles to get to the front. Immediately a friendly young clerk appeared and asked if he could help me find anything.

"Is Mr. Bradley in?"

"He's in his office, but . . . If you're selling something, I wouldn't bother him today."

"How come?"

He leaned forward and said in a whisper, "Bad night. He had me bring him some of what he calls 'hair of the dog' a while ago."

"Well, this is a personal matter. I'll take my chances."

"Back that way." He jerked his thumb toward a door behind the sales counter. "Good luck."

The door was slightly ajar. I knocked and called out to Bradley.

"What?" A shade irritable, but not too bad. The dog's hair must have been working.

"May I come in?"

"If you must." As I moved through the door, he added, "Who the hell are you?" He was a red-faced, fortyish man with a shock of gray-blond hair, and his skin had that flaccid look that a night of hard drinking will produce.

I introduced myself, said I was looking for a friend of his who had been with him at Hobo's in Vernon the night before. "The bartender said you called him Dino."

"Dino Martin. His parents named him for the singer. Funny thing is, he can't hold a note. Sounds like my old hound dog when he tries."

"Where can I reach him?"

"Why do you want to?"

"A friend of mine left the bar with him. She hasn't come home, and I'm worried."

"You must mean Miri Perez."

"Yes."

"Well, she's probably shacked up with him someplace. It's kind of what she does."

"Still, I'd like to talk with him."

He hesitated. "Okay. Try Martin Realty, a block west."

I thanked him and left him to his hangover.

Martin's Realty was a small storefront whose windows were plastered with fliers featuring their listings. There were two desks arranged in the front room, but no one was seated at them. A pair of doors opened to the rear, one of which bore a placard saying DINO MARTIN. I knocked and a gravelly voice said to come in.

Martin could not have less resembled the famed singer after whom he'd been named. He was bald except for a badly dyed fringe of black hair and a short, sparse beard. His eyes were red and puffy; purple veins stood out on his large nose. I judged him to be on the far side of fifty. As I stepped into the office, he picked up a coffee mug with a shaking hand and gulped its contents.

More dog hair?

I introduced myself, said I was a friend of the Perez family.

"And who the hell're they?"

"Miri Perez's relatives. You were with her last night in Hobo's—"

"Oh, that crazy bitch."

"You left with her, said something about going to the Outhouse."

"Yeah. I figured it was the only bar between Vernon and Bridgeport she hadn't been thrown out of yet."

"But you didn't go there."

He put a hand over his eyes like a visor, as if it hurt to look up, and motioned for me to sit down on the chair across from him. "No, we didn't. I was reasonably sober when we left Hobo's, but after what happened, I tied one on when I got back to town. The wife's ready to kill me."

"What happened?"

"Wait a minute. Why're you so interested in Miri?"

"She hasn't been seen since you two left the bar together."

"Hey, I don't know where she is."

"No? Why'd you tie one on after you got back here?"

". . . I . . . She . . . Oh, dammit!"

"Why don't you just tell me?"

"Why should I?"

I took out one of my cards and slid it across the desk to

him. "Legally I'm bound to report what I know to the sheriff's department. The deputies will get around to you soon."

"Oh, God. Okay, okay. We were a ways out of town. She was getting cozy, putting her hands on me, you know what I mean? I thought I was gonna get lucky, take her to a friend's cabin near there that I've got a key to. But all of a sudden she's screaming for me to pull over. I did, right quick—thought she was gonna puke."

"And?"

"Across the highway there's this rundown trailer park. Cop cars all over the place, and an ambulance was pulling out. Miri went nuts. Jumped out of my Jeep and ran across the highway without even looking. Lucky there wasn't anybody coming."

"Did you follow her?"

"Shit, no. I don't mess with cops if I can help it. I've already had two DUIs. And if what was going on was as bad as it looked, I sure didn't want to get involved. The wife—"

"So you just left Miri there."

"Damn right. I didn't owe her a thing. She was just this bitch I picked up in a bar." He took a vodka bottle from the shelf behind his desk, poured into the mug, and drank, flashing me a childishly defiant look. "How much would it cost me to keep you from telling the sheriff?"

"No sale, Mr. Martin. It doesn't work that way."

For some reason my cellular was out of range in Bridgeport, so I found a phone booth—one of the few of that endangered species—and called Drew Warnell, the sheriff's deputy I'd talked with last night at the crime scene. He confirmed that Miri Perez had run across the highway as the ambulance containing her daughter's body was pulling away.

"She went into a total meltdown when I told her what had happened. Assaulted me and another deputy." He sounded as if he were still shaken by the incident. "We had to restrain her, and now she's up here in the Bridgeport psych ward on a seventy-two-hour hold."

I took down the information about Miri, then called the Perez house. Sara answered and said Ramon had come home shortly after I'd left.

"The fool went all the way to Bridgeport and checked out some bars and a few off-hours places he knows about, but Miri hadn't been to any of them. Then he started back, but was too tired to drive all the way and fell asleep in Miri's van at a rest stop."

That was a relief. Now Ramon could deal with the mess I'd uncovered.

I said, "Well, he can stop worrying about Miri. I'm in Bridgeport, and the sheriff's department tells me she's in the psych ward up here." I explained what Drew Warnell had told me. "She wouldn't give them any information about next of kin, so they couldn't contact you."

Sara sighed deeply. "Maybe now she'll get the help she needs."

"Yes." But I doubted that, knowing how our broken health-care system works—especially for the poor.

"I'll let Ramon know," Sara said. "Thank you so much, Sharon."

"I'm happy to help."

But as I hung up, I realized the words were false. The day had cost me, a reminder of too many years of visiting sleazy bars and talking to sleazy characters. Now I had a long ride home, and nothing but an empty evening to look forward to.

* * *

The lights were out in the Perez house when I arrived at the ranch; probably they were up in Bridgeport dealing with Miri. Damn! Amy missing, Hayley murdered, Miri out of control—how could so much bad happen to good people like Ramon and Sara?

I glanced at the stable, wondering if Ramon had had time to feed Lear Jet. Probably not. I might as well do it.

The horse was in his stall. When he saw me he snorted and looked away.

I said, "Look, you damn creature, I'm here to do you a favor."

I went to the bin where Ramon kept the alfalfa, measured out the amount I'd seen him give the horse, and started back toward the stall.

Lear Jet moved restlessly, snorted.

I tensed and stopped. "Hey, there. Take it easy."

The horse reared and let out a high-pitched whinny. His hooves smacked the stall door, splintering its brittle old wood.

I dropped the food and backed toward the outer door.

What you need to do is show them that you're in control.

Ramon's words.

Move away slowly.

Something I'd read in an article about how to behave in an encounter with a mountain lion.

Get the hell out of here.

My philosophy.

Before I could turn tail, Lear Jet kicked free from the stall and charged at me.

I sidestepped, then scrambled backward toward the outer door. The horse came on. I feinted the other way, momentarily confusing him. As he passed I felt a sharp blow on the back of my head. My eyes lost focus. The last thing I remembered was grasping the wall and sliding down. . . .

"Sharon." Sara's voice, commanding. "Wake up."

"Unh." I could hear, but not see, her.

A sharp, unfamiliar scent in my nostrils. One of her native remedies? But why couldn't she let me sleep?

"Wake up." Insistent.

I opened my eyes. Her round face came into focus.

She held up her hand. "How many fingers do you see?"

Stupid question. "Two."

"Good. Do you know where you are?"

"Mmm." I felt the ground around me. Wooden floor with scattering of straw. Now I remembered. That damn horse! "Stables."

"Very good. Let's sit you up now."

She took hold of me under my armpits, eased me up till my back was against the wall.

"Ramon and I saw the horse running free. I thought I'd better check in here."

"What time is it?" I asked.

"Eight fifty-five."

I'd come out here at about 8:45. I couldn't've been out more than a few minutes.

"Let me look at your head."

It was already bowed forward. I felt her fingers probing, winced when they touched a tender spot.

"Not so bad," she said. "No cuts or abrasions, but you could have a mild concussion. I'll take you back to the house in a few minutes and stay with you tonight. If there are any complications, we'll go to the emergency clinic in the morning."

Hooves clopping. I jerked my head up, wrenching my neck. Ramon, leading Lear Jet into the stable.

"Get him away from me!" I said. "He tried to kill me."

Ramon frowned and looked at Sara. She shook her head.

He said, "The horse was spooked—"

"Damn right he was!"

"But not by you," Sara added.

"What d'you mean?"

"The bump on your head isn't anything he could have inflicted. I'd say someone else was here, possibly antagonizing him. When Lear Jet bolted, whoever it was hit you."

"But why . . . ?"

"I don't know," Ramon said.

I thought—fuzzily—of the people whom I'd come in contact with the whole day. Of others who might have felt they had reason to harm me. Of the rippling shadow at Willow Grove Lodge.

No. Not again. That part of my life was supposed to be over!

Thursday

✦

NOVEMBER 1

When I awoke, Sara was sitting in the rocking chair in the corner of Hy's and my bedroom, her hands manipulating knitting needles and red yarn. She looked up when I stirred.

"Good morning, Sharon. How're you feeling?"

I took inventory, touching my head. There was a fair-sized lump behind my right ear, but strangely it didn't hurt much. "Not bad."

"I put some ointment on your scalp last night. It must have helped."

Vaguely I remembered the earthy smell and oily feel of it. "It did. One of your concoctions?"

"Of course. Are you seeing all right?"

"Yes."

"No headache, or sickness in your stomach?"

"None."

"Then I prescribe twenty-four hours bed rest, and you'll be fit as ever." She finished a row of knitting and began putting the needles and yarn away in a brightly colored tote bag.

"Thank God you were there last night, Sara. When I didn't

see any lights at your place I thought you and Ramon had gone to Bridgeport. That's why I was trying to feed Lear Jet."

"We'd planned to go up there, but when we called the sheriff's department they said Miri couldn't have any visitors until this afternoon. And Ramon made the . . . arrangements for Hayley by phone, and then we went out for dinner at Zelda's. We thought we owed ourselves a nice meal—"

A knock at the bedroom door, and Ramon entered, eyes downcast as if he was afraid I might be scantily clad. No chance of that—Sara had enveloped me in a big terry cloth bathrobe of Hy's. She'd seemed somewhat scandalized that I didn't possess a proper nightgown.

"How are you?" he asked.

"Fine. Sara's given me a clean bill of health."

"Only if you stay in bed today," she said.

I raised my hands in a gesture of surrender.

Ramon said, "I've been thinking about what happened last night. I've been around horses all my life. I can feel what they're feeling. Lear's been testing you, but he would never attack—especially when you were bringing food to him. Somebody else had to be there. Somebody he *would* attack."

"Who?"

"One person comes to mind: Boz Sheppard. He did some work up here a while back, rebuilding part of the pasture fence. He deviled the horse, and when I told him to stop, I suspect he kept on doing it behind my back. Lear landed him a good kick on the shoulder the last day he worked here."

"But what would Sheppard be doing here last night? And why would he hit me?"

Didn't add up, any of it.

* * *

I kept my promise to stay in bed until noon. Then restlessness got the better of me. I got up, showered, and dressed. Had some toast and coffee. Sara's remedies had worked their magic, and I decided to do something nice for her and Ramon: I'd spend the afternoon making a casserole for them for when they returned, stressed and tired, from Bridgeport.

Trouble was, I have a limited repertoire of specialties that runs along the lines of garlic bread, spaghetti, stuffed sourdough loaves, and dressing for the holiday turkey. Hy cooks more than I do; we eat out frequently; I'm the expert on prepackaged foods and the microwave.

When I got back to the ranch house I located an old cookbook—*The Woman's Home Companion*—that I recognized as being one of my mother's bibles, my grandmother's before her. There were a couple of simple recipes for noodle casseroles that I decided to combine, but I didn't have the ingredients; I made a list and set out for town.

Day after Halloween: smashed pumpkins in the streets, trees draped with toilet paper; some windows soaped; candy wrappers on the sidewalk. Simple, old-fashioned mischief, the kind we haven't had in the city in some years. For safety reasons, trick-or-treating doesn't happen in most neighborhoods there, and pranks are usually on the vandalous side. Many times Halloween parties end in injuries and fatalities.

Of course, the day before Halloween here had been fatal for Hayley Perez. A reminder that no matter where you are, the world is a dangerous place.

The scarecrow in the Food Mart's parking lot had been dismembered: its head lay on top of the bales of hay, its clothes strewn around. Black spray paint on the white wall said THE DEVEL MADE ME DO IT! No one ever said graffiti artists can spell.

I went inside, made my selections, and took them to the same checker I'd spoken with last Tuesday night. While she was ringing the order up she asked, "Did you find Amy Perez?"

"No, I haven't."

"You hear about her sister, Hayley?"

"The woman who was murdered? Yes."

"I'm wondering: Amy didn't come in to work today, and nobody's seen her. Maybe she and that scumbag Boz Sheppard killed her sister and took off. Nobody's seen him, either."

"Why would they do such a thing?"

"Money. I hear Hayley had a big life-insurance policy."

"Oh, yeah? How much?"

"Not sure, but they say Amy was the beneficiary."

"Who says this?"

"Well, everybody." She swung out her arm to include the whole store, maybe the whole town.

Small-town gossip. One misleading remark, and everybody thinks it's gospel.

Still, I asked, "D'you know what company insured her?"

"There's only one broker in town—Bud Smith. He represents a lot of companies."

"But Hayley had been gone a long time; she must've taken out the policy somewhere else."

"She's been back long enough. Was staying with Boz Sheppard out in that trailer where she was killed. Didn't show her face in town much, though."

"Why not?"

The clerk shrugged. "Ashamed because she ran off and came back with nothing to show for it? Didn't want to run into her mother? I mean, who *does* want to run into Miri? You should ask Bud Smith."

Bud Smith was in his mid-forties and losing his blond hair; a short military-style cut couldn't disguise it. He was lean and wiry, dressed in a loud plaid polyester jacket that was decades out of date and a shirt and tie of the same era. Obviously a fan of vintage clothing. He was on the phone when I entered his office in a lakeside strip mall, but greeted me with a smile and waved me toward a chair.

The smile faded as he said into the phone, "No, stay there. Stay right there. I'll come as soon as I can."

For a moment after he hung up he stared down at the desk. Then he looked at me and said, "What can I do for you?"

When I said I was helping the Perez family deal with the details of Hayley's death, his face grew even more somber: he reminded me of an eccentrically attired funeral director.

"Such a tragedy," he said, "such a waste." His sorrowful expression looked genuine.

"We understand Hayley had taken out a life-insurance policy with you. And that the beneficiary was her younger sister, Amy."

"Uh, yes, she did." He began fiddling with a stack of papers on his desk, tapping them into a neat pile. "Are you putting in a claim? If so, Amy should be the one—"

"Amy's out of town and we haven't been able to reach her. Basically, all we want to know is if the policy exists and what its terms are."

"Hayley should have had the policy in her possession. She picked it up"—he flipped backward through his desk calendar—"on September twenty-sixth."

So she'd been in town for quite a while. Why, as the clerk at the Food Mart had said, hadn't she "shown her face"?

I said, "Perhaps she put it in a safe place. The trailer where she was staying wasn't very secure."

"Apparently not, since she was murdered there." Smith hesitated, running his hand over his clean-shaven chin. "I'm not sure I should be discussing the policy with you. Are you a relative?"

"A good friend. Ramon Perez is manager at my husband's and my ranch."

"Oh, you're Hy Ripinsky's new wife. I heard he got married again. Forgive me. I'll be glad to tell you anything you need to know."

I love to ask questions in small towns where I'm an insider. Hate it when I'm an outsider and they raise the bar against me.

Bud Smith went to a file cabinet and came back to his desk with a slim manila folder. "She came in on September seventh. Said her mother was unreliable—which is true—and that her other siblings, except for Amy, were either dead or in prison. She wanted to provide for Amy should something happen to her. We agreed on a fifty-thousand-dollar whole-life policy, which would accumulate a cash value that could be withdrawn at any time if Hayley, as owner of the policy, needed money."

"Why fifty thousand?"

"The premiums were affordable, and Hayley felt it was enough to give Amy a new start in life."

"She explain what she meant by that?"

"No. And I didn't ask. I don't pry into my clients' personal affairs."

"Did Hayley have to undergo a medical exam to get the coverage?"

"Not at twenty-five. She filled out the usual health disclosure form; that was enough."

"And what address did she give you?"

He consulted the file. "Her mother's, but she asked the policy not be sent there, which is why she picked it up."

"This type of policy—is there a double indemnity clause, in case of accidental death or murder?"

The right corner of Smith's mouth twitched. "Yes. Of course. Unless she was killed by the beneficiary . . . Not that Amy would've done such a thing. The girl's a little wayward, but not bad."

"How d'you know?"

"My avocation is volunteering as a life-skills coach. Helping kids who are at risk. My friend Dana Ivins, who runs the organization, had several sessions with her. She—Dana—thought Amy had great potential."

"This organization is called . . . ?"

"Friends Helping Friends. The name is designed to let troubled teens know we coaches don't consider ourselves superior, but just people who've undergone and overcome the same obstacles they're facing."

"Sounds like a good program."

Bud Smith's smile was a shade melancholy. "We try. That's all we can do—try."

Friends Helping Friends operated out of a dilapidated cottage on an unpaved side street at the west end of town, across the highway from the point where Zelda's was situated. A sign on the door said COME RIGHT IN, so I did. A short hallway opened in front of me. To my left was a parlor full of shabby but comfortable-looking furnishings; in the room to my right, a thin woman with short gray hair and round glasses that gave her face an owlish look sat at a desk. She saw me and smiled.

"What can I do for you?"

I introduced myself. "I'm interested in speaking with one of your coaches, Dana Ivins."

"You are in luck." She got up and extended her hand across the desk to me. "I'm Dana."

"Bud Smith told me you've been working with a girl named Amy Perez."

She frowned. "Sit down, please. I'm afraid Bud shouldn't have revealed that. Part of our success is that we keep our clients' names confidential."

"Would you explain to me how the organization works?"

"Well, the name describes it. We pair young people who are at risk with coaches who have had similar problems earlier in life. They can meet here in our parlor if the clients' homes aren't a supportive environment—which in most cases they're not—or if they aren't comfortable being seen with their coaches in public. Or they can pick another meeting place—so long as it isn't the coach's home; that's inviting trouble from parents who resent our intrusion. We listen to the clients' stories and tell them ours and what we've learned from them. It's strictly a volunteer program with very little overhead, and what there is is funded by donations from local businesses. This is my house, so we don't have to pay for offices."

"Are you licensed therapists?"

"No, just amateurs who've learned from our past mistakes."

So they couldn't legally claim therapist-client confidentiality.

"Ms. McCone," Dana Ivins said, "what is your interest in Amy Perez?"

I told her the same story I'd told Bud Smith, explaining my relationship to the Perez family.

"I see." She pushed away from her desk and swiveled slightly to her left, toward the front window that overlooked the street. "Are you sure Amy is missing?"

I wasn't. Right at this moment she could be with Ramon and Sara, but some instinct made me doubt that. I'd formed a tentative connection with the young woman the first time I looked into her eyes in the Food Mart parking lot, and it had been strengthened by the fear and defiance I saw in them after Boz Sheppard threw her out of his truck.

I said, "She didn't contact her family about Hayley or go to work today." Then I described my encounter with Amy alongside the highway.

Dana Ivins took off her glasses and chewed thoughtfully on one earpiece, still looking toward the window. "I knew your husband's first wife. Julie was a wonderful person; in spite of her health problems, she did a lot for the community. After she died, I was sure Hy was done for—the environmental protesting with a nasty edge, being thrown into one jail after another. Then, because of another special woman, he settled down. That, apparently, was you."

"Yes."

"Then I'm inclined to trust you. And I will tell you about Amy Perez."

Amy, Dana Ivins said, was highly intelligent but struggled with low self-esteem. "Her home life is chaotic—it's not easy being the daughter of the town slut. I know, because that's what my own mother was. Amy's response was the same as mine: she dropped out of school and set about creating the kind of life she thought she deserved, which included alcohol, drugs, and bad choices when it came to boyfriends. She was arrested once for underage drinking and put in an alcohol education program, which did no good whatsoever. There was another arrest for possession of marijuana, but the charges were dismissed because the quantity was so small and Amy claimed it must have been her mother's."

"Great family dynamics working there."

"I'm inclined to think she was telling the truth: the jacket she was wearing belonged to Miri. Anyway, the home situation became intolerable. Amy stopped living there, began moving from one boyfriend's place to another's. She had two abortions in as many years. The boyfriends invariably abused her and then threw her out. When she came to us, she was squatting in one of the cabins at Willow Grove Lodge."

"And how did she come to you?"

Dana Ivins smiled. "Very directly, if unintentionally. I went to my car one morning and found her passed out in the backseat. If there was ever a candidate for Friends Helping Friends, Amy was the prototype. I woke her and took her into the house. Got her cleaned up—she'd thrown up on herself—and loaned her a pair of my sweats. We talked."

"And then . . . ?"

"I found her a place to stay with a friend who rents out rooms. Talked the manager of Food Mart into taking her on part time as a shelf stocker. And she began to work on getting her GED. She stayed clean and sober and didn't see any of her old boyfriends. But then she started to backslide."

"When?"

"It's difficult to pinpoint, because it was subtle at first. A month ago? Maybe even six weeks. At first she'd miss scheduled appointments, but she always had a good excuse. Then she slacked off on her work for the GED. She kept working at Food Mart, but the manager told me her attitude wasn't good. And finally she moved out of her room at my friend's house without giving any notice."

"To go where?"

Ivins shook her head. "My friend didn't know. When I asked Amy, she said she'd moved home because her mother needed her. But she never would have done that; she hates Miri."

"People like Miri are good at emotional blackmail. Maybe—"

"No. Amy had come too far for that. I know; I've been there. Besides, I could tell she was lying. When she lies she gives it away by letting her eyes slide away from yours so they're looking at your left earlobe."

Everybody, except for the most accomplished sociopath, has some mannerism that gives him or her away in a lie. Not every lie, but if the stress level is high enough, it'll manifest itself. I've seen it thousands of times: eye movement, facial tics, changes in vocal pitch, tapping fingers, crossing and recrossing of legs—you name it. Once you pinpoint it, you have a better tool than a lie detector.

"When was the last time you saw Amy?" I asked.

"At least a week ago."

"And how did she seem?"

"I didn't really speak with her. She was stocking the bins in the produce area at Food Mart, and I was in the checkout line."

"This was someone you'd been counseling and had cause to be concerned about, and you—"

"One of the philosophies of our organization is that the clients must be motivated to come to *us*; otherwise the process doesn't work."

I wasn't so sure that was such a good approach, but then, I had no real background in their brand of therapy. Look at how miserably my own recent attempt had failed. "Okay, the time before that . . . ?"

"Weeks before. Amy came here, and we talked in the parlor. She was having trouble with one of her GED courses—algebra—and it was frustrating her. I'm no whiz at math myself, so I advised her to reread the materials and go slowly. I told her if she was still having trouble, I'd locate someone who could tutor her."

"And did you?"

"Yes. I referred her to Bud Smith. Anyone who can figure out insurance-rate tables should be able to explain algebra."

But Smith hadn't mentioned that to me when he spoke of Amy.

"Did she contact him?"

"I don't know. I never heard from her again."

Bud Smith's office was closed. A sign on the inside of the door said he wouldn't return till two. I considered my options, then headed for Zelda's for a burger and a beer, where the owner, Bob Zelda, and I caught up on our personal current events. Afterward I went back to Smith's office. The sign still said back at two, but he wasn't there.

The provisions I'd bought for the Perezes' casserole had been sitting in the Land Rover too long; I drove back to the ranch and cooked. The process of grating cheese, slicing ham and mushrooms, and blending a sauce soothed me. I put the casserole in the oven along with a smaller one for my own dinner, set the timer, and went to the living room to read. After a few pages I dozed off in the comfy oversized chair. It was almost time for the casserole to come out when the phone woke me.

Sara. "Sharon, how are you?"

"Doing splendidly, thanks to you. How's Miri?"

"Going through the d.t.'s. The seventy-two-hour hold is still on; they want to evaluate her and recommend treatment."

"Well, that's good, isn't it?"

"It's happened before, and nothing's worked." She paused. "Ramon wants to talk to you."

Ramon sounded weary. "You're all right?"

"Yes. Did you talk with the sheriff's deputy about Hayley while you were up there?"

"Yeah. There's somebody new in charge of the case—Kristen Lark."

"So she's still with the department. How come I didn't see her at the scene the other night?"

"You know her?"

"From a long time ago."

"Well, she was on vacation. Got handed the case this morning."

"If you like, I can contact her and try to find out more about the investigation."

"Sharon, you're up here for a vacation—"

"It's no problem. I just fell asleep reading. I think I'm getting bored."

"Well, then . . ."

"Ramon, have you heard from Amy?"

"Uh-uh. Don't know where she's gone off to and, frankly,

I'm worried. Her sister's murder has been all over the news; she should've called us by now."

"Did Lark ask you about her?"

"No. Why?"

"She probably will." I explained about the life-insurance policy.

Ramon groaned. "Little Amy. She couldn't've—"

"No, I don't think so. But I'm worried about her, too." To change the subject, I told him about the casserole I'd made and said I'd bring it over.

"Sharon, thank you. Sara's in the kitchen trying to defrost some chicken in the microwave, but it's not going so good. But don't bother to bring the casserole over; I'll come get it when I feed Lear Jet."

"No, let me feed him and then bring the food over." As soon as the words were out of my mouth, I regretted them.

"You sure you want to?"

I couldn't back down now. "Yes."

"Okay. But take him a couple of pieces of carrot if you have any. Treats are the best way to make friends with a horse."

The horse was in his stall, looking dejected. I approached cautiously, and he whickered. When I offered the first piece of carrot, he looked at it for a moment, then reached forward and gently took it from my fingers. I waited, then offered one more. Again he was gentle.

"I'll feed you in a minute," I told him. "I suppose I should clean your stall, but I'd better leave that to Ramon. Tell the truth, I'm afraid of you."

The horse regarded me solemnly.

"Who spooked you?"

Lear shifted his feet, thrust his head forward. And then he

nuzzled my hand. After a moment's hesitation, I stroked his nose. He nuzzled some more. Probably hungry, I thought.

I fed him and left to deliver the casserole to Ramon and Sara.

This dozing off is dreadful.

It was the first thought that came to me when I woke an hour after I'd eaten and sat down to read the book I'd been trying to get through for over a week. I'd dreamed. . . .

Not of the pit or Amy this time—something else, a line of poetry over and over again. It still reverberated in my mind. . . .

I tossed the paperback on the floor. To hell with the former alcoholic and his non-midlife crisis!

In the kitchen I grabbed the keys to the Land Rover from the counter, took down the shearling jacket from its peg in the mudroom. Then, heeding an instinct I'd many times before recognized to be sound, I went to the bedroom, where we kept a .45 automatic—Hy's weapon of choice—in a locked cabinet. Checked its clip. Put it in the jacket's deep pocket, and set out for Willow Grove Lodge.

Home is the place where . . .

The line from Robert Frost's "Death of a Hired Man" was what had echoed in my dream and now filled my mind as I drove.

Amy hadn't had a real home in years—maybe ever—but Willow Grove Lodge, where Dana Ivins had said she'd been squatting in one of the cabins, was the place she'd be most likely to return to after giving up her rented room. And it was only a short way up the highway from where Boz Sheppard had pushed her out of his truck.

I pulled into the driveway there, coasted down the slope, and cut off the headlights as I tucked the Land Rover out of sight behind the main building. Dark and silent there, no lights showing in any of the cabins, not even exterior security spots. I leaned over to take a powerful flashlight from the pocket behind the seat.

The outside air was chill. The moon had waned, but when I looked up I saw a thick cluster of stars that were part of the Milky Way. The wind rustled the leaves of the cottonwoods and willows. I began walking upslope to the lodge's entrance.

It was solidly padlocked, the windows secured by shutters. I walked around the main building, shining my light, then went to the first of the cabins, the one where I'd stayed years ago. Also padlocked and shuttered. Silver phosphorescent letters were sprayed on the wall next to the door: APRIL & KEITH 4 EVER.

I wished the couple luck, whoever they were.

I shone my light around, picking out the shapes of the other cabins. If I were going to squat here, I'd choose one far from the road, but not too near the lake, where passing boaters might spot evidence of my presence. A tiny one-room cabin surrounded by trees stood right over there, not thirty yards away. There was no outward sign of habitation, but that didn't mean anything. Amy would hardly make a fire in the woodstove or open the shutters if she didn't want to be detected.

Slowly I moved toward the cabin, flashlight in my left hand, right hand on the .45. I doubted Amy would be any threat to me, but if someone, say Boz Sheppard, was with her—

Screech!

I started, heard the flapping of wings. An owl speeding away with its prey.

Laughing softly at my edginess, thinking of how such a sound wouldn't begin to penetrate my consciousness in the city, I went ahead toward the cabin.

The shutters were secure, and there was a hasp and padlock on the door, but when I touched the lock, it swiveled open. I removed it quietly, slid back the hasp, eased open the door—

A dark figure rushed at me. I tried to dodge, but the person came on too fast, hunched over, head slamming into my chest so hard that I expelled my breath with a grunt and reeled backward. My feet skidded on the layer of slippery fallen leaves. And down I went on my ass.

Stunned, I took a few seconds to realize that my assailant had run off, was thrashing around in the dark grove. I pushed up, and—holding the gun in both hands—ran toward the source of the sounds. My breath tore at my lungs and sharp pains spread out from my tailbone.

Suddenly the sounds stopped.

I stopped, too, looking around. Nothing moved. The only thing I could hear was my own panting.

Whoever it is, they're hiding. That's all right; I can wait them out.

I crept over to a thick tree trunk, leaned against it, getting my breathing under control. My lower back throbbed, and so did my head. What if I really had sustained a concussion last night, and my heavy fall to the ground had made it worse?

It was frigid under the trees: I could see my breath. Staying still was an invitation to frostbite. After a few minutes I moved in the direction where I'd last heard the thrashing sounds, placing my feet carefully, as silently as possible. I'd dropped my flashlight back at the cabin, but that didn't matter; using it would have given away my position.

The woods are lovely, dark and deep. . . .

Frost again. But these woods weren't lovely. They were silent, full of potential hazards.

The hell with it.

I retraced my steps to the cabin, where I located the flash and shone it through the open door.

What I saw made me raise the .45.

More wreckage like that at Boz Sheppard's trailer: overturned furniture, broken glass, linens pulled from the bed, pillows and mattress slashed, drawers in the tiny galley kitchen emptied. A door to the bathroom stood partway open.

I slipped inside and across the room. In the bath I found more broken glass and a torn shower curtain, its pole slanting down into the tub. The lid of the toilet had been removed and smashed on the floor. Otherwise the cubicle was as empty as the main room.

No one here, dead or alive.

I tried the light switch beside the bathroom door. No power, of course. My flash's beam was strong, but it wouldn't allow me to examine the place thoroughly. Besides, that was a matter for the sheriff's department.

I moved back into the other room. Stepped on something soft. When I looked closely I saw it was the quilted jacket Amy had been wearing the day Sheppard had thrown her out of the truck. My light illuminated other objects that had been strewn around: T-shirts, costume jewelry, makeup, jeans, underwear, other teenage-girl attire.

And on the wall above them, a blood spatter.

* * *

I leaned against the Land Rover, bundled in the shearling coat, watching Lark's team examining what she'd termed a "possible crime scene." For a remote county that was probably operating on an insufficient salary budget, the deputies seemed well coordinated and knowledgeable. I'd seen less thorough initial investigations in the city. Not that that was any surprise: the SFPD has been through up-and-down cycles as long as I've lived there.

Lark finally approached me—a slender woman in her mid-thirties with blonde curls, worn long now, and freckles on her upturned nose. We'd spoken only briefly when she arrived and entered the cabin, not at all since her backup showed minutes later.

Now she said, "McCone, this scene looks bad. The place was tossed, there's blood in the main room, the girl's gone, and you say she's Hayley Perez's sister. How come you came here?"

"Someone told me—"

A man called out to Lark, and she held up a finger. "My forensics guy wants me. When I'm done with him, I'm going off duty. Let's meet at Zelda's, knock back a couple, and you can tell me what I need to know."

The cavernous interior of Zelda's was strangely quiet for a Thursday night. A couple of late diners lingered over coffee in the room to the left, and only a few drinkers gathered at the bar. Bob Zelda was absent—he'd told me he'd turned over the weekday-evening shifts to his son Jamie; Bob worked the weekends because he liked to listen to the country-music bands he employed.

I took one of the tables by the lakeside windows in the bar area and waited for Kristen Lark to arrive. After ten minutes

I went to the bar and got a glass of white wine. Sipping it, I realized why I usually ordered beer at Zelda's. Five minutes later Lark came through the door.

She pointed questioningly to my half-full glass. I shook my head, and she went to the bar; a minute later she was seated across from me with her own drink—a double bourbon.

"So, McCone, I hear you married Ripinsky."

"I did."

"I'm married, too." She held out her left hand; a wide gold wedding ring circled her third finger.

"Who's the lucky guy?"

"Fellow officer—Denny Rabbitt."

"You look good," I said. "Marriage agrees with you."

"Marriage to another deputy, yes. Anybody else couldn't've put up with the crazy schedule. Fly up here with you?"

"No. I'm taking some time off, but he's busy with a corporate reorganization."

She nodded, clearly having asked only for politeness' sake, placed a tape recorder on the table, and asked, "So what were you doing at the lodge tonight?"

I outlined everything that had happened since I spotted Amy Perez outside the Food Mart, while Lark taped the conversation. "I didn't mean to get involved in a police matter," I finished. "It just occurred to me that Amy might be squatting at Willow Grove, and I thought I might be able to persuade her to go to her aunt and uncle's."

Lark shrugged. "Seems we're having a regular crime wave this week. You want to help me on an official basis? You did before, remember."

I solved your case for you and nearly lost my life in the process, you ingrate.

Lark waited for my answer.

I didn't want to help out. I didn't even want to be here talking with an officer of the law. But maybe I could find out some inside information about Hayley's murder that I could pass on to Ramon and Sara.

"Okay, but I told you everything I know; it's got to be a two-way street."

"Deal."

Lark turned off the tape, got up and went to the bar for another drink. When her back was turned I switched on the sensitive voice-activated recorder in my purse. The deputy hadn't asked if I minded being taped, and I wasn't going to ask her, either. She was fair, and a good law officer, but I was aware that our arrangement could backfire if I didn't have documentation.

"Okay," she said as she sat down again. "We didn't have the info on the sister having taken out the life-insurance policy. Hadn't really looked at Amy yet because we were concentrating on the Boz Sheppard angle. So far we haven't located him."

"You have any background on Hayley?"

Lark smiled. "Now *that* is where it really gets interesting."

Friday

✦

NOVEMBER 2

On my drive back to the ranch, I didn't dwell on the facts that Lark had confided to me. She'd insisted on buying another round before we'd left Zelda's at twelve-thirty, and even though I'd left most of my wine in the glass and was under the legal limit, I needed to pay close attention to my driving. High-desert people are generally hard-living folks, but it seemed to me that Lark, a law-enforcement officer and supposedly happy woman, had been pushing the envelope with her three double shots of bourbon.

The country around Tufa Lake is largely devoid of traffic at that time of night, and no wildlife sprang into my headlights, so I arrived home unscathed. There was a message on the machine from Hy: "Just wanted to let you know my ETA tomorrow—four p.m. See you then." Pause. "Does your absence indicate you've been 'sucked in' by the Perez murder?"

Damn! He knew me all too well.

But sucked in I was—and with official sanction. I curled up in the armchair in the living room and listened to the tape I'd made of Kristen Lark's confidences.

Haley and Rich Three Wings ran off nine years ago, ended up in Reno. He dealt blackjack at Harrah's, she worked someplace as a waitress, but pretty quick she started turning tricks on the side. . . .

Around three years after they got to Reno, this high roller came to the casino. Hayley was waitressing there by then, and next thing she ran off with the guy, leaving Rich with only his old car and the clothes on his back. . . .

No, we haven't found out who the high roller was. Rich claims he doesn't know. We've got an inquiry in to the casino, though. . . .

That's another thing we don't know—where she was during the period between when she left Reno and three years ago when she turned up in Vegas. Living off the high roller, no doubt, but it didn't last. . . .

In Vegas, she worked cocktails in a casino—the Lucky Sevens. Kind of downscale and dingy, LVPD says. So she went out on the streets again, got busted a few times, but always brought in a high-powered attorney who got the charges dropped. . . .

How could she afford the lawyer? Damned if we know. . . .

Name's Brower. Frank Brower. With a big firm that's rumored to be connected—Brower, Price and Coleman. Of course, everybody in Vegas is rumored to be connected. . . .

No, we haven't been able to get hold of him. He's on a cruise, or some damn thing. . . .

Yeah, we checked out the address on Hayley's driver's license. A mail drop. We've got no idea where she was living in Vegas. . . .

Apparently nobody here knew she was back in town, except for that insurance agent you told me about. And Boz Sheppard. And maybe Amy. We've questioned everybody, including Rich Three Wings and her high-school boyfriend, Tom Mathers. . . .

Here's something: you might take another crack at Three Wings. I mean, he might open up more to you. . . .

I turned off the recorder. When, I wondered, would people stop assuming that because you're Indian, other Indians will feel a natural connection with you? There are hundreds of tribes in this country; historically some have been mortal enemies, and today they're squabbling over gaming rights. It's like saying any American ethnic group—be it blacks, Chinese, Italians, Irish, Japanese, or Germans—is drawn together because of its background. Ridiculous. The Scotch-Irish family who adopted me at birth frequently fought like they were out to kill each other. Still do, sometimes.

But what the hell, in the morning I'd take a crack at Rich Three Wings. Tom Mathers, too.

It was the least I could do for the sake of the Perez family, I told myself.

Well, yes, for their sake, but also for my own. Cases change both the investigated and the investigator. Maybe one last effort would show me the way to the new life I was reaching for. It wouldn't be any worse than dreaming of trying to climb out of a deep, dark pit.

Elk Lake was a small, placid body of water surrounded by forest, some twenty miles southwest of Vernon. Dirt roads led into clearings where rustic cabins stood. Many of them had cutesy names: Gone Fishin', Bide a Wee Longer, My Lady and the Lake. Rich Three Wings' had no such sign and was one of the shabbier: warped shingles, sagging roofbeam, rusted stovepipe. A large prefab garage sat next to it, and an old International Harvester truck was pulled close to its side. From the rear I could hear the sound of someone chopping wood.

I rounded the cabin, and a spectacular view of the lake

opened up: close to shore waterfowl swam and dove for food, far out two fishermen floated in their rowboat, the opposite shore was rimmed by tall pines. The scene was so peaceful that it stood out in sharp contrast to the man wielding the axe.

Wide-shouldered and narrow-waisted, he was without a shirt on this chilly day, and the muscles in his back were strong and sculpted. He attacked the log as if it were an enemy, with hard, rhythmic strokes and frequent animal-like grunts. He didn't hear me approach until I was halfway to him, and then he whirled, axe upheld. I stopped, braced to run.

"Rich Three Wings?" I asked.

"Yeah. Who're you?" His face was beaded with sweat, his long black hair trapped in a damp red bandana.

I introduced myself, taking out one of my business cards. He lowered the axe and leaned it against a larger log. At that I covered the rest of the distance between us and handed the card to him.

"I'm working in cooperation with the sheriff's department on the Hayley Perez case," I added.

He looked at the card, then crushed it in his large fist. His face twitched, as if he felt a sudden pain.

He asked, "They send you on account of you're Indian too?"

"That was the general idea."

"And you don't like it."

"I hate it. And so do you."

He studied me for a moment, then nodded, having made a judgment. "Come inside, we'll drink some coffee." When I hesitated, he added, "I'm harmless. I didn't kill Hayley and I'm sure as hell not gonna do anything to you."

No, he wasn't. That much I sensed. As to whether he'd killed his ex-wife I couldn't hazard a guess yet.

I followed him to the cabin and into a spotlessly neat room with beautifully hewn wooden furnishings and woven rugs like the ones we had at the ranch. Rich Three Wings noticed my surprise and said, "Appearances can be deceiving, huh?"

"I'll say. This is beautiful."

"Thanks. Have a seat." He motioned at a small table that gleamed with polish and shrugged into a sweatshirt that was draped on a chair. "How do you like your coffee?"

"Black."

"Me too." He went through a doorway, returned with two pottery mugs. "This place, I inherited it from my grandfather, who was a real traditional guy. Material possessions didn't mean a thing to him."

"Sounds like my . . . father." I still couldn't call Elwood Farmer my father without hesitation. "He's an artist and lives very simply on the Flathead rez in Montana."

"You born there?"

"No. It's complicated. This furniture . . ." I motioned around us.

"I made it. I've got a shop in the garage. And the rugs—my girlfriend weaves them. Between the two of us we do pretty well, sell on the Internet and a few shops down in Sacramento and the city."

"It's lovely."

"But that's not what you came here to talk about. Your card says investigative services, and the county sent you."

"I'm a friend of the Perez family, but the deputy in charge of the case said it was okay to talk with you."

"How're you their friend? I haven't seen you around."

I explained my relationship with Ramon and Sara.

"Ripinsky's wife. I'll be damned. He was my hero, back when I was in high school. Real rabble-rouser, but the good kind. If it hadn't been for him, Tufa Lake'd be nothing but mud and crumbling towers by now." He paused. "So what d'you want to know about Hayley?"

"Why don't you give me a chronology of your relationship with her."

"Okay. She was in high school. Dating this asshole, Tom Mathers. I'd come back from a stint in the army; I'm six years older than her. I'd seen her around while I was growing up, but didn't pay her much notice. Then we met at a party. Mathers passed out in the bathroom, so I took her home. She told me how much she hated it here, one thing led to another, and a few weeks later we were on the road to Reno to get married."

"Did you?"

"Yeah. Crappy little wedding chapel, plastic flowers, JP and his wife were both weird. That kind of start, it's natural the wedding vows didn't take. Plus we didn't have much money and fought about it all the time. Three years later she split and I decided to come home. I couldn't take the crap I had to deal with at the casino and this place was waiting for me."

"Kristen Lark told me Hayley was hooking."

"Yeah, she was. I should've realized it, but I didn't—not till it was too late."

"I understand she took off with a high roller, but you don't know his name."

"I just told Lark that to keep the guy from getting in trouble. I mean, he couldn't've cared enough about Hayley to follow her here and kill her. His name was Jack Buckle. From someplace in the Pacific Northwest. I should've guessed what was going on with them, but I never thought . . . well, Hayley was not in this guy's class at all."

"How so?"

"He was rich, smart, and seemed educated. Hayley was just a small-town slut. I know that now, but at the time I was blind in love with her. But a lot of these rich guys, they either don't care or don't look farther than the end of their dicks."

"Did you hear from her again?"

"Only through the divorce papers six months later. By then I'd come back here, started woodworking. After that I never gave a thought to Hayley." He paused. "Well, that's not true. I thought about her some, sure. I hated her for what she did to me, but when I met Cammie—my weaver girlfriend—and things started working out with us, I cooled down."

"You didn't look so cooled down when I got here earlier."

He clasped his hands around the coffee mug, looked into its depths. "Yeah, well, when somebody you once loved is murdered—no matter how much bad they did to you—you get angry. I take my anger out on logs, not people."

"And you didn't know Hayley was back in Vernon?"

"No way. I'm pretty isolated out here. I make a point of going to town only when I need to. Maybe Cammie knew; she lives in Vernon, spends the weekends here, working on her loom in the shop. But if she did, she didn't tell me."

"I'd like to talk to Cammie."

"I'm sure she won't mind. She works part time at the flower shop in town. In fact, she should be there this morning."

There was only one flower shop in Vernon—Petals, on the main street two doors down from Hobo's. When I walked in I breathed deeply of the fresh and fragrant scents; although a bell rang as I passed through the door, no one appeared, so I studied the simple arrangements in the cold case. Roses, carnations, the usual types. Not much variety, but they probably had little call for anything out of the ordinary.

As I was examining a shelf of houseplants, a woman came through a curtained doorway. She was around thirty, blonde, wearing red-rimmed glasses and a sweater to match. Dimples flashed when she smiled.

"Help you?"

"Are you Cammie?"

"That's right. Cammie Charles. And you are?"

I gave my name, handed her my card, and said, "I just had coffee with Rich Three Wings. He said you might be able to help me out."

"Sure. What d'you need?"

"Information. I'm cooperating with the sheriff's department on the Hayley Perez case."

A shadow crept into her gray eyes. "Poor woman. Rich was really upset when he heard she'd been murdered. I mean, they'd had some bad times, but she was his first love."

"He didn't know she was in town. Did you?"

Her gaze slid away from mine, down to an open book of FTD offerings. "Yeah, I did. Bud Smith mentioned it to me when we ran into each other on the street. I figured it was best not to tell Richie."

"Why?"

"Selfishness, mainly. I didn't want him to see her and maybe get involved again. She was so pretty. . . ."

"You knew her, then?"

"No. I'm not from around here. I came up from the Bay Area for a vacation, met Richie, and never left. But Hayley came into the shop a couple of weeks ago—the day after Bud was here—to order a funeral arrangement to be sent FTD. I recognized her name from her credit card. She's not as pretty as the picture of her I found in a box at Richie's place, but still . . ."

"You have a record of that sale?"

"Somewhere. Is it important?"

"Might be."

"Okay." She rummaged in a drawer under the counter for an order book and paged through it. "Here it is—Jack Buckle, address in Olympia, Washington."

Jack Buckle sounded very much alive when I called the phone number from the flower shop's order form. Amused, too.

"Hayley's idea of a joke," he told me. "She's sent me a funeral arrangement each year on the anniversary of the death of our relationship. I pass them on to the local cemetery."

"So you broke up on October . . . ?"

"October nineteenth, three years and some months after she came up here with me."

"And you've received an arrangement every year since?"

"The first arrived five days after the split. But why does your flower shop need that kind of information?"

I hadn't told him I was a flower shop employee, had just given him my name. Now I explained myself.

"Hayley's *dead*? *Murdered*?" He sounded genuinely shocked.

"Yes, Mr. Buckle. I'm sorry."

". . . Poor kid. She was a whore, and greedy like they all are, but she didn't deserve that."

"Tell me more about her."

"Let's see. . . . I was in Reno for an annual high-stakes poker game at a friend's home. Hayley was serving catered food from the casino to us. Pretty little thing, and afterwards

I asked her to come back to my hotel with me. In the course of things she told me that she was with this guy who abused her, that she hated Reno and wanted to get out. So I said, why didn't she come along home with me? When I took her to their apartment she packed her stuff in fifteen minutes. I brought her back here to Olympia and we had fun till the fun ended."

"And why did it end?"

"Like I said, whores are greedy. She behaved for a couple of years, acted like a lady even, but I caught her sneaking cash from my wallet. As if I wasn't footing the bill for everything and also generous with an allowance. Finally, my maid told me Hayley'd been going through my home office, probably looking for the combination to the safe, and practicing signing my signature so she could forge checks."

"So you threw her out."

"No, ma'am. I politely told her to leave and asked her where she wanted to go. To tell the truth, I felt sorry for the kid; she'd had a miserable upbringing. I didn't want to throw her onto the streets with nothing. She said she guessed she'd go to Vegas. So I bought her a plane ticket and gave her a little money to tide her over till she found a job—or another man. She must've done all right on one front or the other, because this year's funeral arrangement was an expensive one."

"Do you know an attorney in Vegas, Frank Brower, of Brower, Price and Coleman?"

"I've heard of him, but I've never made his acquaintance."

"He got Hayley off on a few charges of prostitution."

"Hard to imagine how she could afford that firm. They're corporate lawyers for some of the bigger casinos."

"One other question, Mr. Buckle, and then I won't take up more of your time: what is it you do for a living?"

"I'm chief counsel for the Northwest Council of God."

"The . . . ?"

"Northwest Council of God."

". . . Oh."

He laughed. "I said chief counsel, Ms. McCone. I'm not a member, and I don't abide by their beliefs, nor do they expect me to. They simply want good legal representation and they pay me a significant retainer."

"I see." The pragmatic approach to faith, or lack thereof. "The Mono County Sheriff's Department will be in touch with you shortly."

"I'll cooperate in any way I can."

Immediately after I ended my call to Jack Buckle, my phone rang. Lark.

"We've designated the cabin at Willow Grove as a possible homicide scene," she said. "We're asking local pilots to help us out with an air search for a body tomorrow. Would you be willing to join in?"

I wanted to tell her she'd do better with cadaver dogs. It was unlikely a killer would have placed Amy's body out in the open where anyone could see it, and to a pilot flying at legal altitude over that thickly wooded terrain, a concealed corpse would be damned near impossible to spot.

But to keep on her good side I said, "Sure. Hy's coming up this afternoon: we'll both join in. One more thing: this Tom Mathers—I'd like to talk with him."

"No problem. He's at Tom's Wilderness Supplies and Vacations, about five miles out on the Rattlesnake Ranch Cutoff."

* * *

The terrain off Rattlesnake Ranch Cutoff was barren, like Mineral County over in Nevada. A few volcanically created formations stood out in the distance, but otherwise the land was flat and covered by coarse grass and sagebrush. Tom's Wilderness Supplies and Vacations, an orange-and-purple-trimmed stucco building with racks of rowboats and canoes at the back of the parking lot, was a bright, if gaudy, spot in the surrounding bleakness. A pair of dune buggies were pulled close to the building on the other side from the parking lot.

The building's interior was fairly large and crammed with all sorts of outdoors gear: backpacks, tents, stoves and lanterns, life jackets, fishing equipment, heavy-duty clothing—if you needed it, it was there. Tom Mathers was also a weapons dealer: guns gleamed in locked cases, in others knives glittered evilly under the fluorescent lights.

Guns I know, understand, and respect for their lethal potential. Knives scare the hell out of me.

The man behind the counter was in his mid-to-late twenties: sandy-haired, sun-freckled and -tanned, with wide shoulders and biceps that bulged beneath his T-shirt. A bodybuilder, I guessed, as well as an outdoorsman. A cheerful one, too: he smiled as if his best friend had just walked in.

"What can I do you for?"

"Are you Tom Mathers?"

"The one and only."

I went through my friend-of-the-Perez-family, cooperating-with-the-sheriff's-department routine. Mathers' smile faded and he shook his head.

"Hayley. What a shame."

"Do you have any idea who might have killed her?"

Something moved deep in his eyes. He looked down at

the knives in the case between us. "No idea at all. Everybody loved Hayley."

Bad body language; I didn't believe him. "Tell me about you and her."

"We went together all through high school. She never even looked at another guy. I thought we'd get married, have kids. Then this older guy shows up at a party, and a week later she's gone."

"I understand she left the party with him because you were passed out in the bathroom."

He shrugged. "That was no reason to run off with him. We partied pretty hard in those days. But she knew I would've straightened up. I mean, I've got a great business here, I'm married, own a house on the property." He jerked his thumb, indicating the house was behind the building. "No complaints from the wife, either—"

"A wife who was second choice and you're never going to let me forget it," a voice said from behind me.

I turned. A woman with long reddish-blonde hair had come inside. She was trim and well muscled, wearing only a short-sleeved T-shirt and running shorts. Not pretty, as Hayley Perez had been, but strong-featured. Her mouth was bracketed with lines of disappointment—and she must have been all of twenty-five.

No complaints from the wife. Right.

"T.C.," her husband said, "this is a private conversation."

"Not if you're talking about me." She came over and extended her hand to me. "T.C. Mathers."

"Sharon McCone."

Tom Mathers said, "Ms. McCone's cooperating with the sheriff on Hayley Perez's murder."

T.C. rolled her eyes. "The sainted Hayley Perez. What I wonder is why somebody didn't shoot her years ago."

Tom's face reddened. "Theresa!"

She winked at me. "When he gets mad, he always calls me by my given name. Knows I hate it. When he's really mad, he calls me Theresa Christina. Gets to me because it reminds me of my goddamn reactionary Christian parents who saddled me with it."

I was not at all pleased that I'd walked into this situation. I looked at my watch. Nearing two-thirty, I hadn't had a bite to eat all day, and Hy's ETA was four.

I said, "I'd like to talk with both of you again, but there's someplace I have to be soon. May I call you here or at home?"

"We're in the book. Call or drop in. Just keep following the driveway to the house." Tom Mathers was trying to regain his former composure, but his stance radiated fury at his wife.

"I'll be in touch," I said, and walked away from their domestic conflict.

In town I bought a sandwich and a Coke before I made the drive to Tufa Tower Airport at the northwest end of the lake. It wasn't much: a single runway, a dozen or so planes in tie-downs, a hangar that hadn't housed a resident mechanic in years, and a shack where the manager—a garrulous septuagenarian named Amos Hinsdale—monitored the UNICOM and hoped that some fool would come in and rent one of his two dreadful planes. Normally I tolerated Amos, but today I wasn't in the mood for one of his monologues about the good old days when flying took a real *man's* skill. Forget Amelia Earhart; forget the Powder Puff Derby participants and the women who ferried planes for the military during World War II. Forget the fact that many women, including myself, frequently flew into Tufa Tower. In Amos' mind, aviation was a man's world—although he also thought that the current crop of male pilots, who used up-to-date computerized equipment, were "a bunch of sissies."

I parked behind the hangar where I couldn't be seen from the shack and ate my late lunch. Thought about the case—my absolute last one—and where it was going, where it might lead me. I came to no conclusions about either.

After half an hour I began watching the hills to the north. Hy's and my beautiful red-and-blue Cessna 170B appeared above them; soon I heard the drone of its engine. The wings dipped from side to side, then he executed a barrel roll—showing off, knowing I was waiting for him. Afterward he angled into the pattern, took the downwind leg, and turned for final. I was at our designated tie-down when he taxied over.

He shut down the engine and got out. As always, I felt a rush of pleasure.

This man is my husband; we'll be together the rest of our lives.

Silly thought, because we'd already spent years together before we impulsively flew to Nevada and were married by a judge in Carson City. But those years hadn't been easy. Neither had the past one. I'd had many moments of doubt, and a recent serious crisis that I wasn't sure the union could survive. But through it all, he'd been steady and true and honest. No more doubts. Not now, not ever.

I ran over, threw my arms around him. Kissed him and held on tight. When I stepped back he smiled, even white teeth showing under his swooping mustache. He wasn't classically handsome, with a hawk-like nose and strong, rough-hewn features. His unruly dark-blond hair was now laced with gray. But his loose stride and long, lean body drew the attention of women as he walked through a room. And he possessed one of the finest asses I'd ever seen.

He raised an eyebrow at me and said, "Jesus, McCone, you must've missed me."

"Let's tie down this plane and I'll take you home and show you how much."

"Now, that'll be pure heaven."

That night I did not dream of being trapped in a pit.

Saturday

✦

NOVEMBER 3

Numerous official choppers and private planes from surrounding counties were available for the air search. Hy and I flew together in our Cessna. The morning was crisp and clear, and we'd bundled up in down jackets, jeans, and fleece-lined boots. Hy had brewed an extra pot of coffee, and we took it along in a thermos. I piloted, since he'd had that pleasure on the trip up here.

It had been a while since I'd flown, and on liftoff I'd felt a tremendous rush. It made me realize how important not being earthbound was to me. My depression—these days always a background to whatever I was doing—slipped away, and I settled happily into what felt like a cocoon that only Hy and I could inhabit.

"You realize," I said through our linked headsets as we lifted off, "that this is an exercise in futility."

"Yeah, but you can't tell that to the sheriff's department. And it makes people feel like they're doing something to help. Besides, maybe somebody in one of the choppers'll spot something." Helicopters are authorized by the FAA to fly at lower altitudes than fixed-wing aircraft, and thus are better for searches.

Hy removed a pair of binoculars from their leather case, and I set course toward the area we'd been assigned to search—a barren plain southeast of Rattlesnake Ranch, some ten miles from where Tom Mathers had his wilderness-guide business. The thousand-plus acres, Hy had told me, used to be a working cattle ranch, but had been sold off a decade or more before to a family from the East Coast, who tore down the existing buildings and put up a luxurious vacation home.

As we flew over the ranch, I saw a sprawling house—had to be a minimum of twenty thousand square feet—with a tile roof, various outbuildings, an airstrip, a tennis court, and a swimming pool.

"Who the hell *are* those people?" I asked.

"Don't know their name or much about them. The property sale was handled by a law firm, and the local real-estate agent who represented the sellers is mum on the subject. They fly in on a private jet, don't come to town at all, hire local staff who're sworn to secrecy about what goes on there. It's rumored that they're anything from exiled royalty to Mafia. I say they're just rich people who value their privacy."

"*Very* rich people."

"Well, sure." Hy was scanning the place with the binoculars. "Nobody in residence today—too chilly for them. They're probably off at a similar retreat on St. Bart's or Tahiti this time of year."

"By the way, that trip to Tahiti my travel agent wants to book us—"

"Will happen as soon as I get RI up and running properly. And after you decide what to do about your future."

We'd talked late into the last night about both subjects. Hy was committed to seeing Ripinsky International through the reorganization and then remaining at the helm. I'd told him I still didn't know what to do about my life or McCone Investigations. Maybe wouldn't know for quite some time. He'd reassured me: as long as the agency was running properly in my absence I had no problem.

"You know," he said after a moment of scanning the land beyond Rattlesnake Ranch, "a killer would have to be an idiot to abandon a body out here in the open."

"Exactly what I've been thinking." I switched the radio to the frequency designated for the search. Negative reports on all fronts.

I let the plane glide to a lower altitude, following a southeasterly course, to an area where snow-like volcanic ash covered the ground, peppered with small obsidian outcroppings and Jeffrey pines. Ash and glass, relics of an ancient conflagration; stubborn pines, reminders of nature's life force. Hy and I had often flown over here—

"Take it lower," he suddenly said.

I pulled back on the throttle, raised the nose to slow the plane. "You see something?"

"I'm not sure. Bank left."

I dipped the wing to a medium angle.

"Over there." He gestured, handed me the binoculars.

I peered through them, made out a brownish mass. "Dead pine. Or maybe a large animal."

"Pines and animals aren't shaped like that. Besides, look over there, behind that outcropping. It's a white truck."

I studied the terrain some more. "Right."

"Can you put down someplace nearby?"

"Not too far from the truck, yes. It'll be a rough landing, but—"

"We've made them before."

It *was* a rough landing, the wheels bumping over rocks and uneven ground—the kind that makes your heart race and your adrenaline surge, knowing that you've got whatever it takes to be a good pilot. As I braked to a stop, I thought, So aviation's a man's world, Amos? Hah!

We got our bearings and started off, boots crunching on the ashy, pebbled ground. The watery fall sunlight bore down, but the day hadn't warmed much; I wished I'd brought along some gloves. We topped a slight rise, where Hy raised the binoculars and looked around. "Over that way."

At first all I recognized was a sleeping bag. Olive drab—which had looked more like brown from the air. Then I made out the shape inside it. A large one.

I said, "It's not Amy. She's much smaller than whoever that is."

Hy moved toward it, and I followed. The bag was zipped to the top. I squatted and pulled the zipper down.

Sandy hair, a freckled face—formerly tanned, but now bluish white in death. No marks marred his features; he looked as if he'd crawled into the bag, zipped it up, and gone to sleep.

Tom Mathers, Hayley Perez's former boyfriend.

The man who, the last time I'd seen him, had been engaged in bitter conflict with his wife, T.C.

Hy stayed with the body while I went to the plane and contacted the search team's headquarters. They said they'd have a chopper there in ten minutes.

"When was it you last saw Mathers?" Hy asked when I returned.

"Around two-thirty yesterday afternoon."

"Well, he must've been here since last night or early this morning. There's no odor; the cold's pretty much preserved the body."

"Rigor?"

"I don't know. I don't want to disturb the scene any more than we already have."

I looked around at the ground: faint tire tracks, no drag marks near the body. Of course, the ash had either drifted in the persistent winds or was hardened by thousands of years of exposure to the elements.

Hy said, "I'll check out that truck. Why don't you wait for the sheriff's people?"

"Okay." As he walked away, I stared down at the shrouded body. Tom Mathers had been a big man; in death he would have been hard to move.

I pictured T.C. Mathers. She'd appeared very strong. And then there were all those guns and knives gleaming in their cases at the wilderness supply. What if the argument I'd triggered by asking about Hayley Perez had spun out of control . . . ?

The drone and flapping of a chopper came from the north. It hovered, then set down nearby. Kristen Lark got out and, ducking her head, ran toward us.

It was after six when we finished giving statements to Lark at her office in Bridgeport, nearly seven when we got back to Vernon. We'd had no lunch, so we headed to Zelda's, where a country band whose members must've been tone deaf were playing. Bob Zelda, who had heard about our discovery via the small-town grapevine, gave us a table in the bar area, as far from the noise as possible, brought us complimentary glasses of white wine, and took our orders.

"They turn up any traces of the Perez girl?" he asked.

"No," Hy said, "the search was called off at dusk."

"Bad enough what you found. Tom Mathers was a good kid."

"Somebody didn't think so. He was shot in the back."

"God." He turned toward the kitchen.

Hy swirled the wine in his glass, breathed in its aroma, sipped, and made a face. "I'd rather have paid for a really good vintage," he muttered.

Being one who had spent much of her life opening screw-top bottles, I shrugged.

"Come on, McCone. You've got a better palate than that."

I sipped, and my lips puckered. "You're right. Any potted plants we can pour this into?"

"We'll have a bottle of Deer Hill with dinner."

Deer Hill—my favorite chardonnay, which would go perfectly with the golden trout we'd both ordered. Then my mind flashed back to the night last February when RKI's building on Green Street in the city had been bombed; I'd walked out with a bottle of that particular wine to take to a dinner at my half-sister's place in Berkeley just seconds before the former warehouse blew up, killing three people.

Hy studied my face, accustomed by now to my sudden shifts in mood. He put his hand on mine. "It's over, McCone."

"That threat, yes. But what about the next? I still have nightmares—"

"About that and lots of other things, I know. I have them too. Things like that leave scars, but if you don't have scars, you haven't really lived. Someone like you needs to put herself out on the line."

"I'm not sure that's true any more." I picked up my water glass, drank half, and dumped the sour white wine into it. "You order us a bottle of Deer Hill, and let's forget about crime for tonight."

Sunday

✦

NOVEMBER 4

In the morning Hy slept in and I went to visit Lear Jet, a few carrot pieces in my pocket. Ramon apparently hadn't been there, and the horse was hungry: he took the first carrot eagerly. I offered another, then gave him his morning's ration of mixed hay. While he ate, I watched him. This gentle creature bore no resemblance to the one that had charged me Wednesday night.

I said, "You haven't been getting your exercise, have you, guy?"

A whinny.

"We could go for a short ride, if you cooperate. But if you play games, there'll be no alfalfa tonight."

As if he could actually understand me, he bobbed his head.

It was probably a mistake. No one knew I was taking the horse out, and if he threw me again, I'd have to limp my own way back to the house.

So why're you doing it, McCone? To prove some unimportant point?

No. This one feels important.

Lear Jet allowed me to saddle and mount him with no

problem. He trotted sedately toward the mesa overlooking the lake, and by the time we got there I felt as if we'd tentatively formed a rapport.

"You know what?" I said, stroking his mane. "You need a new name. Lear Jet—even if that's what Hy called you—is undignified. How about King Lear? Now that's strong, speaks of a horse with self-esteem."

Also speaks of insanity, but it's not likely he knows his Shakespeare.

The horse bobbed his head again.

"It's settled, then. I'll call you King for short."

When we got back to the stables, King only stepped on my foot once while I was grooming him. And I was pretty sure that was an accident.

When Hy came out of the ranch house, King was in his fenced pasture and I was cleaning out his stall. Hy stared in astonishment, shook his head, and said, "Never thought I'd see you tending to Lear Jet—or any other horse."

"His name," I said, "is now King Lear. King for short. We're almost friends. In fact, I think he likes me better than you. At least I come to the stable bearing carrots."

"Fickle animal. Since the two of you are on your way to becoming buddies, I just may have to buy myself another nag."

"King is not a *nag*."

"Oh yeah, the two of you have bonded big-time. If I ever get to ride again, I'm definitely going to have to spring for a new nag—I mean, horse."

"King could use some company."

"Do we have onions?" Hy asked.

"Yes, in that wire basket." I sat at the table, thumbing through a report Kristen Lark had faxed me.

"How fresh are these eggs?"

"Check the sell-by date."

"Fresh enough. What's Lark got to say?"

"Not much. Nothing on Boz Sheppard. The sleeping bag Tom Mathers was wrapped in belongs to him; his wife says he kept it in the truck. She's got an alibi for the time of the killing: she slammed out of the wilderness supply a short while after I left; a customer saw her leave, and spent at least an hour afterwards with Tom, talking about a fishing trip he wanted to line up. T.C. went directly to Zelda's, drank and danced for hours, then spent the night with a good old boy at the motel."

"Canned mushrooms all right?"

"They'll have to be; we don't have fresh. The good old boy is Cullen Bradley. I interviewed him at the hardware store he owns in Bridgeport. Glad-handing small-town guy with a serious hangover. Those Bridgeport men really get around. I wonder if— What?"

"Oregano?"

"In an *omelet*? Are you insane?"

"Just trying to get your attention, McCone."

"I'm paying attention."

"No you're not. And that's a sign you're getting better."

Monday

✦

NOVEMBER 5

I spent a good deal of Monday morning on the phone to the agency, going over the week's schedule with Patrick Neilan. Two new clients had set initial appointments with him for the afternoon: one was a deadbeat-dad case, which he'd probably assign to Julia Rafael; the other concerned identity theft. In the past Patrick himself would have taken it on, or it would have ended up on the desk of Charlotte Keim, my chief financial investigator.

But Keim, once my nephew Mick's live-in love, now worked for Hy; after the acrimonious breakup of their relationship, I'd asked Hy to hire her in order to preserve peace within the agency. Her replacement, Thelia Chen, a former analyst for Bank of America, was working out splendidly. She ought to be able to handle the case.

The agency was practically running itself in my absence. Patrick was working out well as a partial stand-in for me. Ted and his assistant, Kendra Williams, were a superefficient pair. Mick and Derek made short work of the increasing number of computer forensic jobs that came in, and weren't averse to doing mundane searches when nothing complex was on the table. Julia Rafael was bilingual and could deal well with Latino clients with limited English; former FBI agent Craig Morland had wide-ranging contacts with government agencies. And for a good all-around operative I could always call on the freelance talents of Rae Kelleher, who was now writing novels with a strong crime element and welcomed keeping her hand in the detective business.

Once this state of affairs would have made me feel distanced, left out. Now I merely felt relieved. I'd created a great team and, if I accomplished nothing else in my career, it had been worth the effort.

Still I felt restless, the empty day ahead weighing heavily upon me. No leads, no new information. Unless . . .

I dialed Glenn Solomon, a high-powered San Francisco attorney for whom I'd done a great deal of work—and who was also a good friend.

"Glenn, d'you know a Las Vegas firm—Brower, Price and Coleman?"

"Sure. They handle the legal work for at least three major casinos."

"What about Frank Brower?"

"Lousy golfer, but a nice guy."

"So you know him well?"

"We get together down there two, three times a year."

I explained what I needed to know and asked, "Can you get him to tell you who was footing the bill for Hayley Perez's legal work?"

"If I go about it the right way."

"Will you do it for me—as a favor?"

"Yes, my friend. But I thought you were taking a long vacation at that ranch you and Hy have."

"I was. Severe case of burn-out."

"And you're over it now?"

"No, I'm just helping out some friends."

I booted up my laptop and Googled Bud Smith. Good luck, with a name like that. I narrowed the search down to insurance brokers, Mono County, California. No Bud, but there was a Herbert in Vernon. His record was clean—no complaints to the state department of consumer affairs. I then searched for more information on Herbert Smith of Vernon, California. Nothing. Apparently he wasn't important enough to the gods of Google. Finally I logged on to one of the search engines that the agency subscribes to—even though I'm averse to availing myself of company resources for personal reasons—and came up with some revealing information.

Herbert Smith of Vernon, California, was a registered sex offender.

To confirm the information I visited a site that posted the whereabouts of registered sex offenders. He was on it.

How, I wondered, had a community of not more than four hundred people failed to pick up on his status? How could Dana Ivins have arranged for him to mentor young men and women?

I dialed Ivins's number. She picked up, sounding crisp and professional. I told her what I'd found out and asked, "How could you put your clients at risk like that?"

Calmly she replied, "Bud's case was unusual. He never confirmed it to me, but even the prosecutor over in Mineral County thought he was covering for someone else."

"So this happened in Nevada."

"Yes, twenty-six years ago. A girl of thirteen was raped, sodomized, and abandoned in the countryside near the munitions storage site outside of Hawthorne. She managed to crawl to the road and flag down a passing car. There was evidence pointing to Bud—tire tracks from his truck in the sand, a piece of cloth she'd ripped from a shirt belonging to him. Unfortunately, the girl was extremely traumatized. She couldn't even speak, much less identify her attacker."

And over a quarter of a century ago, there wouldn't have been any DNA evidence. DNA testing was in its infancy then.

"So why did the prosecutor think Smith was covering for someone?"

"Bud had a younger brother, Davey. He was sixteen, something of a child prodigy—math, I think—but considered strange by his teachers and peers. Bud raised him after their parents died and was overly protective of him. Originally the police focused on Davey because he'd been seen in town talking with the girl, but then Bud confessed. And stuck to it."

"So Bud did his time and . . . ?"

"And moved back here to Vernon, where he was born and raised till the family moved to Hawthorne during his teens."

I was a little surprised that Smith could have gotten a California insurance broker's license. Many types of licenses are unavailable to sex offenders—such as real estate, because the agents have access to keys. But then with insurance, if the person is registered and up-front about doing time, the state is more lenient. And Bud had apparently been honest about his record.

"Is Bud's status common knowledge around here?" I asked Ivins.

"Not really. I suppose some people may have stumbled across it on the Internet. But Bud's very civic-minded and well liked, so if they have they've kept it to themselves. I know only because he confided his past to me when he applied to become a mentor. Then I did some research on his case."

"What happened to the brother, Davey?"

"I don't know that, either. All I'm really sure of is that Bud has been good at mentoring our clients."

"Does he tell them he was in prison, and why?"

"Whatever goes on between friends who help friends is strictly confidential."

It seemed to me she didn't know a hell of a lot of things she should know about what went on between her organization's clients and their mentors.

"Is Bud aware you told me he might have been tutoring Amy Perez in math?"

". . . I mentioned it to him. He called shortly after you left me that day."

"Why did he call?"

She frowned. "I don't really know. I told him about your visit, but then someone called on his other line. He said he'd get back to me, but he never did."

"Is he still living on Aspen Lane?" It was the address listed for him on the registered sex offenders site.

". . . Yes."

"Do you have a phone number for him?"

"I can't give out—"

"Never mind. I'll get hold of him."

Irresponsibility, I thought. Sheer irresponsibility. I'm all for giving sex offenders a second chance, but given the high rate of recidivism, that chance shouldn't be in a sensitive area involving young people. And I wasn't sure I bought the rumors of Bud Smith's false confession—even if the Mineral County prosecutor had had his or her doubts.

I called Smith's office, got a machine. Thumbed through the slim local directory; his home number wasn't listed, under either Bud or Herbert. Better to speak with him in person anyway. I'd drive out to Aspen Lane and—

The phone rang. Glenn Solomon.

"I talked with Frank Brower. His instructions to represent Hayley Perez came from a Mount Kisco, New York, law firm—Carpenter and Bates."

"You know anyone there?"

"No, but Frank was on the *Harvard Law Review* with Bates. He'll get back to me later."

"Thanks so much, Glenn. I'm leaving now and my cellular might not work where I'm going. If it doesn't, please leave a message on the machine here at the ranch."

"Certainly." He paused, the silence full of meaning.

"What?" I asked.

"What I always tell you when you embark on one of your quests, my friend: be clever and careful."

Aspen Lane was three miles out the road to Stone Valley—a place I hadn't visited for years and didn't even like to think about. The horrific events that had happened in the valley back then had ultimately brought Hy and me together, but I didn't want to relive them, even in my head. The vision of the mountain exploding, our frantic flight—

So stop reliving them, all right?

The lane was well named: golden-leafed aspen spread out to either side and clustered around the small, mostly prefab homes. Bud Smith's was at the very end, where the pavement stopped—a double-wide trailer with attractive plantings and a deck with an awning over it. A fishing boat was up on davits, ready to be prepped and tarped for the winter. Usually I think of child molesters as unsavory types who live in squalor and lurk in dark places seeking their prey, but I couldn't reconcile either the man I'd met or his tidy home with such an image.

No one answered the doorbell. I walked around the structure calling out to Smith. No response, but I sensed a presence nearby. Finally I went back to the deck and saw what I hadn't noticed before: the door was slightly ajar.

Not breaking and entering, just trespassing. And trespassing for a good reason: now I'm worried about the man.

The excuses I use to justify my actions . . .

I eased the door open, listening. Silence. Strong smell there, but it wasn't sinister—cooked garlic and onions. Still, I drew Hy's .45 from my bag before I went inside. The living room and galley kitchen were empty. The meal must have been cooked yesterday, since the stove and all the counter surfaces were clean.

I moved along the hallway. Three bedrooms and a bath opened off it, all of them deserted. In one of the smaller rooms, the bed had been left unmade. Otherwise everything was neat.

Why didn't Bud Smith sleep in the larger room with the queen-sized bed? Perhaps he shared the trailer with someone who was tidier than he?

Well, that information could be had online. But while I was here . . .

The master bedroom's closet contained a man's clothing—mostly vintage and odd, as I'd seen Bud wear. So it was his room after all. The bathroom didn't tell me much. A Water Pik and two electric toothbrushes, some first-aid supplies, aspirin, and sinus headache pills. No prescription drugs. A razor and shaving cream on a shelf below a mirror in the shower stall. Third bedroom, mostly empty—a guest room that hadn't been used in quite a while, judging from the layer of dust.

Back to the room with the unmade bed. The closet held some newish-looking woman's jeans. A couple of sweaters were draped across a chair, and there were a few tops hanging in the closet. Woman's underwear in the bureau, and a flannel nightgown tossed on the bed. Makeup items and a pair of earrings on the bureau.

So Smith had a female roommate. She was probably at work.

I moved back to the living area, looking in drawers and cupboards, gave the whole trailer another once-over, then left and started back to the ranch.

I sat at my laptop, thinking about Bud Smith—a convicted child molester who may have been covering for his younger brother. Smith, who had told me he knew Amy Perez and, if Amy had followed Dana Ivins' advice, may have tutored her in algebra. Who had sold a life-insurance policy to Hayley, with Amy as beneficiary. Had he known Hayley before she bought the policy? Probably not, given their age difference.

I logged on to Mono County property records and learned the land and the double-wide had belonged to Smith for seven years. When I went to the state insurance brokers' registry, I found that he'd received his license the same year he'd purchased the land. The California Registry of Sex Offenders showed he'd contacted them within a day of his arrival in the state, and reregistered when required.

Which proved . . . ? Not much.

The *Mineral County Independent News* in Hawthorne

didn't have online issues going back twenty-six years. I could drive over there and check their archives, but it was getting on toward five o'clock. Better to wait till morning.

Well, what about the paper in Reno? A controversial rape case would have warranted mention. I checked, found their online archives didn't go back twenty-six years, either. Tomorrow I'd have to visit Mineral County.

But now I'd take a ride on King, who was probably waiting for me. Tonight I'd cut a path across open land where our small herd of sheep grazed. Hy had told me the sheep had something to do with a subsidy or lower taxes—I forget which—but I suspected he kept them out of sentiment. His stepfather, to whom he'd been considerably closer than to his birth father, had been a lifelong sheep rancher.

The ride was without event, and I felt a growing kinship with the horse. I'd been traumatized by the events of the night when he'd charged me, but so had he. Animals are essentially innocent, until we humans treat them badly and give them cause to fear. King needed my reassurance.

As we retraced our steps, I wondered if this caring for the horse indicated a caring for other things in my life.

Ramon was at the stable when King and I got back, cleaning out the stall. He said hello and went on with what he was doing, allowing me to tend to King on my own.

When I finished rubbing King down and led him into the clean stall, I noticed Ramon's dark eyes were shadowed and puffy. He attempted a smile, but it didn't quite come off.

"How're you doing?" I asked.

He made a wobbly gesture with his hand. "We buried Hayley up in Bridgeport today."

"Oh, I wish you'd told me. I would've—"

"Not necessary; you didn't know her. It was a nice turnout, though. Even that wild man she ran off with and his girlfriend came. The girlfriend brought beautiful flowers. She works at Petals."

So Rich Three Wings and Cammie Charles had paid their respects to Hayley. Rich, because he still loved her, and Cammie, probably because she felt guilty that her imagined rival was dead.

I asked, "Did Miri attend?"

Ramon's eyes narrowed, the lines around them deepening. "No."

"Why not? She was only on seventy-two-hour hold at the psychiatric ward."

"Yeah. And then she checked herself into a rehab facility they recommended. By this morning she was gone. She's probably in Reno or Vegas, helling around or selling herself. I've washed my hands of her. Sara's real broken up about this, but she'll get over it. You gotta go on."

"And what about Amy? Anything from her?"

"Not a word." He leaned in the doorway, and for a moment I thought he'd sag to the ground. "I loved that little girl, Sharon. I should've never let Miri run me off. I should've stayed and fought for the last of my nieces and nephews."

I went to him, took his hand, and drew him over to the nearest bales of hay. As we sat, I said, "You couldn't have known what would happen."

"Anybody could've read the signs that she was headed for bad trouble. But not me, I was too offended at Miri, too dug down into my own unhappiness. Sara and I had two boys, you know—Peter and Raymond."

"I didn't know. Neither of you has ever mentioned them."

"They've been gone a long time. Peter died in a gang shoot-out over in Santa Rosa. Raymond died of a drug overdose. I didn't do so good by them, either."

Sadness welled up inside me—guilt, too. "I'm sorry," I said, "and I understand how you feel. I had a brother, Joey. Always was a rebel and a loner. After he graduated high school, he took off and very seldom came home. Ma—my adoptive mother—got postcards occasionally, but that was it. And then he died all alone of a drug and alcohol overdose in a shack up near Eureka. Ever since then I've wished I'd done more. That any of us had done more. But we just . . . let him go."

"I'm sorry, Sharon. Us people, we're all so careless. I don't want to let go of Amy."

"Neither do I. I promise I'll find her."

That night I dreamed of the pit again—only this time it was bigger. Impossible to place both my hands and feet on its sides and climb into the sunshine like a spider. I woke in a near panic, sat up, collapsed back on the pillows.

Told myself, *I will not allow this to get the better of me.*

Tomorrow I'd keep my promise to Ramon. Start an intensive search for Bud Smith who, my instincts said, was at the center of Amy's disappearance.

Maybe that would keep my nightmares at bay.

Tuesday

✦

NOVEMBER 6

The Nevada sky was cloudless as I coasted past the red-and-white sign welcoming me to Hawthorne, population 3,311. Larger than Vernon by far, and the county seat, but still a small town. Laid out on a grid, so I had no difficulty locating the *Independent News* building on D Street.

The man I talked to was pleasant and friendly. Back issues on microfilm? No problem. They were going to put everything online someday, but who knew when that would be? Soon I was seated in a dusty room fitting reels onto a machine with fumbling fingers. How could I be clumsy at the act I'd performed so many times before I'd become computer literate? Another symptom of burn-out?

I returned the films an hour or so later, having learned too few new details to justify such a long drive, except that Smith's rape victim had remained too traumatized to identify her assailant.

It was after two in the afternoon, so I asked about someplace to eat lunch. McDonald's; everyplace else had stopped serving. I hadn't had a Mickey D's burger in years, and it was a strange experience: not what I now think of as a burger, but a different substance entirely. I blocked out thoughts of what that substance might be and ate it anyway.

Back in the car, I checked my cell to see if it worked here—which it did—and consulted my notes. Got the number for the prosecutor in the Smith case from Information. Warren Mills, now retired, was home and willing to see me once I assured him that I was an investigator, not someone planning to write a book on the case. "Too damn much of that sensational crap going around these days," he told me.

Mills lived only a few blocks away on East Eighth Street. The house was a low-slung rancher, one of a number on that block that were probably built in the late forties before developers realized that the wartime boom in the Hawthorne economy—due to activity at the nearby munitions depot—was dropping off. I parked out front and went up a concrete walk bordered on either side by cacti and polished rock. Westernized, I believe it's called, for yards that don't require much water or maintenance.

Warren Mills answered the door—a tall, erect man with thick gray hair and black-rimmed glasses who, according to the newspaper accounts, must now be in his late seventies but could have passed for mid-sixties. He led me inside to a den with a big-screen TV. The furnishings were overstuffed and looked comfortable; framed photos hung on the walls—color shots of Walker Lake to the north, he told me.

"Coffee, Ms. McCone? A soda?" He had a deep, rich voice that must have resonated in the courtroom.

"Nothing, thanks. I've just come from McDonald's."

"I should have offered you an Alka-Seltzer. Please, sit down."

I sank into a brown chair that enveloped me in an embrace that made it hard to sit up straight.

Warren Mills settled on the couch, propped his moccasin-shod feet on a scarred coffee table in front of it. "You said on the phone that you're a private investigator and interested in the Herbert Smith case. Why?"

"He may have recently been involved in the abduction of a young woman over in Mono County. I've read all the newspaper accounts of his case, but there's so much that seems . . . unsaid. And a friend of Smith's claims that you yourself were uncertain Smith was guilty."

Mills nodded. "His confession was as false as I've ever heard."

"Then why did you accept his plea bargain and send him to prison?"

"It was as if Smith was trying to talk his way behind bars. He insisted on his guilt, refused a lie-detector test when his public defender wanted to order one. I didn't need to build a case against him; he built it for me. And of course the district attorney was hot for a quick trial and conviction. The rape and sodomy of a thirteen-year-old . . . small towns like this need to put crimes like that behind them and move on."

"The victim—"

"I can't tell you her name. But she was a nice girl from a decent, hardworking family. Too friendly and trusting, that's all."

"What happened to her?"

"The family moved away. She was severely damaged by the assault. And as you must know, you can keep the victim's name out of the newspapers and court records but word gets out anyway and then it's blame-the-victim time."

"Smith's friend claims he was covering for his younger brother, Davey."

"The friend's likely right. Davey Smith was a genius, had

just graduated high school at fifteen, with a full scholarship to some college back East. My thinking is that Herbert—Bud, everybody called him—didn't want to see Davey's promising future disrupted, even if it meant going to prison for something he didn't do."

"Why? If Davey was a rapist—"

"You have to understand the way it was with the two of them. The mother died young. Father raised them well, but he had a fatal heart attack when Bud was sixteen. A young man, just starting out in life, and he could have put his little brother in a foster home, but he didn't. Instead he quit school, picked up where the father left off, took whatever jobs paid best to support the two of them. That's sometimes the way some family members are. Bud loved Davey, and I think he saw his brother's promising future as a kind of a way of ensuring the family would go on."

"And where is this genius today?"

Mills shrugged, shook his head.

I said, "Bud Smith is working as an insurance broker in Vernon, on Tufa Lake. He lives in a double-wide trailer in the country—nice property, but nothing fancy. And he's a registered sex offender. I guess his brother—wherever he is—didn't have the same sense of family."

"He could be dead. Or incarcerated somewhere else."

"True."

Mills was silent for a long moment. Then: "I imagine in your profession, Ms. McCone, you've had reason to regret certain of your actions."

Oh, haven't I. Mr. Mills, you'll never know how much I regret them.

"Of course."

"So have I." His eyes, behind their black-framed glasses,

grew pained. "I regret not pushing harder to prove Bud Smith's confession was false. I regret not looking more closely at Davey Smith. Whatever's happened over in Mono County is not Bud's fault."

"And Davey . . . ?"

"My biggest regret: that I may have let a monster walk free."

He paused, seemed to listen to his words. "Talk with an attorney named John Pearl in Carson City." He reached for a pad and pencil on the scarred coffee table and scribbled. "This is his office address and phone number. I'll call ahead to say you'll contact him. He may be able to tell you what I can't."

I took the paper. John Pearl: Bud Smith's former public defender.

The munitions depot occupied a vast expanse of land on the outskirts of Hawthorne. Standard military buildings and cracked and weed-choked pavement were visible from the road, although I'd read on the Net that its golf course and officers' clubhouse had now been turned into a public country club. Storage bunkers covered the land to the east like Indian mounds, and the landscape was stark and uninviting. I passed through the town of Babbitt, which had once been a bedroom community for base workers, and eventually came to Walker Lake.

I drove north along the shore of the elongated body of water that was rimmed by sand-colored hills to the east. It was currently in ecological crisis, as Tufa and Mono Lakes in California had once been, primarily because the waters of its feeder stream, the Walker River, had been overallocated for agricultural use. Hy had done some work with the organization trying to preserve Walker, one of only five deep-water lakes in the world that are able to sustain a good-sized fishery, and had told me that if the water levels continued to drop, increased salinity would destroy its fish population.

Today there were few boats on the lake, and its surface was flat and glassy. The weather had changed: dark clouds hovered over the distant hills—storm clouds that looked to be coming this way. Depression stole over me again, reminding me of all the things I didn't like about my business: the long solo drives and flights; the empty nights in hotel and motel rooms in strange cities; the waiting. Particularly waiting for facts to surface that would allow other facts to materialize and establish the final connection. When that happened, the rush was unbelievable—better, even, than the first time my former flight instructor had put the plane into a controlled spin and the earth had seemed to rush up at us as we plummeted down. . . .

It was an addiction, plain and simple. And addiction, unless it's treated, inevitably ends up in self-destruction.

I wasn't going to become victim to mine. Never again.

So what the hell am I doing here in Nevada?

You promised Ramon you'd find out what happened to Amy.

Carson City: the state capital, and a pleasant town. Not much of a gambling mecca; its big casino, the Ormsby House, had closed down well over a decade ago and since then cast a derelict shadow over the downtown. Renovation by new owners had seemingly been under way forever, as the project hit delays and snags of all kinds. If it hadn't been so late in the afternoon I'd have driven by to see how much progress had been made, but I was more concerned with locating the law firm of John Pearl, on Fairview Drive, a couple of blocks from the state office building where Hy and I had said our vows before a judge.

At first, when I stepped inside John Pearl's office in a two-story stucco house that had been converted into suites for attorneys, I thought no one was there. But when I called out, a high-pitched, nasal voice that reminded me of a cartoon character—I couldn't place which one—answered. With a voice like that, Pearl couldn't have been too successful at trial work.

He emerged from his inner sanctum: a short, chubby man in a rumpled blue suit. His face was round, his hair a grayish-brown mop that flopped over his forehead; his eyes were too soft and kind for a criminal defense attorney.

"Ms. McCone," he said, pumping my hand heartily, "Warren Mills said you'd be stopping by, so I stayed to catch up on some paperwork. Come in, sit down, please."

I followed him into his office. It was in minor disarray, like his clothing.

"I'd offer you coffee but my secretary drank the last cup and forgot to turn the machine off. The carafe's scorched. You can probably smell it."

Now that he mentioned it, I did. "That's okay," I said. "I had lunch at McDonald's and I'm still recovering. Coffee could cause a serious relapse."

"McDonald's." His eyes—so help me—became nostalgic. "I haven't had one of their burgers in years. When they first opened up in the town where I was born, I was in my teens. My friends and I used to go there and order two or three each, and before we'd eat them we'd splat the pickles."

"Do what?"

"You know, splat. Take the pickles—they were terrible—

out of the burgers and try to drop them out the car window so they'd land flat on the pavement. You never did that?"

"Uh, not that I recall."

"Oh, well." Pearl leaned back in his chair. "It was pretty stupid, but so were we at the time. Amazing, though: one of the splatters is now a state supreme court justice; another invented some gizmo that allowed him to retire at thirty-five; a third is a big financial planner in Reno. Then there's me: I was the best pickle splatter, but I'm just a small-time lawyer."

It was a set and well-practiced speech, but I couldn't figure what it was designed to accomplish.

"I doubt that," I said. "You have your own practice; you're your own boss. What type of litigation do you do?"

"Whatever comes my way. Family law, mainly." He paused. "No criminal law. I quit the public defender's office down in Mineral County after the Herbert Smith case. Which, Warren Mills told me, is why you're here."

"Yes." I explained why I was interested in speaking with those who were involved in it.

When I finished, Pearl said, "The opinions of Herbert's friend and Warren Mills are essentially the same as mine. Herbert—Bud, as he was called—struck me on first impression as a badly frightened but innocent young man; he stood by his confession with the tenacity of a bulldog. He resisted all my efforts to help him. Tried twice to fire me."

"And this confession came how long after the rape?"

"About three days, after the investigative officers identified the tire tracks at the scene as having been made by his truck. When they took him in for questioning, he gave them a plausible explanation: he'd been out there taking photographs of the munitions bunkers for an article a friend was writing on the history of the depot. But no one could locate the friend—if he ever existed—and when the sheriff obtained a search warrant for Bud's home, there was only one camera, in a closet, covered in dust and containing no film. And in the trash was a bloody shirt with a piece ripped from it that matched the fabric the girl had torn from her rapist's clothing."

"So they arrested him—"

"Not immediately. The shirt was a size smaller than most of Bud's, and his brother, Davey, had been seen talking to the girl in town that day. The investigators began to focus on Davey and that's when Bud confessed. He didn't ask for an attorney, so the public defender's office assigned him to me. From the beginning he was stubborn and uncooperative. I voiced my doubts to the DA and Warren; Warren was willing to listen, but the DA at that time—he's deceased now—was a real hardnose. I arranged for the best plea bargain I could, but it was still too much prison time for an innocent man."

Like Warren Mills' eyes when he spoke of his regrets, John Pearl's were bleak. "That was the end of my illustrious career as a crusading defender of the poor and powerless. I couldn't stomach the hypocrisy. So here I am." He spread his arms out at his disheveled office.

"Is there anything else you can tell me about the case?"

He considered. "Not really. Except that Davey Smith acted the wide-eyed innocent throughout, and as soon as his brother went to prison, he took off for some college where he'd been given a full scholarship. One thing I do know: if he ever shows his face around here again, I myself may be in need of a public defender."

The rain broke as I was passing the munitions depot. There were a number of motels in Hawthorne, and the man in the newspaper office had recommended a casino that served a great chicken-fried steak—a favorite of mine—as well as an old-time saloon. I'd stowed a small travel bag in the Land Rover, in the event I'd have to stay over.

Well, why not? First the motel, next a good meal, and then a chance to elicit some gossip from the townspeople.

Slim's Tavern, across the street from the casino where I ate, was definitely old-time—decorated with genuine mining, railroad, and military artifacts from the town's colorful past. At ten o'clock it was reasonably crowded and noisy from both the patrons' voices and the clank and whir of the small bank of slot machines. I chose a seat at the bar between two lone men in cowboy hats who looked to be in their mid-forties, and ordered a beer. You don't drink wine in a place like that, not if you want any of the locals to talk with you.

The man to my left stared straight ahead, hunched over his glass of whiskey. Not a talker, I thought, and probably brooding about something. The man to my right gave me a friendly glance, then threw a few dollars on the bar and left.

Well, hell.

I nursed the beer, trying not to breathe too deeply of the smoky air—one of the drawbacks of Nevada casinos and drinking establishments—and checking out the place in the backbar mirror. It was mostly an older crowd, forties on up—my target age group. The brooder ordered another whiskey and continued to stare. A leather-faced, strong-jawed man in a baseball cap squeezed onto the vacated stool to my right and ordered a beer and a shot, calling the bartender by name. Then he looked at me and asked, "You new here, or just passing through?"

"Passing through. How can you tell?"

"I know all the locals who come to Slim's. You want another beer?" He motioned to my empty glass.

"Sure. Thanks. Sierra Nevada."

He waved at the bartender and pointed at my glass, turned to me and, after giving me a long, slow look, said, "I'm Cal McKenzie."

"Sharon McCone." We shook hands as our drinks arrived.

"Where you from, Sharon?"

"I've been staying over at Tufa Lake, trying to figure out where to go next."

He knocked back his shot. "Kind of a wanderer, are you?"

"Kind of. I came up here to Hawthorne looking for an old friend, but I can't find a trace of him."

"Well, I've lived here all my life. Maybe I can help you."

"His name is Herbert Smith, but everybody calls him Bud."

Cal McKenzie's expression became guarded. "How long since you've seen your friend, Sharon?"

"I hate to admit how many years. We lost touch, but I thought since I was in the area . . ."

"Well, Bud's long gone. How close a friend of his were you?"

"Oh, it was just one of those summer things. You know."

"You're lucky that's all it was. Your friend Bud's a criminal. Raped and sodomized the little Darkmoon girl and left her for dead out by the munitions bunkers. She survived and they put him away for a good long time. He hasn't been back here since."

"My God!" I feigned shock, gulping some beer. "When was this?"

"Twenty-six years ago."

"Hard to believe Bud was capable of something like that, even as a kid."

"Some folks around here don't believe it to this day. Nice guy, never in trouble before, everybody liked him. But the evidence was all there, and he confessed."

"This Darkmoon girl—does she still live here?"

"Family moved away right after. Paiutes." He looked more closely at me. "You Paiute, too?"

"Shoshone."

"Well, the Darkmoons were really a nice family. Very religious, too. One of those strict, small sects—I forget which one. Shame what happened to their little girl."

"How old was she?"

"Thirteen."

"D'you recall her first name?"

He thought, shrugged. "No, I don't. They had a bunch of kids, I can't remember what any of them were called." He gestured at my glass. "Another beer?"

"No, thanks. This has been . . . quite a shock, and I think I'd better be getting back to my motel now."

"The evening's young—"

"Maybe I'll see you tomorrow night, Cal. It was good to meet you." I slid off the stool before he could protest and made my exit.

A Paiute family named Darkmoon who'd lived in Hawthorne twenty-six years ago couldn't be too difficult to find. If the Internet couldn't lead me to them, I'd use the moccasin telegraph.

Wednesday

✦

NOVEMBER 7

The moccasin telegraph beat out the Internet.

After I drove home from Hawthorne that morning, I found plenty of listings on Google in the name of Darkmoon—a magazine, a design company, a publisher, even a Wiccan temple—but none of them individuals. There were three on the search engines the agency subscribed to, two in Washington State and one, coincidentally, on the Flathead reservation in Montana, where my birth father, Elwood Farmer, lived.

I could have run more sophisticated searches, but on the moccasin telegraph I could access far more detail. The listings for the three Darkmoons hadn't revealed much about them, other than their whereabouts, and that wasn't surprising: a great many Indians are out of the mainstream and don't own property, have credit ratings, or hold real jobs.

My friend Will Camphouse, creative director at an ad agency in Tucson whom I'd met while searching for my birth parents, had explained the moccasin telegraph as a coast-to-coast Indian gossip network that worked with amazing speed. It was an accurate description. I'd gotten a lead to Elwood from a Shoshone man in Wyoming, and by the time

I reached the Flathead Reservation everyone, including my birth father, knew not only that I was on my way, but also the basic facts about me. Phone calls, interfamilial connections, accidental meetings in such places as the grocery store, and a background check on the Internet had told them a private investigator from San Francisco was coming to town.

For this investigation, George Darkmoon in Arlee, a town near St. Ignatius, where my birth father lived, would be the obvious person to start with. The problem was, I would have to call Elwood.

Elwood was not an easy man to deal with on the phone—or in person. The first two times I'd tried to talk with him he'd rebuffed me—telling me to come back to his house when I'd had time to "assemble my thoughts." Then he'd grudgingly allowed me into his simple log home and acknowledged that I was his daughter. Since then we'd established a tentative relationship, but it had its rough edges: on my part because he'd suspected all along he had a child, but had made no effort to locate me; on his part because I'd disrupted his quiet, traditional life as an artist who volunteered to fund and teach art workshops in the schools at various area reservations.

I steeled myself and dialed his number.

"Elwood, it's Sharon."

"Yes."

"How are you?"

"Doing well. How are you?"

"Doing well."

Long silence. I asked, "How are the workshops going?"

"Excellently." Excitement lightened his voice. "Those young people are amazing. Their enthusiasm . . . it makes me feel young again."

And where were you, when my enthusiasm could have made you feel young?

Not fair, McCone. At the time he wasn't even certain that you existed.

"I haven't heard from you in a while," he added. "Are you sure everything's all right? Those bombings . . ."

Did he really want to know? I decided to lay it on him; talked about my burn-out and my flight to the ranch, my doubts about my professional future.

He didn't speak immediately. I heard puffing sounds—he was lighting a cigarette.

"It may be a time for change, Daughter. That kind of empty feeling is a signal that we need to use our gifts in different ways. Me, when I was making all that money from my art in New York City and living high, I felt the kinds of pressures you were feeling. When I met Leila and we came here, I could let go of the things I thought were important back there, and get on with what really counted."

"Your art, and giving to others."

"Yes, exactly."

"Well, I've taken on one last case, as a favor to friends, and I have a problem. D'you know a man in Arlee named George Darkmoon?"

"No. These days, I stay apart from the community more than I used to. But I can put you in touch with him."

"Moccasin telegraph."

"Moccasin telegraph. I'll find someone to relay the information to George. He'll probably have to call you collect."

"If he calls my cellular, it'll be charged to me anyway." I gave him the number.

"Good. As you know, most of our people can't afford long

distance in the middle of the day. And Daughter, be in touch with me more often."

When I hung up, my eyes were brimming. Elwood had called me "Daughter" twice in one conversation.

"Is this Sharon McCone?"

"Yes."

"I'm George Darkmoon, in Arlee, Montana. Donna Ferguson in St. Ignatius had a call from your father, saying you wanted to get in touch with me. She talked to Jane Nomee here in Arlee, and Jane called me."

It had been ten minutes since I'd spoken with Elwood. The telegraph was working at higher speed than my computer ever had.

"Yes, thank you for calling. Mr. Darkmoon, did you ever live in Hawthorne, Nevada?"

"Never even been there."

"Do you have any relatives who did? Say, twenty-five years ago?"

"Well . . . the Darkmoons have kind of scattered. Family is Paiute, mostly from northern California, but now we're all over the map. Me, I married a Flathead woman, moved here thirty-five years ago. You want I should put it out on the wire?"

"If you wouldn't mind."

"No problem. Don't know your dad personally, but I hear about what he's doing for the kids. Happy to help his daughter."

There was that word again. . . .

"Sharon McCone? This is Phyllis Darkmoon, in Vancouver, B.C. My husband's cousin George says you're looking for a branch of the family who lived in Hawthorne, Nevada, twenty-five years ago."

"That's right. Thanks for calling."

"No problem. My husband wanted me to tell you that he has a second cousin in New Mexico who may have known them. He asked me to put you in touch with him."

"Let me check with some Darkmoon family members in Portland. What number can they reach you at?"

"This is Essie Wilson, in Portland. I'm related to the Darkmoon family. My brother-in-law remembers the Darkmoons of Hawthorne, Nevada. In fact, we visited them once. There was some kind of tragedy with one of their daughters, and then they lost touch."

"Do you recall their first names?"

"The father was Norm, the mother Dora. The kids, no, I don't recall, but a relative in Tonopah, Nevada, might. I'll give you her number."

"Yes, I knew Norm and Dora Darkmoon—they were shirttail cousins. We visited them once, about fifteen years ago when they were living in Yerington. Kind of a sad couple. Their kids had all left home, and he was sick with some kind of lung thing. After that, we lost touch. There's another shirttail cousin in Yerington who might be able to tell you more."

"After the girl was raped, the family moved here to Yerington and stayed for maybe ten years. The girl ran off a short time after they got here. I never knew her name. But her sister, Joellen, still lives in town. You should talk to her."

* * *

"You're looking for Izzy? God, I haven't heard from her since she ran away from home," Joellen Darkmoon Knight said. "No, that's not right. She sent a postcard saying the baby had been born and they were doing fine."

"She had a child?"

"Well, yeah. From the rape, you know."

"And she kept it?"

"Uh-huh, I guess."

"Where was this postcard from?"

"I don't know. Somewhere in California?"

"What's Izzy's full name?"

"Isabel. She hated it because everybody would abbreviate it to Izzy, and she thought that sounded like some weird kind of lizard."

"Is there anybody else in your family who might have heard from her?"

"Well, my parents are dead. Dad had emphysema, and they went down to Arizona, and I swear that hot, dry climate was what killed them both. My older brother, he took off before we moved down here from Hawthorne. Baby brother's overseas in the army, baby sister too. My other sister I don't have nothing to do with, but I've got a phone number for her in Seattle. She was two years older than Izzy, and they were close."

"I'm surprised Joellen gave you my number," Cheri Darkmoon said.

"She mentioned you didn't have much to do with one another."

A laugh. "Try total estrangement. I'm a lesbian, and she couldn't handle it when I came out."

"That's too bad. Families . . ."

"Are not what they show in the TV ads. Take ours: I haven't heard from Isabel for fifteen, sixteen years, since her last kid was born—and we were the closest of us all."

"So Isabel had more children after . . . ?"

"The child born of the rape. Yes, she did. After she ran away she sent me a postcard from Sacramento saying somebody she knew over in California had found her a nice family to stay with."

"Who was this somebody?"

"I don't know. She was only thirteen and had never been anyplace but Hawthorne, so how she had a friend in California I can't imagine. Or how she got there. She didn't have any money of her own; none of us did."

"What happened to her after that?"

"She stayed on with the people, finished high school, got a job. Met a guy and married him. There were more kids—four, that I know of—and I couldn't even congratulate her or send them presents."

"Why not?"

"She would never give me her address. She was afraid that her rapist would find her and ruin her life all over again."

"But he was in prison—"

Another laugh—harsh, this time. "Bud Smith never touched my sister. But his younger brother, Davey, sure did."

"You know this for sure?"

"She told me the night before she ran off. Davey did it, but for a long time afterwards she was so wrecked she couldn't remember, and then she was afraid to tell the truth. I mean, that girl was so bad off she didn't even *speak* for months. And by the time she could, Bud was convicted and we'd moved to Yerington. After she ran away, I never heard anything from her but an occasional postcard and those birth announcements."

"Do you remember the postmarks?"

"Someplace in California that I'd never heard of. I forget."

"Did you save any?"

"I did for a while, but when I moved here to Seattle I threw away everything I didn't absolutely need. Sorry."

Me too.

A pregnant thirteen-year-old rape victim who has no money runs away from home in Nevada to a friend in Sacramento, where she's never been before. The friend introduces her to a family who takes her in, and she lives with them until she meets a man who marries her and gives her at least four more children.

Moccasin telegraph wasn't going to answer the questions raised by that scenario.

Who did I know who might have some insight into the problem? Dana Ivins?

I called her and, because our last conversation had been less than harmonious, she hesitated before agreeing to allow me to buy her lunch at Zelda's. She was waiting outside when I arrived in Vernon, her cheeks pink from the chill wind off the lake. The temperatures had cooled in the last few days; it would be an early winter in the high desert.

We took a table beside the large rear windows in the dining room and ordered sandwiches. Like me, she didn't have to consult the menu; since Zelda's was by far the best restaurant in town, we'd both come there often enough to have it memorized.

As we waited for the food, I explained the Isabel Darkmoon story. When I finished, Dana stared out the window at the lake, where birds huddled against the wind on the offshore islands.

"There's one way she could have managed her escape," she finally said.

"How?"

"Let me ask you this first: was her family abusive to her?"

"I doubt it, but I can't say for sure."

"But they were probably embarrassed by the rape and pregnancy, as evidenced by them moving away from Hawthorne. And they may have taken it out on her in hurtful ways."

"The sisters I spoke with didn't say, but that's entirely possible."

Ivins sighed. "Can you keep this confidential?"

"That depends. I don't have a client; I've simply agreed to help the sheriff's department and the Perez family. I don't even know for sure if the Darkmoon girl figures in the case."

"Well, I don't suppose it matters anyway. The organization's no longer active, and they never kept records. If the authorities contacted any of its members, they'd claim ignorance. I know I would."

"You were involved in this . . . organization?"

"*Loose* organization." She paused while the waitress deposited our plates and withdrew. "About fifty activist women in California and Nevada. We provided money for girls to escape abusive family situations and sent them to homes where they could begin new lives. Many of them, like Isabel Darkmoon, had been impregnated by rapists, often family members."

"Could she have found out about the organization in Yerington?"

"Yes. We had a member there. This would have been

before I joined; I was young and still mired down in confusion about which way my life was going to go."

"Is there any way I could get in touch with this member?"

Ivins hesitated, considering. "If this . . . lead of yours turns out to have something to do with the rash of murders we've been having, her identity would come out in court. As you said, you haven't a client, so confidentiality doesn't apply. She's a highly respected attorney—"

"There you have it. I'll ask her to hire me—for a dollar—to find out what happened to Isabel Darkmoon. Any work I do for her falls under the umbrella of attorney-client privilege."

By four that afternoon I was back in Carson City, this time in the offices of Elizabeth Long, attorney-at-law. The firm was situated only a few blocks from John Pearl's building, but mega-miles away in luxury.

Dana Ivins had called and explained the situation, and Elizabeth Long and I were both prepared. After we sat down in her office, she slid a dollar bill across the desk to me and I presented her with one of the agency's contracts—with the lowest retainer fee we'd ever charged inked in. Once she signed it, we were in business.

Ivins had said Long was a highly respected attorney and she certainly looked the part: beautifully styled blonde hair, expensive black suit, heavy gold jewelry. A face with thin lips, a long nose, and eyes that I was sure could stare down any judge or jury when she was making her case for her clients. She specialized in criminal law.

"Isabel Darkmoon," she said. "She was thirteen, pregnant, and desperate to get away from her family."

"They were abusive?"

"Psychologically. Everyone except for one sister shunned

her. That seems like an old-fashioned word, but they were religious in the extreme and literally would have nothing to do with her. She wasn't allowed to eat at the same table, though she could have scraps from the kitchen. No one spoke a word to her, except the one sister who could only whisper in the night after everyone else had gone to sleep. Isabel had shamed them by being in the wrong place at the wrong time."

"Blame it on the victim."

"Yes." Long leaned back in her chair, eyes narrowed—assessing how much information she could trust me with.

"This is all confidential, Ms. Long."

"Of course." She picked up an oddly coiled paper clip from a shallow container, and began toying with it. Picked up another and linked the two together.

"How did Isabel come to you?" I asked.

"She saw a notice on the bulletin board in the grocery store. We had to be so cryptic in those days: Nevada was not like California. I think it said something like 'In trouble? We can help.' And it gave an unlisted number to call—which was mine. I met her at a drive-in restaurant. Bought her a meal and told her what we could do for her. She needed help badly; she was very undernourished for a pregnant woman and severely depressed. But she wanted the baby."

"Why, if she'd been raped?"

"Because no one loved her and she thought the baby would."

"Bad reasoning, wouldn't you say?"

"Immature reasoning, yes. But by then it was too late for her to abort. And she was very determined for such a young woman. I thought she might be persuaded to put her baby up for adoption, so I sent her to a family in our network who had adopted a number of children."

"And then?"

"I heard nothing. That was the rule of our organization: no further contact, because it might jeopardize the person we'd helped."

Long's eyes had shifted from mine, toward the linked paper clips she was toying with. She was lying, or at least not telling the whole truth.

"No contact ever?" I asked.

She looked at the copy of the contract she'd signed. "No contact until last Monday. She came here, said she'd hitch-hiked from Bridgeport and she needed help."

She paused. I waited. It was one of those moments when I sensed a major connection was about to be made.

"I don't know how she found me. Maybe she's been keeping track of me all along. She was drunk, asking for help. Spun a tale about her daughter from the rape being murdered and she thought the killer was after her, too."

"Who did she think this killer was?"

"The rapist. The daughter's father."

"Did you believe her?"

"I believed she was in trouble. I told her I'd get her into a shelter that also provides psychiatric care. But then she ran out of the office, and I haven't seen her since."

Miri . . .

"Ms. Long, did Isabel have a middle name?"

"I believe it was Miriam."

Right.

"Did you read in the papers about the murder of a young woman over by Tufa Lake last week—Hayley Perez?"

"There was a brief item—"

"She was Isabel Darkmoon's daughter from the rape.

That's why she—now called Miri Perez—is in trouble. And that's why I need to locate her."

Home is the place where . . .

Once again I contemplated the phrase from Robert Frost's "Death of a Hired Man" while Elizabeth Long looked for the notes she'd taken after Miri Perez's sudden appearance and equally sudden departure on Monday.

Miri's oldest daughter, Hayley, had returned to Vernon after years of disappointment and hardship. Miri's youngest daughter, Amy, had returned to the cabin where she'd been squatting at the Willow Grove Lodge.

Where was the home to which Miri would naturally gravitate?

Long sat down at her desk, put on narrow-rimmed glasses, and stared at the notes. "There's nothing here besides what I told you. You can read them, if you like."

I waved the pages away. "These people in Sacramento to whom you sent Miri—who are they?"

"You know I can't—"

"You signed that contract." I pointed to it where it lay on top of a heap of files.

". . . Dean and Jane Ironwood. I don't have an address for them; as a safety measure, we never knew the whereabouts of the people who assisted us."

"Was there anyone else involved in helping Miri—Isabel—escape? She told her sister there was a friend in California who had introduced her to a nice family."

"I can't remember—"

"Try, please."

". . . Hillary King. Also in the Sacramento area."

"Well, maybe I can locate her, or the Ironwoods."

"Why, after all this time?"

"Because, home is— Never mind. Thank you for your time, Ms. Long."

Another dreary motel room, but on this trip in Carson City I'd brought my laptop. And I was on a roll.

I went straight to the expensive search agencies the agency subscribed to. Hillary King. None in the Sacramento area. She could have moved, married and changed her name, or died. I'd concentrate on the Ironwoods.

Ironwood, Dean, Sacramento. He'd been a lobbyist. There was a ton of information on him, but he'd died two years ago.

Ironwood, Jane. She was a registered nurse, license still active. Address and phone number in Carmichael, a suburb northeast of Sacramento. I phoned the number, but reached an answering machine. Left a message asking her to call me on my cellular. Then I settled down to the takeout dinner I'd picked up across the street and a bad made-for-TV movie.

I was asleep before the movie ended. For once it was a peaceful sleep, without nightmares.

Thursday

✦

NOVEMBER 8

I woke in the morning to my cellular's ring and, as I reached for it, was shocked to see that it was after ten.

Hy. "Sorry I haven't called, McCone. I'm in Tokyo."

"A crisis?"

"No, major new client who wanted to meet in person. I tried to leave a message on the ranch machine before I went, but I think it malfunctioned. Squawking noises, like an enraged chicken."

"Damn machines. I swear they make them with a chip that tells them to die the day after the warranty expires. I'll pick up another."

"Good. I had to rush to catch my flight and I've been jammed up ever since, so I haven't had time till now to call your cell. What's doing?"

I explained what had happened since we last talked. "I may have to go to Sacramento. Where's the best place around here to rent a plane?"

"El Aero at Carson City Airport. Ask for my buddy Pete. He'll give you a discounted rate."

Hy had "buddies" in airports throughout the country—

sometimes I thought throughout the world. "Will do. When will you be back stateside?"

"I don't know how long I'll be here, and when I get back home I'll have to play catch-up. Any idea when you'll be coming to the city?"

"I'm not sure. This case—"

"Uh-huh. Now it's a case. Welcome back to the land of the living."

Hy was right, I thought as I stepped into the shower. Since last winter, I hadn't been living—at least not in the sense that I usually did. Although I wasn't yet sure that I wanted to make the reentry, I turned up the water's heat, washed vigorously, and emerged into a new and better day.

There had been a call on my cell while I was in the shower. Ted, with his daily report. I dealt with him, spoke briefly with Patrick, and got off the phone.

Freedom from the tyranny of the agency.

While I was eating breakfast in the motel's coffee shop, the phone rang again. The number on the screen was Jane Ironwood's. While I don't usually talk on the cell in a public place, there were few other patrons and none seated near me, so I picked up.

The voice that spoke was throaty—what in old movies they called a whiskey voice. "Of course I remember Miri," she said after I explained why I'd called. "She was a pleasure to have in our household, more like family than the other children in trouble we usually took in. And we loved Hayley as if she were our own granddaughter. But eventually Miri married Jimmy Perez and they moved to Mono County."

"You sound as if you didn't approve of the marriage."

"When Miri met Jimmy, he'd been around our neighborhood for a little more than a year, doing gardening and handyman work. We never used him because I'd heard that he was unreliable. My husband and I questioned whether he'd be able to give Miri, Hayley, and any future children they might have a good life, but he said he had a brother who owned a ranch outside of Vernon and would give him a good job."

The brother: Ramon Perez. The ranch: Hy's and my small spread.

"Did you hear from Miri after she moved away?"

"A few letters at first. Christmas cards. Four birth announcements. Then nothing."

"Jimmy left her right after their fourth child was born."

A sigh. "So we were right after all."

"Unfortunately, yes. The house where you lived in Sacramento—I imagine you've sold it."

"Oh, yes. When my husband was diagnosed with Parkinson's disease, we had to stop taking in troubled children. And when he died . . . well, it was like living alone in a drafty old barn. I had friends here in Carmichael I wanted to be closer to, so five years ago I sold the house to a company that was going to convert it into commercial space. So far as I know, nothing's been done with it."

"Would you give me the address?"

"Certainly. But may I ask why?"

"Miri's running, trying to escape her life. I have a hunch she might have gone to the one place where she was happy."

"I see." She gave the address and asked me to call again if I had any news.

I set off to rent an airplane to fly to Sacramento.

The former Ironwood home was on Twenty-fifth Street in midtown Sacramento, a block off J Street, in an ethnically diverse area of mixed-use buildings—small shops, restaurants, offices, and private residences. Huge old elm trees and shrubbery that had run wild screened it from the sidewalk, but I could make out a white, three-story shape with a big porch and dormer windows. A flimsy-looking chain-link fence surrounded the deep lot, and a rusted sign proclaimed it as being under renovation for commercial space by Four Star Associates and gave a number for leasing inquiries. It didn't look as if any renovations had ever been made, and I doubted anyone had called the number in a long time. All the same, I copied it down.

Next door was a similarly old but better-kept-up house, outside which a law firm had hung its shingle. On the other side, a big light blue clapboard house with multicolored banners hanging on the porch and a bicycle on the neat lawn—a private home. Across the street a secondhand bookshop, a dental clinic, and another private home.

My prospects for getting onto the property now didn't look good, even though the runaway shrubbery screened it to either side. The attorneys next door might go home at five, but then again they might not. The family on the other side would probably be there in the evening. The bookshop and dental clinic would close down, but the home next to them had large windows overlooking the street.

Why was I even bothering with this? If I was doubtful of gaining entry, how could Miri have done so?

Because she knew the property. She'd lived there for five years.

It was now close to four-thirty. It had taken a while to get a plane from Hy's buddy in Carson City, longer to get a rental car at Sacramento Executive Airport. And then the rental clerk had given me the wrong directions. In a way, the delays had worked to my advantage: it wouldn't be long until dark.

I started the car, U-turned, and drove to a coffee shop I'd spotted along the way. Primarily I wanted to use their restroom, but I also bought a large coffee and a sandwich to go. Then I drove back and parked a few spaces down from where I'd been before. And waited as dusk fell.

Across the street the bookshop and dental clinic were already closed. Lights were on in the private home, but they glowed from behind closed curtains. Lights shone in an upper window of the law firm, but once it became fully dark they went out. Shortly after, a figure descended the front steps, got into a nearby car, and drove away. The private home on the other side of the former Ironwood property remained dark. I waited half an hour longer, then took my small flashlight from my purse, got out of the car, and slipped into the shadows on the side of the property that abutted the law firm's.

The fence continued to the back of a deep lot. A breeze had come up, rustling the leaves of the old elms. I stopped at the fence's rear boundary, saw that it backed up onto a paved space between two buildings on the next street—parking lot, probably, and empty. I moved along, muting the flash's light with my cupped hand. Shone it on the fence and finally saw a place shielded from the parking lot by a disposal bin, where the chain link had been pried up to the height a normal-sized person could slide under.

I looked around, then scrambled under the chain link on my back, headfirst.

The ground was covered with fallen leaves; they clung to my hair and my back. A vine on the other side of the fence took a stranglehold on my ankle and I kicked it free. Then I was inside, sitting on the damp leaves and feeling moisture soak through the seat of my jeans; it must have rained here recently.

I scooted away from the fence and under the drooping branches of a huge cypress. Ahead I could make out unidentifiable shapes and then the house itself. The moon hadn't yet risen—or at least it couldn't be seen from my vantage point—so in order to make my way across the yard I'd have to risk using my flashlight. Small risk, I thought as I turned it on and started out.

The trees ended after a few more feet, followed by an area of waist-high grass that once must have been a lawn. Trees shielded the property to either side. My flash picked out a jungle gym—iron piping, not the colorful plastic ones they have now. Halfway to the house I banged hard into something hidden by the tall grass that was going to leave a nasty bruise on my thigh. I brushed the grass away and found a concrete birdbath, its bowl cracked and crumbling. What else was out here—

"Oof!"

My foot had come down on something round and as it rolled away, I fell on my ass. Jesus, what was *that*? I got up on all fours, felt around, and retrieved the object—croquet ball, the colorful stripe bleached out, covered in cracks and nicks.

Terrific. I'd probably trip over a mallet next, or bugger myself on a wicket.

I straightened and moved more slowly toward the house, feeling around with my hands and feet for other hazards. Arrived unharmed and started up the wide back steps toward a set of French doors.

One of the boards broke under my weight, and I fell through, trapped up to my ankle.

And this is what you used to live for, McCone? Creeping

around in dark, dangerous places in search of someone who's probably heard you flailing about and fled to the next county by now?

I dismissed the questions, extricated my foot from the hole in the boards, and tested each step before I put my weight on it. The French doors proved to be no problem: vandals had broken most of their glass panes, and one side stood slightly ajar. I moved slowly into a large room with a fireplace. The walls were marred by graffiti; beer cans and liquor bottles littered the warped hardwood floors. Used condoms and a pair of woman's lacy panties, too.

Only five years, and all this destruction—courtesy of a company that had bought a handsome, valuable property and allowed it to go to seed. I imagined Miri's distress at finding her former home in this condition. Had she run again—and this time to where? Back to the house in Vernon, where she'd led an unhappy life since Jimmy Perez deserted her—and probably before? I didn't think so.

I moved across the destroyed room and through an archway. This space had not been damaged as much, probably because it faced the street from which lights could be seen by neighbors and passing cars. It was a big, old-fashioned foyer. A staircase ran up either side wall toward the rear, then met in the center and continued.

She'd go up. Up to the bedroom she'd shared with baby Hayley.

I went up, too, along the right-hand branch of the stairs. Turned down the hallway, where open doors revealed rooms empty of anything but more graffiti and trash. Something scuttled across the floor in front of me—a mouse or a rat. Cobwebs brushed my face and clung to my hair. It was cold, and the scents of mold and dry rot clogged my nostrils. Miri couldn't possibly have stayed here. . . .

My instincts prodded me on.

And then I smelled it—faint, but unmistakable. The odor of death.

I moved quickly along the hall to a closed door. Pushed it open and swept the room beyond with my flash. A bare mattress lay on the floor; on it was what looked like a pile of rags.

Not rags. A body.

I crossed the room, shined my light down onto a round face that bore a strong resemblance to both Hayley and Amy Perez. The woman was covered in ratty and torn blankets. She lay on her back, long gray-streaked hair fanned out around her shoulders. Death had removed the evidence of a hard and unhappy life from her features; she looked like a child, deep in peaceful sleep.

I knelt and felt for a pulse that no longer beat. Her skin was as cold as the air around her. I suspected rigor had come and gone.

A shabby purse, an empty liter of a cheap brand of vodka, and an empty vial of pills lay on the floor beside the mattress. I pulled a pair of disposable plastic gloves from my bag, put them on, and checked the purse: driver's license in the name of Miriam Perez, a rumpled card listing Ramon as next of kin, and three dollars. I examined the pill bottle without touching it: a strong tranquilizer prescribed three weeks ago by a doctor in Bridgeport. How many had been left when she mixed them with the vodka I couldn't guess.

So what to do about this? Legally, I should report Miri's death to the Sacramento PD and wait here at the scene. Except I was on the scene illegally. Thus putting my license in jeopardy once again.

But I couldn't just abandon Miri to the ravages of rats, or to be discovered by young people who used the place as a party house. For Ramon and Sara's sake, she needed to be identified and laid to rest. Even though Ramon had said he'd washed his hands of her, he hadn't really meant it. And Sara still cared for her.

Advances had been made in tracing calls to cellular units, so I didn't want to use mine. Where could I find a pay phone?

There was one at a gas station near my freeway on-ramp. I called 911 and made my voice sound young, male, and frightened. Told the dispatcher that I'd found a dead lady at the Twenty-fifth Street address. Second floor, last room on the right. When they asked for my name, I hung up.

It was a clear, starlit night. No wind, easy flying weather. By eleven I'd be back at my motel in Carson City. And as early as possible tomorrow I'd be at the ranch, to help Ramon and Sara through this latest tragedy in the lives of their family.

The flight back to Carson City had somewhat eased my depression about Miri's sad end. There's nothing like breaking free of the earth to mitigate its claims on you. But once I got back to my motel, the gloomy mood descended again and I knew I wouldn't be able to sleep, so I checked out and began driving along the mostly deserted highway.

I thought about Miri. Understandable why she'd had a meltdown upon finding out Hayley had been murdered. Understandable, too, why she'd fled the rehab facility: the prospect of sobriety can be damn scary to a drunk or an addict; I knew all too well because of my brother Joey. But why had she bolted from Elizabeth Long's office? Because Long had offered her only more of the same, a shelter that provided psychiatric care. She'd then gotten a ride—or rides—to Sacramento and returned to the one place she'd been happy, only to find it in ruins.

Accident or suicide? She'd brought along enough vodka and pills to concoct a lethal cocktail. Before I'd left I'd searched for a note and found none, yet many people who commit suicide don't feel it necessary to document their reasons. Miri's reasons were written in the lines on her face, in the history her family and friends could recall.

Vernon was dark and still when I rolled through town at around eleven-thirty, the surrounding countryside even more so. I didn't turn in at our ranch house, but continued to the driveway that led to Ramon and Sara's cabin; it was ablaze with light. I pulled the Land Rover up to the shed that housed Ramon's truck, got out, and noticed an unfamiliar SUV. When I knocked on the door and Sara let me in, I came face-to-face with Kristen Lark.

The Sacramento PD was prompt in having the local authorities notify the relatives of people who had died in their jurisdiction.

"What're you doing here, McCone?" Lark asked.

"I saw the lights and was worried that Ramon or Sara might be sick."

"I see."

"What're *you* doing here?" I asked.

"Informing these good people that they've lost yet another family member."

I feigned shock. "Amy?"

Lark shook her head. "Amy's mother, Miri, was found dead

in a deserted building in Sacramento this evening. SPD asked that we notify the Perezes in person."

"What happened to Miri?"

"Apparent suicide."

I looked past her, saw Sara had left the room and Ramon wasn't in sight. "How did she do it?"

"Booze and prescription drug overdose. Somebody found her and put in an anonymous call—dispatcher thought it was a kid who had been looking forward to an evening of partying and ended up with a corpse on his hands instead."

"That's a shame. Any idea why Miri was in Sacramento?"

"Ramon thinks she used to live there."

"Thinks?"

"He really doesn't know much about Miri's past. His brother Jimmy showed up here one day with a new wife and her four-year-old baby. Miri didn't want to talk about her previous life or the baby's father."

"That baby would have been Hayley."

"Right."

Lark regarded me with narrowed eyes. "Hayley's murdered, her sister disappears, and their mother commits suicide. And there's this other problem of a dead man in the lava fields. Plus you and I are supposed to be working together, but all I get here at the ranch is a machine that makes screaming noises at me, and your cell's always turned off."

"The answering machine has died and I haven't replaced it yet. I've been flying a lot; you can't have the cell on—FAA rules."

"I left messages on your voice mail."

"The mailbox malfunctions a lot."

Again that slitty-eyed look. "Okay for now, McCone. I'll

leave, and you go comfort your friends. But I want to meet with you in the morning."

"Where and when?" I asked, hoping she didn't want me to drive to Bridgeport.

"I'll come to your place, around ten-thirty."

"That's good."

I prefer confronting potential adversaries on my own turf.

Friday

✦

NOVEMBER 9

The phone rang as I stepped out of the shower at around eight-thirty. By the time I got to it, the machine had started: Hy was right—it sounded like an enraged chicken. I picked up, but the squawking went on. Moments later my cell rang.

"McCone, you going to have time to replace that damned machine today?"

"I hope so."

"Good. Try the hardware store. Spare no expense."

"Where are you?"

"Still in Tokyo."

"What time is it there?"

"After midnight, your tomorrow. I'm flying back in the morning."

"Everything go well?"

"Better than well. I'll tell you about it when I get back. How're things with you?"

I didn't want to dwell on yesterday's grim discovery, so I said, "Progressing. I'll fill you in later, too."

We talked a little more, then he told me good morning and I told him good night.

While I was drinking my coffee, the cell rang again. Glenn Solomon.

"Sorry to take so long getting back to you, my friend. Frank Brower had difficulty getting hold of Carl Bates, the attorney back East who asked him to represent Hayley Perez."

"No problem." In truth, I'd forgotten about the inquiry I'd asked Glenn to make.

"The client who asked Bates to contact Brower is Trevor Hanover. He's a major power on Wall Street, owns pieces of Long Island and some of the Bronx, as well as majority shares in several multinational corporations."

"Did this Hanover give any reason for wanting to pay the legal expenses of a hooker in Las Vegas?"

"People like Hanover don't have to give reasons for what they do."

"You know anything else about him?"

"No. I don't follow the Street news much; Bette and I leave handling our finances to someone who does. But Google will tell you anything you need to know."

"What would we do without Google?"

"Probably poke our noses in where they don't belong a lot less often."

Before I began my search I glanced out the window and saw the Perezes' truck drive by. Going to Sacramento to identify Miri's body. Grim task, especially for people as broken up as they'd been last night, but there was no one else to do it. Ramon would shoulder it, though, keeping strict rein on his grief. His responsibility, he'd told me. Even if Amy had been found, he would not have let her do it. He'd already failed to protect her from many of life's harsh realities; if she came back to them—*Dios* willing—he vowed to do better.

Google had plenty of information about Trevor Hanover, although the details of his childhood were sketchy: he'd been born in Erwin, Tennessee, a small town in the northeast portion of the state; his only comments about his upbringing were that it had been "dirt poor" and that he was glad he'd been able to help out his parents in their final years. His rapid rise to the summit of finance was something out of the fabled—and largely false—American dream.

The summer after he turned twenty-one, Hanover was working as a bartender in an East Village club when he broke up a violent confrontation between a drunken young woman and her date, sobered her up, and escorted her home. His demeanor when he delivered her so impressed her father—who was CEO of one of the larger Wall Street firms—that Hanover was invited to come in for a job interview. Again the CEO was impressed, particularly by Hanover's grasp of financial complexities, and hired him as his personal assistant. Later Hanover modestly described his knowledge as "nothing more than anybody could find out from reading the business pages and a few books." From then on his career ran on a fast upward trajectory.

Articles I accessed about Hanover compared him to investment guru Warren Buffett—except Hanover had achieved that status at a much earlier age. Photographs on the sites I visited showed a handsome, brown-haired man with a strong jaw and intense gaze. Hanover was forty-three but looked nowhere near his age—or else he used old publicity photos. He was a skydiver and a pilot, and enjoyed scuba diving. Fifteen years ago he'd married Betsy Willis, a New York City socialite; the union had produced two children—Alyssa, now fourteen, and Trevor Jr., ten.

And then last May the success story had begun to unravel—

I was about to begin a more detailed search when Kristen Lark knocked at the door and called out. I closed the laptop, went to let her in, and poured coffee, and we sat at the table in the breakfast nook.

"So how about you and I bring each other up to speed on what we know," I said.

Lark nodded. "Okay. Start with Boz Sheppard: he's currently in jail in Independence, Inyo County. Got picked up in a drug sting Thursday night. We sent an officer down to interview him. He claims he left Vernon to swing the deal in Inyo County the day you saw him toss Amy out of his pickup, and hasn't been back to town since."

"Has he got people who will alibi him?"

Lark snorted. "Not hardly. His associates're all criminals who're looking for a way to wiggle out of the mess they're in. We'll let Inyo hold him on the drug charges—saves us feeding and housing him—and keep the pressure on. I'm going down there tomorrow."

"Anything on Amy?"

"We've got BOLOs out all over the state and in Nevada, but I don't have much hope."

"And Tom Mathers?"

"Well, that's interesting. The thirty-two-caliber bullet the coroner took out of him is a match for the one that killed Hayley. And it seems T.C.'s alibi isn't as good as we thought. We're going to get a search warrant for her house and the wilderness supply store. She certainly has access to firepower, and she's been one hell of an angry woman lately."

"Toward her husband?"

"Among others. She recently had something going with

Rich Three Wings, but his girlfriend found out and he broke it off. There was a scene between her and Rich at the Union 76 station when they both pulled in at the same time a couple of weeks ago, and she went to Petals and got into it with Cammie Charles in front of two customers."

"May I see your reports on that?"

"I brought copies." Lark tapped her fingers on a file she'd set on the table. "Next we've got Miri Perez. Troubled lady."

"She had reason to be." I explained about the rape over in Nevada, and Miri's family shunning her until she ran away.

"Who told you this?"

"Confidential sources."

She rolled her eyes. "That's what you private operatives always say. It's interesting, though, because it ties in with a local resident—Bud Smith. For years we've known he's a registered sex offender, but of course the details on the underage victim are sealed. Was he Miri's rapist?"

"He was convicted of the crime. But the general consensus, even of the prosecutor, was that he was covering for his brother."

"I've heard rumors to that effect." Lark paused to sip coffee. "So do you have anything else for me?"

"No." I also wasn't about to own up to finding Miri's body and phoning in anonymously. And I didn't want to hand Lark the Trevor Hanover lead till I'd checked it out thoroughly. Once an approach by law-enforcement officials is made to someone that powerful, the avenues of communication become a traffic jam of gatekeepers and attorneys.

After Lark left I went back to the computer, read accounts of the latest chapter in Trevor Hanover's story. In May several of his investment clients had lodged complaints against him with the Securities and Exchange Commission. Excessive trading without their permission, obviously looking to score a big home run and enrich everybody, especially himself. A criminal indictment against him in August. Divorce papers served upon him in early September. Since then he'd become increasingly reclusive, going to ground in an apartment he owned in Manhattan. His family and financial empire were falling apart and, according to an anonymous friend, Hanover "wasn't too well wrapped" these days.

I went to the agency's search engines to dig deeper into Hanover's background. A child named Trevor had been born to Ina and Clay Hanover on the date the bios indicated, in Erwin, Tennessee. But there were no further public records on him or his parents.

I tried neighboring states. Nothing. Widened the search. Still nothing. By then my eyes were aching from staring at the screen, and I realized it was after three and I hadn't eaten. I also realized why I paid Mick and Derek such handsome salaries for their expertise.

I shut off the machine and went to make a sandwich.

Agency business intruded with a call from Ted. "You've been on the phone all day," he said.

"Online. There's only dial-up here. You should've called my cell."

"Maybe you should check its charge."

"Oh, hell, did it discharge again?"

"Yes."

Ted sounded clipped, irritated. I said, "I'm sorry. I'll charge it up right away."

"That would be helpful."

"Is something wrong?"

"Wrong? Nothing except we got a notice from the Port

Commission about a big rent increase. As did all the other tenants. I think they're trying to force us out so they can demolish the pier."

Twenty-four and a half was one of a string of piers along the southern waterfront occupied by businesses; none of them measured up to the glitz of the refurbished Ferry Building and upscale restaurants; the city had plans for the area and they didn't include us.

"When do we have to respond?" I asked.

"Not till after the first of the year."

"That gives us some leeway."

A pronounced sigh. "Shar, can I be frank with you?"

"Of course."

"This is urgent. It's hard to find decent space for an operation of our size in the city. And there're other things here that need your attention."

"Such as?"

"Adah Joslyn is fed up with the SFPD and considering a move to Denver." Adah was an inspector on the department's homicide detail and the live-in love of my operative Craig Morland.

"So if she goes, Craig does, too," I said.

"Right. Also, morale is at an all-time low here. Mick and Derek have put up a sign on their office door saying 'genius room' and it's pissing off everybody else."

"For God's sake, Ted, it's a joke."

"It would be if you were here. You'd put an X through the 'genius' and write 'asshole' instead, and that would be the beginning of a long string of jokes. But without you, everything's kind of edgy. The staff meetings suck; Patrick's so . . . earnest."

They need me.

But do I *need them?*

"Look, Ted, just tough it out a little longer. I'll talk to Mick, tell him to tone down the nonsense."

"You need to talk to him about more than that. He's kind of in a bad place."

"I thought he was over the breakup with Charlotte—"

"No, he's not. And he's engaging in self-destructive behavior."

"Such as?"

"Booze. Long, dangerous motorcycle rides at night."

Shit. "I'll call Rae and Ricky. Maybe they can straighten him out."

"Wouldn't it just be better if you came back and talked with him yourself? I don't know anybody he respects more."

Why me? Why am I always the go-to person in a crisis?

"Okay," I finally said, "I'll come down and talk with him. Attend Monday's staff meeting, too. But I'm working on something up here, and I'll need to get back pretty quick."

"When're you planning on coming down?"

"Well, it's almost the weekend. I could drive there tomorrow, talk with Mick on Sunday, attend the staff meeting on Monday." An idea occurred to me. "Actually, I have a project for Mick which may take his mind off his misery."

"Good. Because he's becoming a major pain in the ass."

After I ate my neglected sandwich, I went for a ride across the meadow on King. In spite of the splendid, clear day, I couldn't keep my mind off the Perezes: Ramon's strength in the face of various tragedies, past and present; Sara's love that enabled him to go on. Amy's disappearance, so long ago now that the sheriff's department had effectively back-burnered it. I'd promised Ramon and Sara I'd try to find her and had run around gathering information, but all that had resulted in was the unearthing of yet another tragedy.

And now things were falling apart in the city, and I'd promised to go down there and try to set things right. . . .

King seemed to sense my melancholy mood. He stopped by some shoots of green grass that were pushing their way through the brown, put his head down, and munched. I stared out across the meadow. Even as winter was closing in, new life was claiming the high desert. After a while I clicked my heels against King's flanks, and he trotted obediently toward the stables.

What was it Ramon had said to me about horses?

What you need to do is show them that you're in control, and that you respect them. Then comes the love.

I was in control, and I respected King.

But love? For a *horse*?

When I returned to the house, the answering machine was still doing its chicken imitation but my cell had recharged. It rang soon after the machine gave a final shriek that sounded—to mix a metaphor—like the chicken's swan song.

"McCone? No new machine yet?" Hy.

"Sorry. Busy day. Where are you?"

"SFO, about to grab a cab for home."

Home. I could sleep next to him in our own bed tomorrow night, see our cats . . .

"I need a favor."

"Anything."

"Will you fly up here tomorrow and take me back?"

"Absolutely."

"Thanks. There're some things I need to take care of in the city. And I really want to see you."

"Me too. Here's a suggestion: why don't I come up to-night?"

"Aren't you tired after that long flight?"

"Not any more."

"Well, if that's the case, just phone with your ETA."

"I'll do that, darlin'."

Saturday

✦

NOVEMBER 10

We lazed in bed till almost noon—it had been another nightmare-free sleep for me—and then Hy went over to see how the Perezes were doing. He came back quickly; no one had been there, but he'd left a note of condolence.

"They're probably still in Sacramento," I said. "This is so much for one couple to bear. I wish I could help more. . . ."

Hy hugged me. "You already have, McCone."

"I feel bad, leaving at a time like this. But the situation in the city—"

"I know. And Ramon and Sara will understand."

"But, Ripinsky, what about King?"

"Who?"

"King Lear."

"Lear Jet?"

"No, King. Who's going to take care of him?"

"One of the sheepherders. They know when Ramon's gone, and they pick up the slack. How d'you think Lear . . . uh, King's survived all these years?"

"Are you sure the herders know Ramon's not home?"

"In territory like this, everybody knows what's going on."

"Not everybody. Not by a long shot."

We arrived in San Francisco at around seven that evening. The cats, Ralph and Allie, were happy to see us, and while Hy was ordering a pizza, Michelle Curley, the teenager next door who tended to them and the house when we were away, came over to give us a report and an arrangement of pyracantha berries from her mother's garden.

'Chelle was an amazing young woman: all-A student; star basketball player; budding entrepreneur. She'd told me only a month before that her dad had volunteered to match the funds she had saved to rehab a wreck of a house in the next block; the purchase had been sealed, and Curley & Curley were in business. I wasn't to be concerned about losing her as a house-and-cat-sitter, she'd reassured me, because projects like this first one always went over budget and she'd need the cash flow.

Real-estate mogul in the making—purple hair, tiger-striped fingernails, multiple piercings and all.

'Chelle's report was good: the cats were eating well, the ficus in our bedroom had responded to the new food she'd been giving it, the chimney sweeper had come out and cleaned both fireplaces. We invited her to share the pizza, but she declined, admitting shyly to having a date.

That night we slept peacefully in the new bedroom suite we'd had constructed on the lower level behind the garage. Just before we drifted off I said to Hy, "I can fix these things with Mick and the agency. With you guarding my back, I can fix anything."

Sunday

✦

NOVEMBER 11

Wrong again, McCone.

The phone woke us before eight that morning. Ricky, saying Mick had been involved in a motorcycle accident and was in critical condition at SF General's trauma center.

I didn't ask for details, simply said we'd be there as soon as possible. As I drove, white-knuckled, to the hospital, Hy said, "This is not your fault. You know that."

"I've been up at the ranch wallowing in me, me, me. If I'd been here it wouldn't've happened."

"Maybe, maybe not. You're not that powerful."

I glared at him, and he shrugged, looked out the side window.

The waiting room at the trauma center was quiet at almost nine; presumably most of the victims of a San Francisco Saturday night had been cared for and released or admitted, and their loved ones—if any—sent home. Rae and Ricky sat on a sofa, holding hands. Her face was pale beneath its freckles. His eyes were bloodshot, his hair unkempt; given that and the beard he was growing for a film role he'd accepted, you'd have thought him a derelict who had come in to escape the fog, rather than a country-music superstar.

We all hugged, and I sat down on the sofa with them while Hy went outside to use his phone.

"You hear anything yet?" I asked.

"He's still in surgery," Rae said. "Broken bones, ruptured spleen, all sorts of injuries."

"Damn kid," Ricky muttered. "Charlene and I never should have let him talk us into that moped."

Ancient history. When he was in his teens Mick had run away at Christmastime because Ricky and my sister had refused him the scooter; as my luck would have it, he'd come to the city and my Christmas Eve job was to find him. And later, as overly well-off and permissive parents will do, my sister and Ricky granted him his wish. A string of more and more powerful bikes had followed.

"He'd have pursued his passion anyway," I said.

"Yeah, that's what the Savage men do—pursue their passions. I should've set a better example—"

"Stop it, Ricky," Rae said. "You've been a good father to him."

"Have I?"

"Yes." She stood. "I'm going to try Charlene again."

Ricky watched her leave the waiting room, then said to me, "This is about Keim, isn't it?"

Charlotte Keim, the operative I'd lured away from Hy's firm years ago, only to have to ask him to lure her back when she broke up her relationship with Mick. "Probably."

"A passing driver found him under his bike on the shoulder of Highway 1 at five this morning, reeking of alcohol. What the hell was he doing there?"

Playing with his death wish.

I didn't voice the thought. "Apparently he's been in a pretty self-destructive mode lately."

"You knew this? And you didn't warn us?"

"I only found out yesterday. It was one of the reasons I came down."

He nodded, grasped my hand. I followed his gaze as a doctor in scrubs approached us. The doctor looked too young to be so tired; he smiled reassuringly at Ricky.

"Your son's a lucky man, Mr. Savage. He'll be in casts for a while—left arm and leg—but he's young and he should heal completely. He'll need physical therapy, and I'd also recommend counseling. Has he been drinking heavily for long?"

Ricky looked at me, shrugged. "I haven't seen much of him lately."

I said, "I think his drinking may have been escalating since last winter, when his woman friend broke up with him."

The doctor looked questioningly at me. Ricky introduced me as Mick's aunt and employer.

"Well," he said after we'd exchanged greetings, "he's still in recovery, but you should be able to visit with him soon for a few minutes. One of the nurses will take you to him."

Then he was gone and Rae was back, saying Charlene and her husband Vic were on their way up from Los Angeles. Hy followed her in, asked about Mick's condition; Ricky reported what the doctor had told us. At that point Charlotte Keim rushed through the entrance.

"What's *she* doing here?" Ricky asked.

"I called her," Hy said.

"Why the hell did you do that?"

"She has a right to know. And he has a right to see her if he wants to. It may even help him."

"Get her out of here."

Hy kept silent, his gaze level with Ricky's. After a moment, Ricky looked away. "Ah, what the hell. Just keep her away from me."

Hy went over to Keim, who was pale, her brown curls disheveled, and guided her to the opposite side of the room.

Rae said to Ricky, "You can't blame Charlotte. Mick did this to himself."

". . . I know that. Like I did a lot of things to myself. And like me, I suppose he'll try to blame it on everybody else."

"I don't think so. Over the past few years you've set a good example for him."

"Whatever. I just want to see him."

I moved away, went over to Hy and Keim. She looked at me, eyes moist. I put my arm around her and said, as Hy had to me earlier, "This is not your fault. It's good of you to come."

"I wouldn't be here if I didn't care for him."

"I know." I looked at Hy. "Why don't you guys get some coffee? I'm going to drive over to the pier for a while."

The pier was always occupied, even on a Sunday. This morning, two cars belonging to the architects in the second-story suite opposite ours were parked in their spaces on the floor. I went up the stairs to the catwalk, and ripped down the GENIUS ROOM sign from Mick and Derek's door, before I continued to my office. I shuffled through the papers in my inbox till I found the Port Commission's rental-increase notice.

They had to be crazy.

No way we could afford this. And even if that hadn't been the case, I'd feel I was being extorted every time I walked through the door.

But where the hell would we find comparable space?

Maybe it was confirmation that I'd be better off out of this business. But maybe not . . .

I settled down to do some hard thinking.

Mick had been moved to a private room when I returned to the hospital. He was awake, his parents and their spouses beside his bed. His left limbs were in casts, the leg elevated; cuts and bruises marred his features and his nose was taped where it had been broken; both eyes were black. And he was angry—with himself.

"I'm such a stupid shit—" He saw me in the doorway. "Hey, Shar, you didn't have to come down here."

"I was already in town when you pulled your genius act."

He smiled weakly. "I guess I better take the sign down."

"I already did."

Charlene hugged me and said, "I think the four of us should take off, so you can talk with Mick before he gets his next pain shot and falls asleep. Meet us at Rae and Ricky's later."

After they'd all exited, I said, "What did you think you were doing?"

He grimaced. "Jesus, I hurt. I don't know. To tell the truth, I don't remember anything except thinking I could fly on the bike."

"Be glad you couldn't."

". . . Charlotte was here. Dad was pissed, but he let her see me."

"And?"

"She told me we'd talk later. I know that probably doesn't mean much, but at least she came."

"And you got the attention you wanted from her."

He closed his eyes. "Not now, Shar."

"Okay. How long're they going to keep you here?"

"Dad's having me moved to a private hospital ASAP."

"Will you have computer access there?"

"Yeah, I'm sure. Why?"

"I don't want your skills atrophying while you recover." I reached out to take his right hand.

Again he grimaced. "I feel half dead. Only dead people don't hurt this much—I hope."

"They'll give you a shot soon."

"I'm counting the minutes."

"Don't talk any more now."

We sat holding hands till the nurse came with the shot and asked me to leave.

The hard thinking at the pier had paid off. Now I detoured on the way home to the Spanish-style apartment my operative Craig Morland and SFPD homicide detective Adah Joslyn shared in the Marina district.

Adah came to the door wearing blue sweats. God, how did she manage to look elegant even when her armpit area was streaked with perspiration?

"Craig and I just got back from our run on the Green," she said, catching with her fingertips a drop of moisture from one of the cornrows she'd recently taken to wearing. Her smooth, honey-tan face creased between her eyebrows. "What's wrong?"

"Nobody called you two about Mick?"

"No. What happened?"

"It's bad, but he'll live. If you'll invite me in and give me a drink, I'll tell you both. And then I have a proposition for you."

* * *

It was after five, and Hy and I were relaxing in front of the fireplace in the parlor, a cat in either lap, when Glenn Solomon returned my earlier call.

I cut from pleasantries to my main question: "How much influence do you have at city hall these days?"

"If you mean, do I have something on the mayor? No. But I've got the goods on some very highly placed officials."

"What about the Port Commission?"

"One of those highly placed officials has influence there, yes."

"You willing to call in some markers in exchange for a free pass on the next few cases you bring to the agency?"

"Always willing to call in markers for you, my friend."

"Okay, here's what I need. . . ."

When I replaced the receiver, Hy toasted me and said, "You're back, McCone. All the way."

Monday

✦

NOVEMBER 12

The Monday-morning staff meeting had gone well. In fact, a kind of giddiness had prevailed. The boss was back—even temporarily. But as I soared above Oakland's North Field on my way back to Mono County, following the ATC's instructions, once again I felt remote from the everyday concerns of the agency.

Hy had suggested I take Two-Seven-Tango. He didn't have time to deliver me and was sure he wouldn't need the plane for a while. I was more than glad to do so. As I set my course toward the Sierra Nevada, I fell into that strange state that I sometimes enter when flying: alert on one level, contemplative on another.

Contemplative about the new direction my life was taking. Contemplative about my current case. All other concerns slipped away as I planned what to do when I arrived.

As I passed the shack that served as Tufa Tower's terminal, Amos Hinsdale gave me one of his "Female pilots—bah!" looks through the window. I waved cheerily in response.

I drove to the Ace Hardware in town and looked over their

limited selection of answering machines. Hy had said to spare no expense, but I bought the cheapest. It would serve for the length of time I remained here, and before we came up again I could pick up a better one at a lower price at Costco.

When I reached the ranch I checked the old machine to see if it had somehow resurrected itself. Not even a peep out of the thing. I disposed of it in the trash bin, set up the new one, and called Kristen Lark for an update.

"Not much to report," she told me. "My interview with Boz Sheppard went nowhere. I'm sure he knows more than he's saying, but he's stonewalling."

"How about if I take a stab at him?"

"If you want, I can set it up. Tomorrow afternoon?"

"Sure."

Otherwise Lark had nothing else to report. She referred to the cases as "dead ends."

I knew otherwise.

I was checking my e-mail when my cell rang. Mick.

"Thought I'd let you know that I'm in this convalescent place Dad had me moved to. It's posh—gourmet meals and pretty nurses and great therapy facilities."

He'd mentioned them in the order I would've expected. "That was fast."

"SF General likes to free up beds."

"You sound good."

"Well, I'm on these terrific pain meds. You asked if I'd have computer access here, so I assume you need something."

"I've got a situation to run by you." I told him about my interest in why a man like Trevor Hanover would hire a high-priced attorney to represent a Vegas hooker.

"Let me play with this awhile," he said. "Back to you later."

* * *

I felt restless, so I drove into town. Petals was open; the clerk told me Cammie Charles and Rich Three Wings were due home from a camping trip in the Toiyabe National Forest that afternoon. Cammie always let her know where they were going and when they'd be back, in case there was a problem such as their vehicle breaking down. When I asked for Charles' home address, the woman gave it to me without hesitation. Small towns—you gotta love them.

The address was a cinder-block house two blocks down on the same street where Miri Perez had lived. An old Toyota with peeling paint and various dents sat in the driveway. I rang the bell, but no one was home.

It was a long drive to Rich Three Wings' place at Elk Lake. I decided to wait a while, see if Cammie came home.

That left T.C. Mathers. Was I up to tackling her? Sure. I'd dealt with tougher, more hostile women in my day and come out with the upper hand.

The wilderness supply store was closed when I got there. Tom Mathers had told me they lived on the property, so I followed a dirt driveway around the store and across a barren acre till I spotted a prefab house nested in the shade of a grove of cottonwoods. A Ford SUV was pulled up outside.

I knocked on the door. For a moment there was no reply, then T.C.'s voice called, "Go away!"

"It's Sharon McCone, T.C. I met you at the wilderness supply last week. I wanted to check and see how you're doing."

"The hell you say." She slurred the words.

"That's what I say."

The remark seemed to confuse her. There was a silence, and then she opened the door.

Drunk, all right: her long reddish-blonde hair was tangled,

her eyes unfocused, and there were stains on her sweatshirt and jeans. She reeked of alcohol and cigarette smoke. She stared at me for a time before motioning me inside. I watched her stumble across the room to a sofa and flop down. She picked up a pewter mug from an end table and raised it to me.

"Welcome," she said. "You here to tear my home apart like those fuckin' deputies did?"

I shut the door and sat in an armchair opposite her. "I only want to talk. Tough time, huh?"

She shrugged. "I've seen tougher."

"I don't know. I was married last year, first time. I can't imagine how I'd deal with having my husband murdered."

"Tom? That asshole. I only married him because all the good guys were already taken."

"Like Rich Three Wings?"

She drank from the mug, replenished it from a vodka bottle tucked beneath the table. "How d'you know about us?"

"In a place like this, everybody knows everything."

"Ain't that the damn truth? That Cammie—little Miss Priss—found out about Rich and me getting it on. Then the shit hit the fan."

"I thought Rich was pretty much committed to her."

"*Pretty* much, yeah. But she was pressuring for marriage, wouldn't even move out to the lake to be with him unless they tied the knot, for Chrissake. He was starting to feel trapped and manipulated when I showed up to buy one of his rocking chairs. I wasn't in any position to trap or manipulate him and he knew it, so he took me to bed. Again and again, till the silly little bitch caught on."

"And so you confronted him and Cammie—"

"Give it a rest. I got a bad temper, but they're both alive, aren't they? And I didn't kill Tom. He had another woman, you know. Maybe you should check her out. Lives in that trailer park where Hayley Perez bought it. Little mouse of a woman. I happen to know he was with her that night, they always got together on Tuesdays."

"That make you angry, T.C.?"

"Annoyed, but I didn't care enough about Tom to kill him over any woman."

"This 'mouse'—you know her name?"

"Judy Perkins. She works as a hair stylist at the Vernon Salon. Little skank, wouldn't hurt anybody. And Tom came home alive and well that Tuesday."

"Any other ideas about who might've killed your husband?"

"I don't know. He was such a nothing. I can't imagine why anyone would bother." Her eyebrows pulled together. "He had something else going, though. Knew something he wasn't telling me."

"For how long?"

"Not very."

"And how do you know this?"

"Tom wasn't subtle. He'd been strutting around acting smug and arrogant, talking about all the money he was going to have, and if I was nice to him he'd share."

"But you have no idea where this money was coming from?"

"Uh-uh." She reached for the bottle, refilled the mug. "It must've been something big. But before he could collect, he went and got himself killed. Stupid bastard. Now what am I gonna do?"

I, I, I . . .

Me, me, me . . .

A prevalent mindset in contemporary society, and God knew I'd recently been guilty of it myself.

So Tom Mathers had had something big going. What, possibly, could that be? He was a wilderness guide; good money in that, and in the supply business, but it wasn't going to make him rich—not unless he'd discovered Bigfoot or a vein of gold during one of those treks.

It sounded to me like blackmail.

There are three kinds of major-crime felons who are too stupid for words: bank robbers, kidnappers, and blackmailers. The first two because they almost always get caught; the last one because they are frequently killed by their own victims.

But who could Tom Mathers' prospective victim be? A wealthy client who had committed some indiscretion on one of his wilderness tours? I'd like to get my hands on Tom's calendar and invoices. Perhaps tomorrow when T.C. would—hopefully—be sober.

But right now, onward to see Judy Perkins.

I drove through the trailer park until I found Perkins' space, one row down from Boz Sheppard's. It was small but well kept-up, with her name painted on a cheerful yellow mailbox. I got out of the Rover and started along a path of flagstones.

A woman's voice called out, "If you're looking for Judy, she's not home."

I turned. The speaker was elderly, wearing shorts that exposed well-muscled legs; for some reason, she was watering her graveled yard.

"You know where she is?"

"Out of town. Someplace near LA. Her mother's taken sick. Probably'll have to be put in a home."

"That's too bad. When did Judy leave?"

"Almost two weeks ago, Sunday. I been picking up her mail."

Almost two weeks ago, Sunday. The day after Hy and I had found Tom Mathers' body.

"You have her mother's address or phone number?"

"No. Why—?"

"That's okay. I think I have it in my book at home."

I started back to the Rover, but the woman said, "Sure has been a lot of tragedy in this place lately."

"You mean Hayley Perez?"

"Yes. And now I hear they've arrested Boz Sheppard. Such a nice young man; he used to help me take out my garbage."

Well, everybody has a few good points. "The night Hayley was killed—did you hear the shot?"

". . . Yeah, I heard it. Everybody did."

"But nobody called 911."

"Not that I know of. Or if they did, they're not saying. I didn't; I locked my doors and kept the lights low. I'm old and so're a lot of the other folks here. Not easy to defend ourselves."

"Did Judy hear it?"

"She didn't say. You'll have to ask her yourself." She turned back to watering her gravel lawn.

The old Toyota was still in Cammie Charles' driveway, but its trunk lid was up. I parked behind it, glanced inside on my way to the house's propped-open front door. Boxes and plastic garbage bags. The backseat contained more boxes and a couple of suitcases.

As I reached the door, I came face-to-face with Charles. Her arms were loaded with a comforter and pillows, her pert face flushed with exertion.

"What's happening, Cammie?" I asked.

She stared, not recognizing me.

"Sharon McCone. We met at Petals—"

"Oh, right. Would you mind . . . ?" She motioned with her head that she wanted to get around me.

I took a couple of pillows from the top of the bundle, stepped back, and followed her to the car. "You moving in with Rich—?"

"No. That's over. I'm going back to the Bay Area." She stuffed the comforter into the trunk, took the pillows from me.

"What happened?"

She didn't reply, punching the pillows into place as if they were defying her.

"Does this have to do with Rich's affair with T.C. Mathers?"

She slammed the trunk lid shut and turned to face me. "God, how many more people have to remind me of that? No, it does not."

"What, then?"

"None of your damn business."

"The two of you were on a camping trip. What went wrong?"

"What can go wrong on a camping trip? A bear ate our food? We burned the s'mores? Rich didn't catch any fish? Take your pick!"

"Seriously . . ."

"Seriously, I'm out of here. Go away!"

"Cammie—"

She straightened, balling her fists. "You want to know what's wrong? This place. People talking and prying into your life. People who don't really care about anybody but themselves, and will do anything to avoid responsibility. *Go away!*"

No sense in antagonizing her further. I went.

Rich Three Wings was chopping wood again. The sound of the axe smashing its target rang out over the quiet waters of Elk Lake. Given the sorrow and aggravation he'd suffered recently, he'd soon have enough logs to fill all the fireplaces of Vernon.

He heard me approach and turned, eyes reflecting the fire from the late afternoon light off the lake.

"What do *you* want?" he demanded.

"I saw Cammie—"

"Fuck Cammie!"

"What went wrong, Rich? You were camping in Toiyabe—"

"Who said we were in Toiyabe?"

"The clerk at Petals."

"Verna? Stupid bitch doesn't know one camping place from another. We were over in Yosemite."

But the clerk had been sure that they'd gone to the national forest.

"Whatever," I said. "Something went wrong, though."

"Damn right it did!" He turned away, resumed his chopping.

"You want to talk about it?"

No answer, just the ringing of the axe.

"Rich?"

"No, I *don't* want to talk about it."

"But she's moving back to the Bay Area. It must've been serious."

He pivoted, the axe held high, the sunlight making its metal blade shine as fiery as his eyes. "What part of 'no' don't you understand?"

I began moving away, watching him carefully. "I understand you're hurting. You know where you can find me if you need a friend."

It was nearing dusk and Petals was closed. I walked two doors down to Hobo's and asked the friendly bartender with whom I'd spoken nearly two weeks earlier if he knew where Verna lived.

"This got to do with Miri?" he asked.

"In a way. I want to buy some flowers."

"Poor Miri. But I don't think there'll be a service. Just cremation and her ashes scattered on the lake."

"These are for Sara and Ramon—to try to cheer them up."

"Nice idea. Verna's out at that trailer park where Miri's daughter got herself killed."

"You know which space?"

"Just look for the Airstream with all the rosebushes outside."

The rosebushes were blooming. I could see their huge blossoms even in the dim light. Verna must be some gardener, I thought. Rosebushes could be coaxed to bloom year-round at California's lower levels, but I'd never seen them this late in the fall at such a high altitude. The trailer was one of those streamlined silver ones. Light glowed behind its closed blinds, and music filtered out—something soothing and classical that I didn't recognize. Maybe Verna's choice of music was what made the roses grow so well. More likely it was her green thumb: some people just have the knack. For others, like me, the thumb is black.

She answered my knock after a few moments, wearing a Japanese-style robe, her hair wrapped in a terry cloth turban. I gave her my card, said I had a few questions about Cammie Charles' and Rich Three Wings' camping trip.

"Why?" she asked.

"I spoke with Cammie about an hour ago. She's moving back to the Bay Area."

"I know. She called and asked me to cover for her at the shop tomorrow."

"What happened?"

Verna didn't answer the question, but she let me inside. She turned off the music, motioned me to be seated in one of a pair of armchairs facing a small TV.

"I'm worried about Cammie." She reached for a pack of cigarettes on the table between us. "You mind?" she asked.

"No," I lied. "Were she and Rich camping in Yosemite or Toiyabe?"

She flicked a lighter, inhaled deeply, and blew out a plume of smoke. "Toiyabe. I told you that before."

"You did, and that's what puzzles me. Rich claims they were in Yosemite."

"No way. Cammie's still an urbanite—deathly scared of 'something bad happening'—as if it wasn't more likely to happen in the Bay Area than here." She paused, probably reflecting back on the events of the past weeks. "Well, it *used* to be more likely. Anyway, we were good friends, so she always let me know where they'd be going and when they'd be back. Usually she'd call to tell me they'd gotten there okay."

"Did she call this time?"

"Yeah. They were at a combination gas station and convenience store off of 395."

"Was Rich with her when she made the call?"

"I don't know— No, wait. She said he'd forgotten to bring beer and was inside picking up a couple of six-packs."

"You know where they went in Toiyabe?" From what I remembered of my only visit to the forest, there were a number of places where you could enter: some led to secondary roads, others only to trailheads.

"Devil's Gate, a few miles before Fales Hot Springs. There's no overnight parking or camping there, so they'd pull the car off into the trees and hike in to some favorite place of theirs." She stubbed out her cigarette, which was only half-way smoked. "Trying to quit. Figure if I only smoke part . . . But that's bull and I know it."

"Did Cammie explain what went wrong on the trip?"

"Not really. She said something they saw up there and Rich's reaction to it that told her he wasn't the man she thought he was."

"Something they saw?"

"That was all she said." Verna shrugged. "If you ask me, Cammie's trying to throw a scare into Rich."

"Why?"

"Because he won't marry her. She gave me a phone number where I could reach her in the Bay Area. Probably she thinks I'll pass it on to him and he'll come after her."

"May I have it?"

She read it to me from a scratch pad on the table. Area code 510—East Bay, a lot of territory.

"I'm worried about her," Verna said again. "I know for a fact she's broke—probably doesn't have ten bucks on her."

"Well, she gave you that phone number. It must belong to a friend, somebody who'll help her."

"Hope so."

"If she gets in touch, will you let me know? You can call me on my cell."

She looked at my card, nodded again. "Cammie's a nice woman. She deserves better than Rich Three Wings."

"Why d'you say that?"

"Well, he cheated on her and now he doesn't want to get married. In my book, that makes him pond scum."

I drove directly to Tufa Tower, where I fetched the San Francisco aviation sectional that covered this area from the plane. Then I went to Zelda's, took a table in the bar area, and ordered a burger and a beer. I'd also brought with me the *Thomas Guide* from the Rover. While I waited for my food, I sipped and studied them both.

The guide showed me where the Devil's Gate entrance to the Toiyabe National Forest was. A short way inside, the road stopped in the middle of nowhere. Well, that didn't tell me anything. Next I studied the sectional. It showed that the area where the couple had camped was about three miles from the trailhead, southeast of Mount Patterson, altitude 8,500 feet. There were some buildings nearby—probably maintenance sheds or other rudimentary facilities.

Well, great. That helps a lot.

My food came. I ate, contemplating the situation. They'd gone up toward Mount Patterson and stumbled across something. Rich had reacted in a way that told Cammie he wasn't the man she thought he was.

People who don't really care about anybody but themselves, and will do anything to avoid responsibility.

What had Rich Three Wings done to avoid responsibility?

After I left the restaurant I called the number in the Bay Area that Verna had given me. A machine told me I'd reached the Clarks. I decided not to leave a message; Cammie couldn't possibly be there yet and wouldn't return my call anyway.

On the new machine at home I found—among others—a message from Kristen Lark: "I've arranged for you to see Boz Sheppard down in Inyo at one o'clock tomorrow."

I returned the call, got her machine, and left my own message about my day's activities. Then I curled up in the old, saggy, spindle-posted double bed and pulled up to my ears the quilts that Hy's mother had made for it. In minutes, I was asleep.

No more dreams about pits for me. Other grotesque and disturbing things might haunt my mind in sleep—and probably always would—but somehow I'd climbed my way into the sunlight like a clever spider should.

Tuesday

✦

NOVEMBER 13

Inyo County is one of the largest in California: ten thousand acres that encompass Mount Whitney, the highest point in the U.S. outside Alaska; Owens Valley, the deepest on the American continents; and one of the most beautiful, forbidding, and awe-inspiring places in the world, Death Valley.

Inyo's size makes it a difficult county for its sheriff's department to patrol: a person on the run can easily hide out there; the remains of victims of violence are frequently not found, if at all, until they're reduced to bone fragments; residents of small, hostile enclaves are clannish, impervious to the law, and outright dangerous. An extreme example is the Manson family, who conducted their murderous forays from an isolated ranch east of Death Valley.

In the interest of saving time, I opted to fly Two-Seven-Tango to the county seat of Independence, then call a taxi to take me to the jail at the opposite end of town. I'd driven through there on the highway before, but always in a hurry to reach another destination; now, as the cab took me along the main street, I noted motels and small businesses, false-fronted buildings, side streets on which modest homes were tucked. Independence reminded me of Bridgeport: an old-fashioned courthouse, definite Western feel, and at its limits the empty, sage-covered desert stretching toward distant purplish hills. Today was clear but cold; snow dusted faraway peaks, and few people moved along the sidewalks; those who did hunched inside their heavy outerwear for warmth.

The driver dropped me at the starkly functional-looking jail and said he'd probably be there when I came out. "Nothing much happening today. You're my first fare. If I'm not here, call and ask for Troy." He gave me his card.

Lark had paved the way for me and, after the usual security checks, I was ushered into the visitors' room; shortly afterward a guard brought in Boz Sheppard.

Now that I had a close-up look at him, I decided Sheppard looked as if he were descended from rodents—white lab rats, perhaps. His nose came to a sharp point; his teeth were long and yellowed; he sported a scraggly mustache and an even more scraggly beard; his greasy brown hair was drawn back into a ponytail. Under the orange jail jumpsuit there would be tattoos—usually are on men like him.

He smiled at me, showing more of those teeth than I'd've liked to see, and said, "So Mono's sent in reinforcements, huh?"

I studied him until his smile faded and he shifted in his chair.

"I don't know what you mean by 'reinforcements,'" I said, "but if it's any comfort to you, I don't think you killed Hayley Perez."

He cocked one eyebrow—interested.

"I do think you know more than you've told the deputies. You're interested in cutting a deal on the drug charges, so you're holding something back."

He shrugged.

"Okay, listen to this, Boz: I don't give a rat's ass about the drug charges. And I'm not a cop. I'm not even acting in my capacity as a private investigator. I'm here as a friend of the Perez family, Ramon and Sara. They've had a lot of grief lately and I want to give them some closure."

"How?"

"By finding out what happened to Amy and who killed Hayley."

He considered, tapping his fingers on the table. "What's in it for me?"

Nothing, you asshole.

"If you cooperate with me, I could work on your case, find you a way out of here." Silver-tongued devil McCone.

"Yeah?" More interested. "You're from some big agency in San Francisco, right?"

"I'm the owner of the big agency."

"Huh." More finger-tapping. "It's not like I know anything. I mean, *really* know."

"But you suppose something."

"More like it."

"And that is . . . ?"

He shook his head. "I gotta have guarantees, man. I can't do any more hard time—"

"Well, there *aren't* any guarantees. I don't know if I can help you. But what I can do if you don't cooperate is go out there"—I motioned at the door through which I'd entered—"and tell the deputies that you're bluffing. And then I can go back to Mono and tell the authorities there that in my opinion you're guilty of both Hayley's and Amy's murders. There's also your trespassing on my ranch Halloween night, spooking my horse, and then knocking me unconscious. To say nothing of your second visit to Willow Grove the next night."

What I'd said left him speechless, but not for long. "I didn't kill nobody. Amy was alive and kicking last time I saw her. Hayley, too. And I haven't been on your goddamn ranch since I did a fencing job there a while back. Thursday night I was down here getting busted."

"Well, Hayley's dead, and Amy hasn't surfaced since I saw you throw her out of your truck. I'm the one who can put both deaths solidly on you."

"Amy ain't dead. She's probably out whoring around someplace."

"You ever heard of a no body conviction? I can provide enough evidence against you for one on Amy. Hayley, that's probably open and shut. The jury wouldn't be out an hour."

"Shit, you wouldn't—"

"Try me." I folded my hands on the table and waited.

It took seven seconds—something of a record in my experience.

"Okay," Sheppard said, leaning forward and lowering his voice, even though no one was listening. "I don't know about Amy. But I told Hayley I had business down here and was gonna leave the morning of the thirty-first, Halloween. She asked me to go on the thirtieth. Said she had an important meeting with somebody and it was better if I wasn't around."

"And?"

"I drove down early. Next thing I hear, she's dead."

"Any idea who this person was?"

"No, but I think it involved money. She said the meeting could change her life if it worked out, and if it didn't she'd go to the media and get famous."

"Was the person male or female?"

"Male, I think. She said 'he' once."

"Where was she meeting him?"

"Well, at the trailer, where else? That's why she wanted me away. That's where she was killed."

I remembered the dress Hayley had been wearing: black silk, expensive-looking. What else? Ridiculously spiked red sling-back heels. Garish red costume jewelry that was supposed to simulate rubies. The shoes and the jewelry were junk, probably what she'd worn for her johns in Vegas. But that dress was stylish—possibly a leftover from her time with Jack Buckle in Oregon. And there'd been a shaker half full of martinis and two glasses on the breakfast bar. One of the glasses had been broken.

So she'd worn her best clothing and made drinks for an important meeting that could change her life. All dressed up for whoever it was. And the man had put a bullet through her finery and into her heart.

Life-changing meeting. Certainly was.

Boz Sheppard was still holding something back, but he'd given me a few ideas. I could tackle him again if those didn't work out.

I flew north, but instead of landing at Tufa Tower I kept going to the northeast, studying my sectional, until I found the Devil's Gate entrance to Toiyabe National Forest. I spiraled down low and slowed the plane. There was something unusual—although not alarming—about the way the engine was running, and I remembered the plane was due for its hundred-hour inspection next week. Our mechanic would diagnose the problem then.

The entry road ended in a parking area. No cars on a weekday this late in the year. I glimpsed a trail leading through browned grass to the northeast, but it soon disappeared under a stand of scrub pine. I crested them, found a mountain meadow ringed by sunbaked hills, and flew in a circular pattern, hoping to pick up the trail again. No luck. Only a dark wood structure with a tumbledown roof—not one of the buildings indicated on the sectional.

Something hidden out there, I thought. Something that made Cammie Charles leave her lover.

The sun was waning when I drove up to Sara and Ramon's cabin. Their truck was there; I went to the door and knocked.

Ramon greeted me, his face heavy with sorrow. "Thanks for coming, Sharon," he said. "Did somebody tell you?"

"Tell me . . . ?"

His shoulders slumped. An old man before his time.

I said, "I came to see how you and Sara are doing," I said.

"That's more than anybody else has."

"I don't understand."

"We're scattering Miri's ashes on the lake in half an hour. I put out the word in town, said folks should come here first for a drink or some coffee. You're the only one."

Sad. So sad. "Well, I'd love some of that coffee."

We went into the living room, where a fire blazed on the stone hearth. Sara came out of the kitchen, moving slowly; the past weeks had aged her, too. She hugged me and then sagged onto the sofa.

"Have you heard from Amy?" I asked.

"No. I doubt we'll ever see that girl again."

"Don't give up; I'm still looking for her."

"Thank you, Sharon." Sara put her hand on my arm.

Ramon looked at his watch. "You really want coffee, Sharon?"

"Not if you'd rather get going. Whose boat are you using?"

"Bob Zelda's. We're casting off from his pier."

"Then let's go."

Ramon and Sara exchanged surprised looks. He said, "You want to go with us?"

"I'd like to, unless you'd rather keep it private."

"No, no . . ." He looked away. "But why?"

Because I don't want you and Sara to be alone out there.

"I didn't know Miri, but I feel as if I had. I want to pay my respects."

Because I was the one who found her and left her body all alone till the police could come. Because I owe her.

Tufa Lake: deserted, its waters catching faint fire from the sun disappearing behind the mountains. Silent, too, once Ramon shut off the outboard motor. The birds were tucked into their nests, or had migrated along the Pacific Flyway to their winter homes. Wavelets rocked the boat gently as the three of us sat there, not speaking.

After a moment Ramon cleared his throat. "I don't know how to do this."

I thought of when my brother John and I had scattered my father's and grandfather's ashes from a rented plane—my grandfather's also, because our family has an unfortunate tendency to avoid dealing with its dead. I didn't remember if John and I had said any words.

Sara said, "Tell her what's in your heart, Ramon."

"Do I have to say it out loud?"

"No."

He bowed his head for a few moments. Then he took the box that lay on the seat next to him, opened it, and emptied it downwind.

I thought I heard him say, "Goodbye, Miri," before he started the motor and headed for shore.

Wednesday

✦

NOVEMBER 14

I was out of bed before dawn and in the Rover by first light, heading for the Devil's Gate entrance to Toiyabe National Forest.

I'd spoken with Lark the night before, reporting on my interview with Boz Sheppard, and telling her the scenario of Cammie Charles and Rich Three Wings' camping trip. Lark had allowed as it wasn't enough of a lead for their overworked department to pursue, but said I was welcome to go ahead myself. So here I was, off on another fool's errand.

The Toiyabe is a huge forest with eight designated wilderness areas, some of whose ranger stations are as far as five hundred miles apart. It stretches over the Great Basin from the Sierra Nevada to the Wasatch Mountains of Utah, and encompasses snowcapped peaks, prairies, and granite canyons. The changes in elevation are sudden and extreme, making for a tremendous variation in climate, wildlife, and scenery. The Bridgeport Ranger District, where I was headed, is one of the largest in the forest—an area formed by millions of years of glacial, earthquake, and volcanic activity.

I easily found the turnoff I'd seen from the air and drove to the parking area. No cars today, either. I got out of the Rover, shouldered my backpack. The pack was light—a couple of bottles of water, a sandwich and an apple, and a pair of binoculars. After a moment's hesitation I reached back into the vehicle and took out Hy's .45, which I'd stowed in the side pocket.

Rattlesnakes, I'd told myself at the time.

Snakes of any kind—particularly human, I told myself now.

I tucked the gun into my belt and set off toward the trailhead.

Cold under the trees, piney smell strong. The trail was good, frequently traveled. It was quiet here too: only an occasional birdcall. I looked for evidence of where Cammie and Rich might've camped, but found nothing.

Finally I reached the brushy meadow. At its far side was the tumbledown log building that I'd seen from the air and more trees, beyond which the sand-colored hills rose into the clear blue sky. I crossed the meadow toward the building—once a barn, from its appearance. Probably a leftover from the days when this was private ranchland. The roof had partially caved in, but the near wall was intact. I slipped up to it, feeling foolishly dramatic in the bright light of day, and peered around the side. Boards were missing there; I moved along and did some more peering through the openings.

Nothing but the play of light and shadow inside an empty structure.

I kept going to the other side. Most of the wall there was gone, ravaged by time and the elements. Cautiously I stepped inside.

And stopped, sniffing the air. Something had burned here

recently. When I moved forward I located the source of the odor—a doused campfire near the far, mostly intact, wall.

Rich and Cammie had camped at a favorite place. What better than a falling-down barn? Shelter from the night cold, a cozy nest at this time of year. The park service had probably left the barn to collapse rather than demolishing it, not thinking it could serve as a haven for unauthorized campers—and be a potential fire hazard.

Okay, then, whatever Rich and Cammie had found here must be reasonably close by. I headed for the stand of trees along the hill's base.

Cold. Dark. You wouldn't think the pines could grow so thickly at this elevation. I batted back branches, avoided exposed tree roots. No trail, just acres of forest.

Would Rich and Cammie have come here? I doubted it. There was no sign of human visitation. I turned back, went the wrong way, and came to a place where a large section of branches had been broken away, so large that through it I could see the meadow and the barn. There were tire tracks in the damp earth here. I followed them, ducking under the fractured branches.

There it was: an SUV, tucked way back under the trees. Filthy white, with a trailer hitch. As I moved forward, I identified it as a Subaru Forester. It was dusty and stained with pine sap and the right rear tire had gone flat. Branches cascaded over its roof.

Christ, not another body?

I peered through the Forester's dirty rear window.

Empty.

I circled it, peering through the side windows.

Empty.

The passenger door was unlocked. I leaned inside it to

open the glove box. Maps and some utensil-and-napkin packages from Kentucky Fried Chicken. A pencil flashlight and a bottle opener. Small pack of Kleenex. And, under it all, the Subaru's registration and insurance card.

Herbert Smith, Vernon, California.

I was standing outside the convenience store by the highway when Lark pulled up in her cruiser. She waved at me and yelled, "Come on, McCone!"

I'd driven to the store where Cammie and Rich had stopped for beer on Friday, to use the pay phone because my cell wouldn't work in the area. While I waited for Lark I asked the clerk if he remembered the couple. Yes, he said, they'd come in around three. The woman had made a call, the man had bought beer and beef jerky.

Now I slid into the cruiser next to Lark. "Are your technicians on the way?" I asked her.

"By chopper. You got some kind of divining rod?"

"What?"

"You know, like what they used to use to find water—only *you* find dead people."

"There was no dead person in the SUV."

"You want to bet that we won't find one within a few hundred yards of it?"

"I'm not a betting woman."

"You're lucky. I am."

I sat in the cruiser after I'd shown Lark where the Forester was hidden and watched her technicians arrive by a sheriff's department helicopter. Then I got out and went to the far side of the barn, where I sat on the dusty ground and ate my sandwich and apple and sipped bottled water. Contemplated the mountains and the pines.

I was feeling at peace again, taking pleasure in the natural world in spite of my discovery in the forest. I'd taken steps toward my future; I'd taken steps to find out what had happened here, however grim. I thought of Amy. A certainty stole over me: I would find her, dead or alive, and set Ramon's and Sara's minds at rest.

About an hour later, Lark found me there. She sat on the ground too, took out her own water bottle, and drank deeply.

"My people've gone over the vehicle and the surrounding scene. We'll have it towed to the garage so the techs can go over it again. I've got deputies on the way to conduct a search."

I looked at my watch, was surprised to find it was only a little after two. Still, the light couldn't be good under those tall trees, and dusk would fall early in the shadow of the mountains.

Lark sensed what I was thinking. "They'll search as long as they can, then come back tomorrow."

I nodded. "You have time to run me back to the convenience store? There's nothing more I can do for you here."

"Sure." She stood up, dusted off her pants. "Just let me tell them I'm going."

On the drive back to Vernon, I thought some more about Amy.

Waiflike woman, standing outside the Food Mart in the dark, pulling her flimsy clothing around her against the cold. Big eyes, and somehow I'd sensed her fear.

Tossed-away woman by the roadside, too proud to accept my offer of help.

The derelict cabin at Willow Grove Lodge, her meager possessions scattered around. The blood.

Dana Ivins had been a mentor to her. Bud Smith had tutored her. But somehow she'd fallen through the cracks.

The miles slipped by and soon I was in Vernon. I pulled to the curb across from the Food Mart, intending to walk over there and buy something microwavable for dinner. Sat there instead, my hands on the wheel, listening to what my subconscious had been trying to tell me while I sat on the dusty ground in the mountain meadow. Recalled the phone conversation Bud Smith had been finishing in his office when I went to see him. And got the message—loud and clear.

I'd have to move fast, before the sheriff's deputies found Smith's body.

Aspen Lane was deep in shadow when I reached it. I thought I saw a light shining faintly through the trees from Bud Smith's double-wide, but when I turned into his driveway all was dark. I parked the Rover next to the boat that was up on davits and got out, my feet crunching loudly on the gravel. No other vehicle in the yard, yet I could smell the aroma of cooking food coming from inside the mobile home.

None of which was unexpected.

I moved up onto the deck under the awning. Knocked.

No response, but there was a soft scurrying noise. I sensed someone on the other side of the door, breathing shallowly.

I knocked again. Called out, "Amy, open up!"

The breathing stopped, then resumed at an accelerated pace. I tried the doorknob. Locked.

"Amy, I'm a friend of your Uncle Ramon. Please open the door."

Gasping now; she'd begun hyperventilating.

"Please, Amy!"

A click as the lock turned. When I pushed inside, I found her crouching on the floor to the right of the door, her arms clasped across her breasts. Her shoulders heaved; she looked up at me with wide, frightened eyes.

"It's okay," I said. "Stay there."

In the kitchen I found a drawer full of folded grocery bags, took the smallest back to her. "Breathe into this."

She stared, not understanding. I put the bag over her nose and mouth and repeated, "Breathe."

The bag helped her get herself under control. Then she was able to stand, lean on me as I led her to one of the chairs.

"I know you. . . ."

"Yes. I saw you outside the Food Mart, and then again on the highway when Boz Sheppard threw you out of his truck."

". . . You asked me if you could help."

"And you walked away."

Silence.

"I don't think you want to walk away again." Dusk was gathering outside, so I turned on a lamp. Amy was pale and much too thin; I could see her ribs outlined by her tube top.

A burning smell from the kitchen. I went in there and took a saucepan I hadn't noticed before from the stove. Turned a control knob off. Ravioli, courtesy of Chef Boyardee. The empty can sat on the counter.

When I returned to Amy, she had pulled her legs up onto the chair and was wrapping herself in an afghan that had been slung across its back.

I tucked it around her, sat in the other chair.

"You've been here since whatever happened at Willow Grove Lodge?" I asked.

She nodded.

"Amy, talk to me."

"Okay, I been here since the day after. I was asleep that night when somebody broke in. I fought him, and he stuck me on my forehead with a knife." She touched a bandage above her right eyebrow. "So I kneed him in the balls and got away and hid in the grove. Next day, when I thought it was safe, I used the pay phone and called Bud. He brought me here. That night he went back to get my stuff from the cabin, but before he could pack it all somebody almost walked in on him, and he had to run off."

So it had been Bud Smith, not Boz Sheppard, I'd chased through the grove. But whose presence had I sensed while I was having my picnic there? Not Amy's or Boz's; they'd been in his truck on the highway. Probably some trespasser who saw me and thought I belonged there.

"Where's Bud now?"

Amy shrugged.

"Answer me. We don't have much time."

"Why?"

"I found Bud's Forester this morning in the Toiyabe National Forest. The sheriff's people are searching for his body. When they find it, they'll come here."

"Bud? Bud's not dead."

"Then where is he?"

She shook her head. "He said he'd come back. I been waiting every day. . . ."

"Where did he go?"

"I don't know." She pulled the afghan up to her chin. "He

had a phone call and he left in a big hurry, didn't even unhitch the empty boat trailer from his SUV. Said something about a relative. . . . I don't know!"

I considered my options. None of them were good. Finally I said, "You go get whatever stuff you need. Two minutes, no more."

Big dark eyes filling with suspicion. "Where're you taking me?"

"Home, to Ramon's."

Home is the place where . . .

Ramon and Sara fussed over Amy, crying and hugging her and bundling her up in front of their fireplace. Sara fetched homemade soup and the four of us sat around the coffee table to eat it.

After we were finished, I asked Ramon and Sara if we could speak privately. We went into the kitchen.

"She's been living in Bud Smith's mobile home since the day after the attack on her at Willow Grove. It happened the same night her sister was killed. I should've figured it out sooner: I sensed somebody was close by when I first went to the trailer looking for Bud. Amy heard my car and hid in the trees. The door was unlocked, so I went in and found clothing in the guest room—Amy's. At the time I thought it belonged to a roommate."

"Poor kid," Sara said. "Why was she living at the lodge in the first place? She had a perfectly nice room here in town."

"From what she told me on the way here, I gather it had to do with Hayley. Amy used to worship her big sister, even though she hadn't seen her for years. But when Hayley came back to Vernon, Amy found out she was a prostitute. It tore up the fragile new life she'd built for herself. She regressed and, essentially, went home to the lodge."

"But after the attack, why didn't she come to us?"

"Because it was the logical place for whoever attacked her to look. She was scared, though she didn't know Hayley was dead till Bud told her."

Ramon's face darkened. "That pervert had our Amy—"

"Smith's not a pervert, and he didn't do anything to Amy but give her shelter. The problem is, he's likely been murdered up in Toiyabe. When the sheriff's department finds his body, they'll go to his trailer and discover somebody else besides Smith has been living there. After that, it's only a short step to finding out it was Amy."

He glanced helplessly at Sara. "What should we do?"

I said, "Do you have a lawyer?"

"Yeah, but I don't think he's up to handling something like this."

"Well, then, just make sure that she gets a lot of reassurance and a good night's sleep. Chances are they won't find Bud's body till tomorrow—the light in Toiyabe was already bad when the sheriff's people started searching. I'll be back here around eight in the morning, take Amy to talk with the deputy in charge of the case. If she needs a lawyer, I can call one."

Ramon asked, "What was this business with Boz Sheppard throwing her out of his truck?"

"On the way here we passed the spot where it happened. She told me he picked her up in town and came on to her, wanted her to go down to Inyo County with him. She refused, things got ugly, and he threw her out. I'd say there's a good possibility that Sheppard was the one who attacked her in the cabin."

"Did he rape her?"

"No."

"But he cut her—the bastard!"

"If he's the one who attacked her, he won't get away with it."

Two pairs of hopeful eyes looked back at me; Amy was all they had left of their family, and they needed me to sort this out.

Please help me. You can make this horrible thing right.

I don't know what to do. Please help me.

I always wanted to say to clients, "Maybe I can, maybe I can't."

I always said, "I'll give it my full attention. Don't worry."

There were various messages on my machine when I got back to the ranch house: Hy, Ted, Adah Joslyn, Ma, Patrick, Mick. I noted them down and began returning them in order of importance. Mick, since he'd said it was urgent, came first.

"I did a nationwide sweep on this Trevor Hanover, using some really sophisticated software Derek and I have worked up."

"You've been creating sophisticated software on *my* time?"

"No, on *ours.* At night and on the weekends. Derek's between women and, well, you know where I'm at. Anyway, today was the first time I'd put it through its paces and judging by its performance, I'd say he and I are due to make a bundle on the licensing. I'd've gotten back to you sooner, but the nurses keep taking my laptop away and telling me I should rest."

"Well, you should. What have you got on Hanover?"

"I concentrated on the gap between when he was born and when he was rewarded with the cushy job for bringing the investment broker's drunken daughter home. But Trevor Hanover—the one born in Tennessee—never lived in New York City or worked as a bartender. He and his folks died in an apartment house fire in Chicago when Trevor was thirteen."

"The old stolen-identity trick. Our Trevor was in his twenties when he surfaced as a lucky bartender. Back then you could still easily get away with that kind of scam. Any details on the fire or the parents?"

"Typical tenement fire. Too many people, too many appliances, bad wiring. The father worked as a security guard. Mother described as a housewife. Trevor was in eighth grade. There's not much information."

"In short, they weren't anybody, so no one cared." Sad, bad truism of our society: we can cry over a movie star's marital crisis, but we give scant attention when an ordinary family is wiped out in an accident that could have been prevented. "Anything else?" I asked Mick.

"I'm going to run a nationwide search on Hanover's personal life as soon as Kelley here will return my laptop to me." He paused, and then I heard him saying, "Kelley, please. Please, please, *please.* I'm going into withdrawal!" He came back on the line and added, "She's relented, thank God. Talk later."

Next I called Adah back. Only the voice mail at any of her numbers. I hoped her message meant she was seriously considering my proposition.

I decided to call Ma next, reserving Hy—the best—for last. The business calls could wait till tomorrow, after I'd taken Amy to Bridgeport to talk with Lark.

Thursday

✦

NOVEMBER 15

Lark was in her office when I called to say I'd located Amy and was bringing her in.

"I thought you'd be supervising the search in Toiyabe," I added.

"Nope. That's in good hands."

"Anything yet?"

"No. So what's the Perez girl's story?"

"I'll let her tell you in person."

I left the sheriff's department after delivering Amy into Lark's hands, and started back toward Vernon. Halfway there my cell rang. Lark.

"We've located Bud Smith's body," she said. "Few hundred yards from his vehicle, in a ravine. Told you it'd be that close."

"Cause of death?"

"Shot in the back. Same as Tom Mathers."

"Estimated time of death?"

"A week at least, probably longer, the ME says. Body was badly decomposed. We tentatively ID'd it from a backpack that was lying next to it. Thing is, Smith's wallet and a bottle of water were inside, but not his car keys or any of the other stuff you'd take along if you were hiking in such an isolated area."

"I'd say whoever killed him wanted him identified and tried to make it look like an accident. He may have been shot elsewhere, then driven to Toiyabe and dumped."

"How'd the killer get back to wherever he came from?" Lark asked. "It's a long way out of there on foot."

"An accomplice, maybe?"

"Maybe."

Lark switched tacks. "The Perez girl was forthcoming about what happened to her. My guess is that Sheppard waited around till after dark, then broke in thinking she wasn't there."

"And tossed the cabin after she got away?"

"Probably. Before he came on to Amy in his truck, he was asking her about something Hayley might've given her for safekeeping. He didn't know what it might be, but insisted it had to do with her sister asking him to clear out of the trailer that night."

"She have any idea what it was?"

"She said no. That's the only point where I felt she wasn't being candid with me."

"So now what?"

"I'm driving down to Inyo tomorrow morning, and taking my best interrogator along."

"Good-cop bad-cop, huh?"

"Yep. And that interrogator is you."

"Then you're flying down."

"McCone, I hate small planes!"

"As I recall, you appeared at the crime scene in the lava fields in a chopper."

"I keep my eyes closed when I'm in one of those things. Really, we can drive—"

"You want to get this job done soon, or what?"

"All right, I'll keep my eyes closed . . . again."

When I got back to Vernon, I drove to Willow Grove Lodge and sat down at the end of the dock to think.

Remembered a night years ago when Hy and I had drifted there in a rowboat, sipping beer while I confessed to things I'd never told another living soul.

This past year, I almost blew two people away. . . . Each time I really wanted to do it. . . . I wanted to act as an executioner.

Our relationship, then so new and fragile, had saved me from those dark feelings. And given rise to the dedicated resolve to quell any and all such inhuman urges. To maintain control. To let go of the idea I could right every wrong and instead settle for righting only a few. So far I'd been able to keep my promises.

But at this moment there were a large number of wrongs that needed righting.

Hayley, all dressed up, offering a martini to her visitor and being shot in return.

Amy, brutally attacked.

Tom Mathers, left dead in the desert.

Miri, a suicide, as the inquest in Sacramento had determined, but equally a victim of the person who had killed her firstborn.

Bud Smith, decomposing in a ravine in a national forest.

Yes, quite a few wrongs.

Time to go see T.C. Mathers, a woman who had free access to guns.

The parking lot of the wilderness supply looked the same as when I'd first visited it. I was about to take the driveway to the Mathers' residence when I saw that the OPEN sign in the window of the store was lighted. I parked and went inside.

T.C. sat on a stool behind the counter, going over some pages in a thick binder. Her face was haggard, her eyes bloodshot—but she appeared to be sober.

"McCone—just who I've been wanting to see," she said, but without rancor.

"How you doing?" I asked.

"Terrible. I think I know what the d.t.'s feel like."

"And what're you doing?" I motioned at the binder.

"I thought maybe Tom had something on one of his clients that he was using for blackmail. He kept a log on each trip he guided. But there's nothing here."

"Well, he wouldn't necessarily have written it down if he planned to cash in on it."

"True. These logs go back years, so I started reading the most recent ones first. Most of the entries are trips with longtime clients. I know them; a lot had their entire families along. I can't imagine . . ."

"Why don't you let me borrow the log? Look it over from an outsider's perspective."

She sighed, shut the binder, and pushed it toward me. "You're welcome to it."

I set it aside, leaned on the counter. "T.C., I spoke with Kristen Lark. She says your alibi doesn't look so solid."

"Oh, Christ, she's probably been talking with Cullen Bradley. I need a drink."

"No, you don't."

"You're right, I don't. At least that's what I've been telling myself all day. Last night I promised myself I'd stay off the stuff, concentrate on running this business. But it's like people think the plague lives here; nobody's come in." She paused. "I guess *I'm* the plague. Everybody thinks I killed Tom."

"Did you?"

"No."

Her eyes looked candidly into mine; she didn't display any unusual body language. I believed her.

"Tell me about Bradley," I said.

"That night I was furious with Tom. So I stomped out of here and had myself a big evening, went to the motel with Bradley. I must've been insane. But then he passed out, so I left his fat ass in bed and came home."

"Was Tom here?"

"No. Right away when I drove in I saw his truck was gone."

"What did you do then?"

"Took three aspirin and went to bed."

"You weren't worried about Tom?"

"No. We fought a lot. One of us would leave, then come home and act as if nothing had happened. That's the way it was with us. We just never thought one of us would leave and never come back."

After I left T.C. I called the number in the 510 area code that Cammie Charles had left with her friend Verna. On the third ring, a familiar voice picked up.

"Cammie? Sharon McCone, the private investigator—"

"I know who you are. Who gave you this number?"

I ignored the question. "I found Bud Smith's SUV in Toiyabe yesterday. And today the sheriff's department found his body."

"Oh, God. When we saw the Subaru I recognized it. I told Rich we should report it."

"And he didn't want to get involved."

"No. Rich, there was some problem between him and Bud. He said it looked like Bud had been killed and he didn't want anything to do with the cops. I told him we couldn't just walk away from this . . . thing. But we did."

"Why didn't *you* report it?"

Silence.

"Because Rich said not to?"

". . . Yeah. I didn't want him to get in trouble."

"But you left him."

"I thought if I did, he'd shape up, take responsibility for his life, and then we'd get back together."

Verna had been right about Cammie's motives. "So what was this problem between Rich and Bud?"

"I don't know. You'd better ask Rich."

"I'll do that. Any message you want me to pass along?"

". . . No. Well, yes. Just tell him I love him."

I drove to Elk Lake, but Rich Three Wings wasn't there. Finally I caught up with him at Hobo's around eight o'clock that evening. He was sitting at the bar, the two stools to either side of him vacant, as if the other patrons feared the aura of gloom he exuded might be contagious. I sat down to his right.

"Rich, I spoke with Cammie tonight."

He started, his eyes jerking toward me. "Jesus! You scared me."

"Sorry. As I said—"

"You talked to Cammie. Where is she?"

"Some friends' house in the East Bay."

"That would be Kendall and Dan Clark. They visited up here a couple of times. How'd you get their number?"

"Verna, from the flower shop."

"Is Cammie okay?"

"Yes. She asked me to tell you she loves you. I think she's waiting for you to call and make nice."

"Yeah, that's her style. She knows I've got the phone number."

"Are you going to?"

He considered, turning his glass between his hands. The bartender looked questioningly at me, but I shook my head.

"I don't think so," Rich finally said. "Cammie's better off without me. I'm an asshole."

"Because of what happened in Toiyabe?"

Silence.

"She told me about it."

"Then you know why she's better off. Bud Smith was probably out there struggling to survive, and I didn't want to get involved. What kind of a shit does that make me?"

"It makes you human. And you couldn't've done anything for Bud; he was long dead by then. The sheriff's search party found his body today; he'd been shot in the back, probably somewhere else."

"Jesus, all this killing." He shook his head. "Why would somebody shoot Bud?"

"Well, there was trouble between the two of you. What was that about?"

". . . We got into an argument in here a few years ago. One

of those pushing and shoving things. Nothing unusual, but people in this town have long memories."

"What was the argument about?"

"Miri wrote a letter to Hayley and asked Bud to hold it for her, in case she ever came home. Bud said he hadn't read it, was keeping it in his office safe. But I could tell he was lying."

"How did you know about the letter?"

"Miri got drunk in here a lot. When she drank, she couldn't hold her tongue; she talked about the letter, but she never would say what was in it. About that she wouldn't say a word."

"And why would she entrust something that important to Bud?"

"Miri had a small insurance policy with him. When it was going to lapse because she couldn't make the payments, Bud took them over. He was nice to her in other ways. She said he never judged her."

Well, that fit with what I knew about Miri's rape and Bud covering for his brother. Guilt, plain and simple. "So you asked Bud about the letter and that led to this pushing and shoving."

"Yeah. Another example of what an asshole I am. I mean, Hayley wasn't any of my business any more. We were divorced. I'd made a new life for myself. But I couldn't let it rest."

"As far as you know, when Hayley came back to town, did Bud give her Miri's letter?"

"I didn't even know Hayley was here till she was killed."

"She took out an insurance policy with Amy as beneficiary. Do you think Bud would've passed on the letter then?"

"Probably. He knew Hayley would never go see her mother. She hated her. Once told me she wished she'd die."

After eleven. I pushed Tom Mathers' log book aside and rubbed my eyes. I'd come back and answered my business messages, then called Ma, and finally Hy, who was in Chicago "cleaning house." Which meant that, as part of his reorganization plan, he was firing and hiring personnel for RI's most inept and corrupt branch office. He was tired, frustrated, and disappointed that he couldn't get back for the weekend. I told him no worries, my case was coming to a conclusion, and I'd probably be in San Francisco when he arrived next week.

I sounded more confident than I felt.

I microwaved myself some mac and cheese, and then, feeling guilty about my recent poor eating habits, made a small salad. Ate while watching an old episode of *All in the Family* on TV. The show held up, even in this tumultuous first decade of the twenty-first century. Come to think of it, not much had really changed since the nineteen-seventies; technological advances, yes, but not matters of the human conscience and heart.

The rest of the evening I devoted to Mathers' log. T.C. was right: there were no notations to indicate trouble on any of the trips. I jotted down names and addresses of the clients for searches to make after I got back from Inyo County tomorrow.

Now, even as tired as I was, I got some carrots from the fridge and took them out to King Lear. The horse whickered when he heard my footsteps, nuzzled my hand as he took his treats. I stood petting him for a while, then said, "You know what? We've got to get you a companion. Being an only horse is not a good thing."

Friday

✦

NOVEMBER 16

There was frost everywhere when I looked out the kitchen window in the morning. Frost so heavy it mimicked the snowcapped peaks of the mountains. I was glad Lark and I weren't due at the Inyo County jail till two, when the day would have warmed some; cold-weather flying is something I prefer to leave to Hy.

I called the agency. Ted told me he'd taken matters into his own hands and was researching copy machines. He was fed up with calling the repairman for our present one, and had been lobbying for a replacement for months.

"I'm getting to know the repair guy so well, I feel like I should invite him to Thanksgiving dinner," he added. "Speaking of which, are you and Hy gonna make it this year?"

Ted's annual Thanksgiving party. God, I'd forgotten all about it! I glanced at the calendar on the wall by the fridge; I hadn't changed it from October.

"Uh, when is Thanksgiving?"

Ted let out a despairing sigh. "Next week. What planet are you living on?"

"A very strange one. Count us in." Even if I had to fly back for just the one day.

"Good. Is it okay to go ahead with the new copier?"

"Yes. But don't finalize the sale till you okay the price with me. And now let me talk to Patrick, please."

Patrick sounded tense. "Six new clients yesterday, Shar. All corporate. Derek and Thelia and I have split them up among us, but there're other cases that're backlogged. What with Mick in rehab . . ."

"Thelia needs an assistant."

"I know."

"Find her one."

"Me?"

"You. First, call around to the agencies we cooperate with and ask if they have any recommendations. If not, run an ad. You know what kind of person we're looking for. Then interview the most promising ones."

"But I just can't go ahead and hire—"

"By the time you complete the interviews, I'll be back to make the final decision and negotiate salary and benefits."

"Okay," he said, "I can do this."

"Of course you can. If you get really swamped with new cases, call on Rae. She delivered her latest book to her publisher last month."

We discussed a few other matters, and by the time we ended the conversation, Patrick seemed more confident and in control than ever.

Way to delegate, McCone.

Next call: Mick. I hadn't heard from him about his deep backgrounding on Trevor Hanover since Wednesday. There was no answer at his extension at the rehab center. Probably in therapy, I thought. But it wasn't like him not to keep me posted, so I called Rae.

"Oh, God, I should've let you know!" she said. "Yesterday afternoon he had an episode of internal bleeding and they had to transfer him to UC Med Center to perform more surgery."

"Is he okay?"

"He will be. I'll tell you, this experience has taught him a lot. Us, too. We should've kept in closer touch after his breakup with Charlotte, given him the support he needed."

"I should've, too. I was so mired down in my own situation I didn't realize how bad off he was. When's he going back to the rehab center?"

"This afternoon." She paused. "Oh, I just remembered—before he went into surgery he told Ricky that there was some information on his laptop that ought to be forwarded to you. But Ricky forgot, and he had to go to LA this morning. He only called a while ago to tell me about it. Do you want me to go over to the rehab center and try to access it?"

"No, don't bother. I assume when Mick's back there he'll send it along. Give him my love when you see him."

"Frankly, I'd rather give him a good slap upside the head. God, I'm glad I never had children!"

"Yeah—and instead you became stepmother to six of them."

"Independence traffic, Two-Seven-Tango, turning for final."

"Two-Seven-Tango, Three-Eight-Niner. I'm still behind you. That's a damn pretty plane you've got."

"Thank you, Three-Eight-Niner."

I glanced over at Lark. She had her eyes closed. She'd closed them when we'd taken off from Tufa Tower, then kept them rigidly focused on the instrument panel during most of the trip. She was capable of speech, however, and we'd discussed the scenario for our interrogation of Boz Sheppard.

Lark had spoken with her superiors and the DA in Mono County, and then the sheriff and DA in Inyo. Together they'd worked out a plan that would ensure Sheppard's cooperation without either jurisdiction giving up very much. While we were aware that Sheppard—like any criminal or, for that matter, anyone who watched crime shows on TV—knew the good-cop bad-cop routine, very few of them failed to be rattled by it.

"Are we there yet?" Lark asked.

I leveled off, then set the plane down on the runway without so much as a bump.

"Are we—?"

"We're there."

"What?" She opened her eyes and looked around as I braked and turned off toward the tie-downs. "When did—?"

"That was one of my better landings. And since you had your eyes closed, you couldn't tell where we were at."

"No way! I could feel every motion—"

"I'll demonstrate on the way back."

"The hell you will!"

An Inyo County Sheriff's Department car took us to the jail, and a guard led us to an interrogation room that was much smaller than the visiting area where I'd earlier spoken with Sheppard.

Lark pulled out a chair from the metal table and looked around. "The ambience is perfect. Very claustrophobic."

"And scenic." I nodded at an ugly water stain on the ceiling. "Where do you want me?"

"Stand over there by that big crack in the wall. Fold your arms and look relaxed."

"Yes ma'am."

Seconds later Sheppard was brought in. He looked pretty bad—drug withdrawal, I supposed. His face was pale and pinched, more like a lab rat's than ever.

"Hello, Boz," Lark said. "You remember me? And Ms. McCone?"

Sheppard grunted and sat down across from her.

"I'm going to be taping this session," she said, activating the recorder on the table. "I've been talking with the authorities and DA's offices down here and up in Mono. I can offer you a deal, depending on the information you're willing to give up."

Flicker of interest in his eyes. "Yeah? What kind of deal?"

Lark began ticking off the items on her fingers. "No charges in the Hayley Perez murder. No charges in the attack on Amy Perez—"

"Amy? She didn't know I was the one—"

Snared. Snared and stupid. But Mono wasn't giving up anything, because they had no evidence Boz had killed Hayley, and Amy really couldn't identify him as the perp.

"Yes, she knows," Lark lied. "And she's willing to testify to that effect. On the other hand, McCone is willing to forgive you on the trespass on her ranch and assault charges. You tell us what you were looking for in Amy's cabin, it all goes away."

"... A letter from Miri Perez. Something Bud Smith gave Hayley. What this meeting the night she was killed was all about—the one she was gonna profit from. I tore the trailer apart, but it wasn't there. So I figured she'd given it to Amy."

"You have to beat up and cut Amy to search for it?" I asked.

Sheppard started. He'd forgotten I was there. "I didn't know the little skank was in the cabin. She woke up and tried to hit me with a lamp. Real fighter, that one."

"Don't browbeat the man, McCone," Lark said, glaring at me. She turned back to Sheppard. "Tell us about your history with Hayley."

"What about the rest of my deal?"

"This information is to cement the deal with Mono."

"Okay, okay. I met Hayley in Vegas. She was hooking."

"And you were . . . ?"

"Working in a casino."

"Which one?"

"Same one she was."

"The name?"

"I forget."

I said, "He was probably dealing—but not cards. Or pimping. Were you her pimp, Sheppard?"

"Leave him be, McCone," Lark said.

"He wasn't doing anything legitimate in Vegas, that's for sure."

Again Lark glared at me. "Not relevant." She turned her attention back to Sheppard. "Okay, you knew Hayley in Vegas. When?"

"When she was first there, I don't remember how many years ago. Then I did a stretch for possession. I was railroaded."

I said, "That's what they all claim."

"And after you got out?" Lark asked him.

"I decided to go to Vernon. I had connections—"

"Drug connections," I said.

Lark gave an exasperated sigh. "You see Hayley in Vegas beforehand?"

"Yeah. I stayed with her a few days till my parole officer gave me permission to leave the state. She said she had family here and might visit me sometime. And she did—late September, I think. She needed a place to stay. She'd come up HIV-positive, was already feeling sick."

So that was why she'd taken out the insurance policy with Amy as beneficiary. The county's pathology reports hadn't showed any evidence of her illness because they hadn't been looking for it. Which meant the life-insurance policy benefiting Amy would pay off.

"And?" Lark asked.

"I let her stay. Next thing I know, she's talking about cashing in on something, living out the rest of her life in luxury."

"Something that was in the note Miri left for her with Bud Smith."

"I guess."

"Did Hayley own a gun?"

"Hayley? Jesus, no. What would she need a gun for?"

"Violent johns?" I said.

"McCone, I'm warning you!"

"Sorry."

"Okay, Boz, do you own a gun?"

Silence.

"Part of your deal."

". . . Okay, I've got a thirty-two I bought off of a guy in Reno."

"Where was this gun the night Hayley was killed?"

". . . In the trailer."

"So Hayley had access to a weapon of the caliber that killed her."

"Yeah, she did."

All three of us were silent. Then I said, "Don't you want to discuss the deal you've got here in Inyo?"

He shot me a look of pure rage. "Who the hell're you, coming in here and trying to take over from *her*?" He motioned at Lark.

"Somebody who thinks you're pond scum. All right if I tell him about his deal down here, Lark?"

"Sure, be my guest."

"There isn't any."

"But she said—"

"She said that she talked with the authorities and DA in Mono and down here. She said 'I can offer you a deal.' Not we—I."

"You stone bitches!" He started to rise from his chair, but the guard, who had been standing by the door the whole time, stepped in quickly to restrain him.

Lark and I exchanged glances. Then she extracted the tape from the machine on the table, and we left Sheppard in the hands of the Inyo County authorities.

"Amazing!" Lark said. "I thought we were headed straight for Tufa Tower, but that's June Lake down there. I didn't even notice when you turned."

"Because you had your eyes closed again. You didn't notice that it was a steep bank, either."

"No kidding."

"Want to close your eyes one more time?"

"Uh, why?"

"It'd be interesting to know if you could tell when we were upside down."

"No way!"

"Just one little spin."

"Spin! Jesus, like a tailspin—?"

"Then I guess you'll have to keep your eyes open and enjoy the scenery."

Back at the ranch house, I found a message from Mick: "Call me ASAP. I'm at the rehab place and Nurse Ratched has confiscated my laptop. Says I can only speak to you for three minutes."

I dialed, and a woman's voice answered. I almost asked her if she was Nurse Ratched, then realized it was Charlotte Keim.

Well, well . . .

She passed me along to Mick.

"Charlotte's forwarding you the information on Hanover that I accessed—*she's* allowed my laptop—but I thought you'd want to hear this."

"How're you feeling?"

"Okay. But listen, they really mean it about the three minutes. What I found out is that Trevor Hanover owns property in Mono County. A lot of it—one thousand acres." He gave me the parcel number, adding that a map was on the way via e-mail.

I booted up my laptop in preparation for Keim's incoming file, while asking Mick more questions about his health. The nurse wrested the phone from him as the e-mail arrived.

The map showing the location of Hanover's property didn't really surprise me. I guess at some level I'd suspected it all along: Hanover was the owner of Rattlesnake Ranch.

A wealthy man from the East Coast, who flew to his private airstrip in his own jet. A man who had been a New York City bartender who happened to get lucky because of his ingratiating manners and impressive knowledge of finance. A man whose financial empire and private life were now crumbling.

A man who, under his real name, held a degree from a prominent Eastern business school. Who had ceased to exist shortly after attaining that degree because he couldn't risk the future possibility of being named a rapist, if for some reason his brother decided to tell the truth.

A man who used to be called Davey Smith.

Time to proceed slowly and cautiously. Build a case that no high-priced defense attorney could tear apart.

I couldn't confide what I knew to Lark. In spite of her elation at our handling of Boz Sheppard, the woman seemed on the ragged edge. In fact, she'd called earlier from her home to tell me her superior officer had told her to take a day off. Her voice had been slurred, and I'd heard ice tinkling in the background. I didn't want her alcohol-impaired judgment to get in my way.

Ramon was at the stable when I went out there, cleaning King's stall. I asked if Amy was still at his house. Yes, she was. I said I was going over there, I needed to talk with her.

Before I left, I slipped King the carrots I'd brought for him.

Amy was clad in a bathrobe that enveloped her petite frame; I assumed it was Sara's. She sat on the living-room couch, listlessly watching a game show while her aunt bustled around in the kitchen. I turned the TV set off and sat down next to her.

"How're you doing?"

She shrugged.

"I hear everything went well with Kristen Lark."

"Yeah, I like her."

"I understand Hayley gave you a letter for safekeeping."

"More like a big, thick envelope."

"Did you open it?"

"No."

"One thing in the envelope is a letter Boz Sheppard was looking for when he came to your cabin and cut you. I think he was going to look for it here too, when he saw the light on in the stable, spooked the horse, and hit me. He didn't find it either place. Where is it?"

". . . At Mrs. Ivins' house. Dana Ivins, who runs Friends Helping Friends. I knew it wouldn't be safe at Willow Grove or here, so I snuck over there and hid it in her garage."

"Why didn't you entrust it to Dana?"

"She's nosy. I knew she'd read it."

"But you didn't read it."

"I told you no. Hayley asked me not to." Her eyes welled up and tears spilled down her cheeks. "I was upset with Hayley when I found out she'd been hooking all those years, and when I found out she was living with that loser Boz I felt even worse. But I still loved her, I would never pry into her private business. Now I wish I had; maybe she wouldn't've gotten killed."

I didn't tell her that Hayley probably would have died of AIDS anyway since she apparently had forgone treatment. Amy didn't need that kind of memory of her big sister.

Instead I said, "The other thing that's in the envelope is a life-insurance policy Hayley took out on herself, with you as beneficiary. Since she was murdered, the double indemnity clause goes into effect. Eventually you'll receive a hundred thousand dollars."

Amy stared at me, her mouth opening in a little O.

"It's up to you what you do with the money," I went on. "Blow it on expensive cars and clothes and bad boyfriends. Or use it to give yourself a much better life than your mother and sister had."

For a moment she looked away at the blank TV screen, envisioning any number of scenarios. Then: "I could finish up my GED and go to college."

"Yes."

"I could do something that would've made Mama and Hayley really proud of me."

"That, too."

Amy put her hands over her face and shook her head. "Oh, God!"

"What?"

"Oh, God, I'm all of a sudden so afraid."

"Of what?"

"I'm afraid I'll fuck up like I have over and over again."

I grasped her wrists and pulled her hands from her face, looked into her eyes. "You have Ramon and Sara. You have Hy and me. You can be sure if you start to fuck up, one or the other—or all four of us—will tell you."

Dana Ivins opened the side door to her garage, snapped on an overhead light. I followed her inside.

"There's the storage cabinet," she said, motioning to a hulking white assemble-it-yourself piece of the sort you can buy at Home Depot. Its doors were misaligned: one was at least two inches higher than the other.

I went over and reached behind the cabinet. Wedged against the wall beams exactly where Amy had described to me was a thick nine-by-seven envelope.

When I pulled it out, Ivins said, "Why, for God's sake, did she hide it there, rather than give it to me? I could've put it in my safe."

I shrugged. "She's young and she wasn't thinking too clearly, I suppose. Or maybe she thought your safe was too obvious a place and this envelope's presence might've made you a target."

"Amy always was a considerate girl. I'm so happy she's safe with her uncle. What's in the envelope?"

And she's right, you are *a nosy woman.*

"I don't know. Amy just asked me to retrieve it."

"Maybe, for her sake, we should open it."

"No, it's her private property."

"But it could shed some light on these killings—"

"If it can, Amy will turn the information over to the sheriff's department. She's been talking with them."

"About what?"

"I haven't been in on the conversations."

Ivins looked disappointed. For a person who insisted on her organization's right to confidentiality, she certainly played fast and loose with other people's.

I drove a couple of blocks along the main street before I pulled to the curb and opened the envelope, as Amy had given me permission to do. It contained the insurance policy Hayley had taken out with her sister as beneficiary, and a smaller pink envelope with Hayley's name written on it in erratic, badly formed penmanship. It had previously been opened, then closed with the flap slipped inside. I slid the letter out.

Dear Hayley,

I know you never want to lay eyes on me again and I dont blame you. I been a bad mother and a bad woman but that dont mean I dont love you. Bud Smith has been good to me. So I'm leaveing this with him in case you ever come back home or he hears where you are. What you need to know is Jimmy Perez wasnt your father. I was raped when I was 13 by a bastard named Davey Smith. Thats Bud's little brother. He got off scotch free because he was some kind of genius and Bud took the rap for him so he could go away to school. My family wouldnt let me have an abortion, but they treeted me real bad so I ran away and had you. And I kept you—thats how much I loved you. The other thing you need to know is Davey Smith is a rich man now. Goes by the name of Trevor Hanover and lives back east someplace tho he has a big ranch outside of Vernon. Rattlesnake its called. I found out from the woman who cooks for him when he's there—Linda Jeffrey, she lives on Yosemite Street. You can ask her if you want to. The way she knew he was Bud's brother is that Bud went there to dinner once and she heard them fighting. I guess Davey tried to give him money, but he wouldnt take it. Bud told him to put the money in the bank for you and hire a lawyer to help you out because you were bound to get in trouble in Vegas. I guess you must of kept in touch with Bud because he knew where you were. But baby, Davey owes you more than that. Talk to Bud and have him set up a meeting with Davey. Your his daughter.

You have rights, you claim them. I know I'll never see you again baby, but you deserve a good life.

All my love,
Mama

Okay—slowly, cautiously. First I'd talk with this Linda Jeffrey.

Her tidy home was in the center of one-block Yosemite Street. A TV flickered in the front window. I rang the bell. After a moment the porch light came on, and a tall, slender woman in sweats, whose gray hair was pulled back into a ponytail, looked out at me.

"Yes?"

I said my name, gave her my card.

"Oh, you're Hy Ripinsky's wife. You've been helping out the Perezes. Come in, please."

The room she led me to was cluttered, but in a clean, comfortable way. Books and magazines stacked on tables, a hand-knitted afghan thrown carelessly over the large sofa, videotapes and DVDs piled high atop the TV. Jeffrey turned off the program she'd been watching and said, "Sit anywhere, but before you do, look for cats."

The chair I went to did contain a cat—a light-gray shorthair, whose sleepy gaze dared me to move it. I did, picking it up and setting it on my lap; instantly it curled into a ball and started purring.

"They run our lives, don't they?" its owner said, taking a place on the sofa and pulling the afghan around her.

"Yes, they do."

"I figured you for a cat person. And I assume you're here to ask about what goes on at Rattlesnake Ranch."

Her statement surprised me. It showed, because she added, "I know who Trevor Hanover is—or was—and I've been debating whether to go to the sheriff's department about him. Your visit has more or less resolved that issue."

"Why were you only 'debating'?"

"For two reasons. When Mr. Hanover hired me to cook for the family, he had me sign a contract with a confidentiality clause. I was not to talk about him, his family, or anything that went on at the ranch."

"But you've already broken that agreement by talking to Miri Perez."

"How do you . . . ? Well, that doesn't matter. I did it for Miri's safety; it was only right that she know her real rapist had property so close by."

"And the second reason?"

"I don't really *know* anything—at least not about the times when Hayley, Tom Mathers, or Bud Smith were killed. The way my arrangement with Mr. Hanover worked, someone would call and tell me when the family would be there and what to prepare. But as far as I know, the Hanovers haven't visited the ranch for five or six months."

"Who else works there while they're gone?"

"My neighbor: she did the housekeeping. But Mr. Hanover called her in October and told her her services would no longer be needed. He gave no reason, but did send a large severance check. She used the money to take a trip to Philadelphia to spend Thanksgiving with her daughter. And there was a gardener and handyman, but he recently moved to Arizona."

"How recently?"

"A month ago. Around the time Mr. Hanover fired my

neighbor. I don't know who's doing the outdoor work out there now."

The timing was interesting. Another generous severance check?

"Did the Hanovers always arrive by private jet?"

"Always. He's a pilot, you know."

"Did you ever hear anything that would explain why he chose to buy a ranch here?"

"I once heard him tell his daughter Alyssa that he'd grown up in Vernon and had always loved it here, but then his family moved to Nevada and his life was never right again. He said he was happy to come back as an important man to the place where he was born."

"But he bought the ranch in strict secrecy and never showed his face in town."

"Probably afraid somebody would find out who he really was. And he seemed content sitting out on that big old terrace and looking down on Vernon. I guess it was enough for him."

Until his daughter Hayley showed up and wanted him to acknowledge her.

"When did Bud Smith come to the ranch for dinner with Hanover?"

"Two years ago, the last Saturday in July. I remember because it was quite an evening. . . ."

It had started out pleasantly enough, Linda Jeffrey told me. Hanover had been alone on the trip and in an expansive mood, ordering her to serve special hors d'oeuvres and wine on the terrace; the dinner menu was similarly elaborate. Bud Smith, who was Linda's insurance broker, arrived about five o'clock and was given a tour of the property by Hanover.

Bud called Hanover Davey, and Jeffrey assumed it was a nickname. The two men seemed reserved but were getting along well enough through drinks and hors d'oeuvres and the soup course of the dinner.

"Then their voices got louder. I was shocked to hear Hanover call Bud his brother. Hanover wanted to pay Bud half a million dollars for what he called 'his trouble.' Bud said he preferred to earn an honest living, that no amount of money could make up for those lost years in prison."

Hanover then began pressuring Smith to take the money, and Smith blew up at him.

"He said he had been in touch with Izzy Darkmoon's and Davey's child from the rape, Hayley Perez. She called Bud periodically to ask him about her little sister, Amy. Bud told Hanover to put the half million in trust for Hayley and also retain a good lawyer for her, because she was a prostitute in Las Vegas and headed for serious trouble."

"What was Hanover's reaction?"

"He said he didn't want anything to do with his trailer-trash bastard. That's when Bud threw a glass of wine in his brother's face. He told him he'd better establish the trust and retain the lawyer as soon as he went back to New York, and provide him with confirmation. Otherwise he'd go straight to the authorities over in Nevada and tell them the truth about the rape. And then he stormed out of the house."

"What did Hanover do?"

"Wiped the wine off and called for me to serve the next course. He asked if I'd heard any of their conversation, and I said no, I'd been listening to my iPod. He believed me because there's a light in the kitchen that flashes when somebody presses a button in the dining room, and a lot of times I do have my iPod on while I work. So I served him the roast.

He didn't eat much or ask for the dessert course. Afterward he gave me a hundred percent tip on top of my usual fee, which is fairly generous to begin with."

"To ensure your silence, in case you *hadn't* been listening to music."

"Yeah." Linda Jeffrey smiled wryly. "But me, I'm like Bud: I prefer to make an honest living. I wrote a check next morning to Friends Helping Friends for the amount of the tip, and then I went to see Miri Perez."

So Linda Jeffrey hadn't been summoned to Rattlesnake Ranch in five to six months. And the housekeeper had been let go and the handyman and gardener had suddenly moved to Arizona.

I had nothing if I couldn't somehow prove Hanover was at the ranch on the date Hayley died.

Who would have the information I needed?

Amos Hinsdale. He practically lived in that shack at Tufa Tower. Monitored the UNICOM constantly. No one in a private jet could land in this territory without Amos knowing about it—even if the pilot didn't broadcast to other traffic.

Now, if I could only get the old coot to talk with me . . .

"Canada Dry ginger ale," the bartender at Hobo's said. "Amos hasn't had a drink of alcohol in his life that I know of. But he comes in here every Saturday night and always has three or four Canada Drys. Likes company and conversation that one day of the week. I keep a supply of the stuff on hand for him."

"Would you sell me a cold six-pack?"

"Sure. You planning on seducing him?" He winked.

"If only what I have in mind were that simple."

* * *

Hinsdale gave me a suspicious look when he opened the door of the shack at the airport. "We're closed, lady pilot."

What on earth could be closed? There were no avgas or mechanic's services here, just the UNICOM and a rudimentary landing-light system that had ceased to work reliably years ago.

I held up the six-pack of Canada Dry. "I thought we might share a couple. It's my favorite, and I hear it's yours, too."

Now he scowled. "I'd think a woman like you, married to Ripinsky, would prefer beer."

"I like a brew sometimes, but not tonight."

"So you decided to visit an old man and sip some ginger ale. Hard to believe."

"Hell, Amos, you've nailed me. I need help."

"Something wrong with that plane of Ripinsky's? What did you do to it?"

"Nothing's wrong with the plane. But something's very wrong in this town."

His eyes narrowed, wrinkles deepening around them. "What d'you mean—wrong?" But his downturned mouth told me he already knew the answer.

"Hayley Perez, her sister Amy, and her mother Miri. Tom Mathers and Bud Smith. And a private jet that landed at Rattlesnake Ranch around the day Hayley was murdered."

His features seemed to fold inward, and his eyes grew bleak.

"Please, Mr. Hinsdale . . ."

He opened the door wider, motioned me in. "I'll take that Canada Dry, thank you."

* * *

Surprisingly, the shack was comfortably furnished, with two overstuffed chairs beside the table that held the UNICOM. Yellowing rental forms for Amos' clunker planes, scribbled slips of paper, old newspapers and magazines, and even older aviation sectionals were scattered beside the unit.

I sat in the chair he indicated, opened two cans of ginger ale and handed him one. He sipped and stared silently at the opposite wall, where a framed photograph of a young man in a U.S. Navy flight suit was hung; he stood beside a fighter plane, his gaze stern, jaw thrust out aggressively.

Amos caught me looking at it and said, "Me. Down at Miramar before we shipped out for 'Nam on the *Enterprise*. December second, 1965."

"You fly a lot of missions?"

"Yeah. I was one of the lucky ones: I lived to tell about them. A lot of my buddies didn't."

"My father was a Navy man—NCO. In fact, we lived in San Diego and could hear the planes out of Miramar." The sonic boom from one had cracked our swimming pool so badly that my parents had filled it with dirt and turned it into a vegetable garden.

Amos nodded absently, sipped more ginger ale. "Wasn't a private jet."

"What . . . ? Oh, you mean at Rattlesnake Ranch."

"That's what you're asking about, isn't it? That jet, I don't even have to see it approach the ranch; I can hear it. You wouldn't think my hearing could be so keen after all these years around aircraft, but it is. No, that day I was standing in the door trying to work myself up to cutting the grass alongside the runway when this Cessna 152 flew right over the field. Damned low, and the pilot didn't even announce himself to traffic. UNICOM was dead silent. I watched the plane make its descent at the ranch."

"You get the plane's number?"

"I did. Was going to report it to the FAA, but"—he shrugged—"things get away from me these days." His eyes strayed to the photograph on the opposite wall. "It's hard to admit that you're not as energetic or clearheaded as you used to be. But it's a fact, you can't challenge it."

"It was clearheaded to take down the Cessna's number. You still have it?"

"Somewhere." He sifted through the items scattered on the table, came up with a blue Post-it note. He was more clear-headed than he gave himself credit for; I was willing to bet he knew where every item in that clutter was. "Yours," he said, handing it to me. "How about we have another ginger ale?"

"Sure," I said, surprised at how mellow he'd become toward me. I popped two more tabs, passed a can over to him.

"How'd you get interested in flying?" he asked.

"Ripinsky. I'd been at the controls of a plane a few times, years before I met him, when I was dating a Navy pilot stationed at Alameda, but I didn't enjoy it all that much. He was a hotdog pilot and liked to scare people."

"Guy was an asshole then. Ripinsky breaks a lot of rules, but never at the expense of a novice passenger."

"That's true. And he's a terrific pilot. Once I got comfortable flying with him, I asked him to teach me—he's got his CFI, you know. But he didn't think it would be good for the relationship, so he found me an instructor near San Francisco. And I've been happily flying ever since."

Amos pursed his lips; I suspected he was trying not to say something. But the desire to speak won out: "You been flying happily and beautifully. Nobody around here—male or female—makes the kind of landings and takeoffs you do."

I was genuinely touched, but I said lightly, "Not even Ripinsky?"

"Not even him. And I'm not bad-mouthing your husband, because he admits you're the better pilot."

Somehow I—and Canada Dry—had won grouchy Amos Hinsdale over. I'd been promoted from "lady pilot" to just plain "pilot"!

From the FAA's Internet site, I found the Cessna whose number Hinsdale had noted down belonged to a flight service in Fresno. I called the service, got a machine. By then it was nearly eleven. Hy hadn't called today. No one had, except for Patrick and Ted with terse reports they'd left on the machine. Hy's silence didn't bother me; I could sense him urging me on.

I flipped the TV on to the national news. The recent happenings in Mono County had become a major story. Apparently they had been for nearly two days, when the media smelled links between the murders. Come to think of it, I'd seen a CBS van in town the previous afternoon, but had been too distracted to take much notice. Tonight's follow-up said the sheriff's department was searching for both Bud Smith's boat trailer and the keys to his Forester, so far with little success.

After watching the weather report—more snow—I poured myself a glass of wine and sat down to think.

Trevor Hanover—wherever he was—would be monitoring the news. He'd be aware of the interest the cases had generated. But would he suspect someone had also linked the events to him?

Maybe, maybe not.

I began to construct my view of what had happened.

Hanover had been intimidated by his brother Bud's threat to tell the truth about Miri's rape to the Nevada authorities. He'd retained the attorney for Hayley and probably put the half million dollars he'd offered Bud in trust. When Hayley returned to Vernon and took out the life-insurance policy, Bud gave her her mother's letter. After reading it, she asked Bud to set up a meeting with her father; again the threat hanging over Hanover had worked, and he'd agreed. Perhaps he'd expected some kind of trouble, since he'd flown his jet to Fresno and rented a small plane that wouldn't be recognized as belonging to him.

Still, I couldn't believe even as cold and calculating a man as Hanover was reputed to be would have planned his own daughter's murder.

An accident, then. Hanover refusing Hayley's demands for money and recognition as his child. Hayley taking out Boz's .32. A struggle, and the gun going off and killing Hayley. Happens all the time when irresponsible people untrained in the use of firearms have access to them.

Hanover left the scene, taking the gun with him. And someone saw him leaving. . . .

Tom Mathers. T.C. had told me her husband had a woman friend in that trailer park—a woman friend who'd left to care for her supposedly ailing mother shortly after Hy and I found Tom's body. Mathers could have heard the shot and followed Hanover. After that, he did some checking and made a phone call to the ranch, thinking he had a big deal going.

Blackmail—the fool's crime.

From this point on, my thinking became more speculative.

Bud Smith knew as soon as he heard the news of Hayley's death that his brother had killed her, but for some reason he didn't go to the authorities. Lack of proof? Shock? The habit of lifelong loyalty and protectiveness? The hope he could persuade Davey to turn himself in? Family ties could be that strong: I'd seen it over and over again, in my own life and those of others.

Did Bud try to talk with his brother, but found himself unable to because Hanover had forted himself up at the ranch?

No way to tell.

On November second, a meeting between Hanover and Mathers at the lava fields. More demands on Hanover. His financial empire is crumbling, his wife has left him, he's killed his daughter, and now this. He snaps, and when Mathers turns away from him, he shoots him in the back with Sheppard's .32.

Premeditated? Yes. Maybe he wasn't expecting the meeting to turn out that way, but the possibility must have been in the back of his mind, or he wouldn't have brought along the gun.

Now he's panicked. He's in the lava fields with a dead man and two vehicles. He doesn't want to leave the body there—the proximity to his ranch. He can put the body in its owner's truck, drive it to some remote place, and dispose of it, but then how the hell does he get back?

The answer is the same as it always has been with the former Davey Smith: he calls on his big brother Bud for help.

Bud comes to the ranch in response to Davey's plea, not even taking time to unhitch his boat trailer from the Forester. But when Davey tells him what he wants done, Bud flat-out refuses. Davey's killed his own daughter as well as Tom Mathers, and Bud confronts him with the facts, threatens to call the sheriff's department. Maybe he even goes to the phone.

It's the first time Bud has ever refused Davey a way out. Davey snaps again, shoots his brother in the back.

Now he's got two bodies on his hands. The one in the desert—which he's zipped into a sleeping bag from the victim's own truck—doesn't matter, he decides, since the only other people who knew he was at his ranch are also dead. And the boat trailer provides a perfect solution for hiding his brother's corpse: put Bud's body into his—Hanover's—own car, the car onto the trailer, drive the Forester up to a remote spot in Toiyabe National Forest, dispose of both. Hitch the trailer to his car—because a vehicle with a boat trailer and no boat would attract a lot more attention when found in the forest than the SUV of a hiker who apparently went astray—and return to the ranch. Then get the hell out of there.

If that was what happened, the trailer might still be at the ranch. Maybe the keys to Bud Smith's Forester, too. Since Hanover had driven it into the woods, he might have pocketed them.

And the ranch house was a probable crime scene. There could be material evidence—blood, fibers, fingerprints . . .

So?

Check out the property from the air, make sure it was deserted. And then get onto it and into the house. Look for something that would give Lark probable cause to obtain a search warrant.

Of course, those actions were totally illegal. Trespassing, breaking and entering. I could lose my private investigator's license, go to jail. And I didn't want to hinder the authorities in building a case against Hanover. While Lark was willing to bend the law when circumstances merited it, no way she'd be able to get a warrant based on information gleaned during an illegal search.

Well, what if my plane's engine went out, and I had to make an emergency landing on the ranch? Wasn't able to make radio contact with anyone? Was forced to hike to the house to ask to use the phone? Found no one there, but looked through the windows and saw something suspicious? Left and reported it to Lark?

Lark didn't know enough about planes to realize that when you had an engine out, it didn't suddenly start up again. She'd assume it was like a car's flooded motor. And the roughness of the landing could explain the loss of radio contact.

Thin, but Lark wouldn't be inclined to ask too many questions if a multiple murderer was brought to justice as a result.

Okay. I'd sleep on it. But first I'd run a search for the license plate number of Bud Smith's boat trailer.

Saturday

✦

NOVEMBER 17

The morning air was crisp, the sky clear. The projected snowstorm had blown past in the night and was currently blanketing parts of Tuolomne County.

Amos Hinsdale arrived at the UNICOM shack as I was preflighting Two-Seven-Tango. "You leaving?" he asked, genuine disappointment in his voice.

"No, just going out to take a look around."

"At that ranch, you mean."

I hesitated. Could I trust him? Yes, I could: in Amos' world there was a brotherhood of pilots, and last night he'd allowed me to join it.

"That's my approximate destination."

The lines around his eyes crinkled. "Be careful. You got plenty of fuel?"

"Yes. I filled up at Independence yesterday."

"Stop in when you get back. I've still got a couple of Canada Drys on ice."

"Will do."

"And keep tuned to the UNICOM. If there's any unannounced incoming traffic, I'll contact you. Code word Reptile."

We smiled at our little intrigue and shook hands before I climbed into the plane.

I turned the key in the ignition. The engine coughed and then a warning light flickered. Electrical system failure. There was a backup battery, but I didn't know how much charge was left on it; recalling the way the engine had sounded when I'd returned here after my overflight of Toiyabe, I realized I might have been flying on battery for some time. Would I have missed the warning light then and also on the flights to and from Independence? Doubtful, but lately I never knew. . . .

Well, I couldn't take Two-Seven-Tango up without a certified mechanic's okay. And I was no mechanic; neither was Amos.

I removed the key from the ignition, got out, and said to Amos, "Which of those rental planes of yours is the better?"

It was a thirty-seven-year-old Cessna 150—the type of plane I'd trained on—with a banged-up exterior, ripped-up interior, and crazing—small fractures—on the windshield. It preflighted well, though, and started strongly. The gauges were all functioning, and no warning lights flashed. I gave Amos a thumbs-up sign and taxied toward the runway.

A thousand acres of ranch land is a lot of territory to explore, even from the air, but I'd devised a plan. First I checked the house and outbuildings, putting the plane into slow flight, scanning for signs of habitation. None visible. Then I flew over the long airstrip—well paved and equipped with all the bells and whistles of a small municipal airport, including a large hangar. The hangar's doors were closed; a faded orange windsock at midfield drooped limply. Easy landing day, no strong crosswinds. But I wasn't planning on using this runway.

I kept flying to the southeast, looking for a landing place that was far enough away from the house that I wouldn't attract attention in case someone actually was in residence, but also within a reasonable hiking distance. A long ridge crossed the terrain, rough-surfaced and dotted with small obsidian outcroppings. On the other side of it I found a flat, open area that once must have been cattle graze. I could put down and take off easily there. It would be a fair hike to the house, but I was wearing sturdy boots and had bottled water in my backpack.

Bottled water, binoculars, and Hy's .45.

I didn't want to land just yet, though. Instead I headed back toward the airstrip and house, thinking a second slow overflight might scare up anybody who hadn't been curious enough to come outside the first time.

No one.

Okay, back toward my selected landing place. I spoke into the radio's microphone. "Tufa Tower traffic, Reptile. Anything?"

"Negative, Reptile."

Midway between the ranch compound and the jagged, rocky ridge, something strange caught my eye. I glanced forward at the engine cowling. Nothing. Maybe I'd glimpsed a black bird narrowly missing the plane.

A few seconds later I saw it again: a smoky curl drifting from the edge of the cowling. The paint there looked bubbled. Suddenly bright orange flames flickered upward.

Engine fire!

Fuel-fed, not oil-fed—had to be from the color of those flames.

Panic made my limbs rigid, fused my gaze to the flames. I'd been in a serious emergency situation once before, but long ago—

Time telescoped as fear turned to rage. My life was back on track: I'd made my decisions and was set to enjoy the future. And now maybe I was going to die because Amos Hinsdale hadn't properly maintained his crappy airplane.

Focus. Do what you were trained to do.

Stubborn determination gripped me as I looked at the instrument panel. I was *not* going to die—not now, not like this. Emergency procedures from my old training manual flashed through my mind.

Forced landing, engine fire: Shut off the fuel supply. Keep the ignition switch on to clear the fuel lines. Lower the nose to maintain your airspeed.

My hands moved mechanically through the actions I'd practiced many times in simulated situations.

Now look for a place to bring this piece of shit down.

My altitude and airspeed were not enough to crest the ridge ahead to level ground or return to the airstrip. And that ridge was the worst possible place to try to land.

"Okay," I said aloud, "I don't care about saving the plane. What I need to do is keep the cockpit—and me—intact. Screw the wings, tail section, and landing gear."

The terrain was treacherous, but I could use it to my advantage. Rock was an energy-absorbing medium; even the scrub pines would help stop the plane once it was down. *If* I landed correctly, allowing only the outer parts of the Cessna to be mangled . . .

But what if the plane exploded on impact? I'd never see Hy again. Never see the other people I loved, never—

Focus, dammit!

Lower flaps. That increases mobility. Bank a little here, not too much. More right rudder. Lift the nose slightly. Now hold it level.

I was almost to the ridge now, its black, glassy rocks seeming to jump up at me.

Hold it level.

Slow it down.

Slower . . .

There was a stand of scrub pines near the ridgetop. Perfect. The right wing would hit them, slow the plane before it hit rock.

Brace yourself!

Jarring impact. A shearing sound. Metal screaming. The plane slewed violently to the left.

My seat belt tore loose and I slammed against the door, then forward onto the yoke. Pain shot through my chest, but I clung to the yoke as if it were a life preserver, my eyes squeezed shut, steeled for the *whoosh* of igniting fuel.

The plane dropped downward, its landing gear crushed. Then, with a sound like a great sigh, it settled. Stones rattled, metal groaned, the windshield rained down.

The silence that followed was almost as deafening as the crash.

I raised my head and looked around. The right wing was gone, the plane's nose buried into the ground, facing downhill. But the cockpit and I were intact.

You did it, McCone. You brought it down.

The voice in my mind sounded like Hy's. As if he'd been there all along, urging me on.

Exit and get clear of the aircraft promptly, in case of explosion.

I grabbed my backpack from the passenger seat and pushed through the half-sprung door. Tumbled to the ground, pushed myself up, and took off running and skidding down the ridge.

At its bottom I looked back at the twisted wreckage of the Cessna. The elevators on the tail section had also been sheared off, the tail itself bent. The slope above it was littered with metal. There was still no fire or explosion, but I wasn't going to wait around for either. As I moved away, I took out my phone: no reception.

Behind me I heard popping and crackling sounds. Then a loud bang. In a few seconds the wreckage was engulfed in flames.

Exit and get clear of the aircraft promptly. . . .

Yeah.

Quickly I turned away. I'd walk to the ranch house and ask for help, playing out my cover scenario for real.

I set out for the ranch compound. In spite of the cold, the sun beat down and soon I began to sweat inside my heavy parka. I unzipped it and went on.

The pain in my chest was becoming more bearable, but every now and then a sudden, vicious stab would make me stop and catch my breath. I wondered if I had a cracked rib or pelvic bone.

The hiking boots weren't ones I frequently wore. My toes and heels began to chafe against them. I promised myself a pedicure when I got back to the city.

As I approached the compound, my backpack tugged uncomfortably at my shoulders. I stopped, took it off, and removed Hy's .45 to reduce the load. Time to have the gun at hand, anyway. I stuck it in the waistband of my jeans, had a drink of bottled water, put the pack back on, and kept going.

When I got to a small stand of Jeffrey pines, I dropped down onto my knees and took out the binoculars. Surveyed the bleak land that stretched in front of me, the cluster of simulated adobe buildings with red tile roofs. No motion, no life.

The sun was glaring down now. Sweat oozed along my rib cage. I shed the parka and left it on the ground. Began to creep along—alert for the presence of other slithering creatures. After all, Rattlesnake Ranch had been aptly named. This was the predators' natural habitat.

House, hangar, and outbuildings clearly in sight now. Drained swimming pool showing through a long, tall hedge of hardy-looking evergreens. I picked up the pace.

Halfway there I paused to raise the binoculars. Empty landscape.

Last hundred yards or so. Parched, but unwilling to stop for water. Hand on gun. If someone had heard the crash, he could be lying in wait.

Emptiness.

I reached the hedge that screened the house and pool.

A hissing sound.

Snake!

I drew the .45, tensing—and then saw droplets clinging to the plants and realized the hiss came from an automatic sprinkler system.

Come on, McCone—after what you've just been through, an encounter with a rattler is nothing.

I slipped up to the hedge. The spray from the sprinklers felt cool on my face and bare arms. I moved through the prickly branches till I could see the house.

Patio on the other side of the pool, furniture covered. French doors, with blinds closed. Other windows, also covered from within.

No one here, but that was what I'd hoped for. I needed to get inside and call for help, so I might as well carry through with my original purpose.

Where was the garage? Not on this side. Try the other.

I followed the line of the shrubbery. More covered windows. Other small patios. A garden, mostly turned earth and weeds, with a border of dried-out sunflowers. Finally a garage, large enough to hold at least three cars. There was a window in the rear, blocked by what looked to be cardboard.

The dead sunflower border of the garden provided shelter. I went to the garage window.

Cardboard, yes. A flattened carton with the words WOLF SUB-ZERO REFRIGERATOR printed on it. A box the appliance had been delivered in, not yet discarded. It didn't quite fit the window; I peered through the crack to its side.

A wall of shelving. A gray SUV; I couldn't make out what kind.

Chances were Hanover had a security system on the house. What would be the responding agency? The sheriff's department? Not likely; they were too shorthanded to provide emergency services every time the system malfunctioned and set off the alarm, as sensitive ones are inclined to do. And none of the big outfits like ADT operated in this area; I knew because Hy and I had considered security for the ranch, then dismissed the idea. The ranch buildings hadn't been subject to a break-in in all the time Hy had owned the property. If Hanover had any kind of security, it would probably be a loud alarm to repel intruders. Or a private patrol that came by once or twice a day.

Take a chance, McCone. If that boat trailer of Bud Smith's is in this garage, you've got Hanover nailed.

Still, I hesitated, thinking of the damage I could do myself and the legal case against him if I was caught.

I felt around the window frame. Flimsy aluminum. Billionaires will spend a fortune on the most ridiculous things, such as toilets that wash and dry your butt, but when it comes to the basics, like a garage window . . .

I tugged at the frame. And the window slid open.

No clanging alarm. Nothing but silence.

I pushed the cardboard aside, peered into the garage.

Door leading into the house. The SUV I'd partially seen earlier—a Saab. Gardening supplies and tools. Hot-water heater and furnace.

And an empty boat trailer.

First piece of evidence.

I pushed the window open wider and climbed—wincing at the pain in my chest—into the garage.

First I looked around to see if there were any junction boxes to indicate I was wrong about a silent alarm. None, and the circuit breakers were all on and clearly labeled. I turned my attention to the trailer. The dusty license plate secured to it was Smith's, all right.

Next I checked out the Saab. It too was dusty but nearly new, its interior clean and smelling of good leather. In the glove box I found a registration card in the name of Trevor Hanover. There was a trailer hitch, also nearly new, but with scratches that showed it had been used to tow something.

Gingerly I got down on my hands and knees and examined the tires. Well-defined tread. I ducked to look at the undercarriage. Pine needles caught there, similar to those in the grove where I'd found Smith's Forester.

That was hard evidence.

It's a little-known fact that, like humans, trees possess distinctive DNA. I'd once been involved in a murder case in the White Mountains, where a cone from one of the ancient pines that grow there was the star witness that ultimately convicted the killer.

Now for the house.

I tried the knob on the door leading to the interior. It turned smoothly and silently. Beyond was a large laundry room, with tile counters and top-of-the-line appliances. Through a connecting door I stepped into a kitchen that would have been the envy of any celebrity chef.

Another pain in my chest. I braced myself against a counter till it subsided. Even though the house's interior was cool, I was sweating profusely. For a moment I felt disoriented, my sight blurring.

I'd covered a lot of terrain in bad shape. I was dehydrated and could have internal injuries.

There was a wall phone; I should pick up the receiver and call—

A sound came from somewhere deep in the house.

I shook my head, thinking I'd imagined it. The sound came again. I drew the gun, haltingly crossed the kitchen to a swinging door, and pushed it open. Beyond was a huge formal dining room. I stood in the doorway, steadying myself and listening.

The sound continued, a kind of faraway drone. And now I could identify it: someone talking—in spite of the deserted appearance of the house. Hanover? He could have flown in again, stashed the plane in the hangar.

I waited till my equilibrium returned. Then, gripping Hy's .45, I went through the gloomy dining room full of heavy, antique furnishings that might have come from one of the state's original land-grant haciendas, and paused at an archway on the far side. The voice had stopped.

Several seconds of silence. Then I heard a thump and a cry of frustration. It sounded as if it had come from the other side of the hallway I was facing.

I checked out the room opposite: a formal parlor, full of the usual uncomfortable furnishings and a grand piano. Empty.

The hallway was long and tiled, running from a large foyer by the front door, with many arches opening to either side; at its end, a wide staircase swept up to the second story.

I moved along the tiles, back against the wall, both hands steadying the weapon.

First archway: a den. Real he-man's room, with stuffed animal heads, a TV that took up a whole wall, and a pool table. No one there.

Second archway: kids' room. Toys, games, another big TV, jukebox—contemporary replica of those from the fifties—and comfortable furnishings.

Third archway: crafts room. Sewing machine, easel, paints. Canvases stacked against the wall. Supplies arranged in plastic storage boxes on shelving. The topmost painting was a good, though bleak, portrait of the surrounding high desert. It was signed "B. Hanover." Betsy, the soon-to-be ex-wife.

I heard the voice again—subdued, more a mumbling now. Coming from behind the wide staircase. I glanced briefly into the rooms beyond the other archways as I moved ahead.

At first I saw nothing but the high backs of a leather couch and chairs and a wall whose French doors were covered with blinds; probably they were the ones I'd seen overlooking the pool area.

The mumbling continued. I moved into the room, slipped

along the wall to the right. The furnishings were arranged in a U, with a handsome distressed wood coffee table in the center. Magazines were fanned out on it, next to a cordless phone unit whose handset was nowhere in sight. Beneath the table was a white, intricately woven area rug.

And on the other side of the coffee table, a man was down on all fours.

A bucket lay on its side next to him; water pooled on the hardwood floor between the rug and the French doors. The man was rubbing at a rust-colored stain on the rug. Back and forth, back and forth, pressing hard. Like a male version of Lady Macbeth.

"Buddy, Buddy, Buddy . . ."

I brought the gun up but didn't speak.

"Why'd you say no to me, Buddy?"

He kept rubbing.

"Why, Buddy?"

I thought he sensed my presence then, because he looked up. But it was just reflex. The handsome face I'd seen in his publicity photos was crumpled and his mouth worked spasmodically. His eyes were dark, bottomless pits. I'd seen that look on people in shock, but never so extreme as this.

This was a man whose interior had been totally shattered.

Slowly I relaxed, lowering the gun. Neither Trevor Hanover nor Davey Smith was a danger to me or anyone else. Wherever this man had gone, he wasn't coming back.

His mouth worked some more, and then he lowered his head and continued scrubbing.

"Buddy, Buddy, Buddy . . ."

Thursday

✦

NOVEMBER 22

The crowd of Thanksgiving Day revelers overflowed Ted and Neal's spacious third-floor apartment on Telegraph Hill's Plum Alley. They filled the living room and dining area, standing beside or sitting on the nineteen-thirties-style sofas, salon chairs, and ottomans, or hovering over the wine bottles and hors d'oeuvres spread on the long table. They sat on the spiral staircase or leaned against the chrome-railed catwalk that connected the apartment's front and rear bedrooms above the dining area. They congregated on the deck, where a sweeping view of Alcatraz and the Bay provided a dramatic backdrop. The only room we'd all been banished from was the kitchen that was tucked under the staircase, where Ted and his life partner, Neal Osborne, were putting together another of their famous Thanksgiving feasts. Wonderful aromas drifted out: roasting turkey, tangy cranberry sauce, sweet apple-cider yams, and stuffing that I knew contained a powerful combination of spices and sausages.

Hy was on the deck, talking with Ricky. From my vantage point in the living room I watched the glint of sunlight on his dark blond hair and thick mustache. Felt a rush of pleasure at covertly observing the man who held my world together and supported me in everything I did.

I made my way through the crowd and rejoined Rae, balancing my wineglass on a plate laden with Neal's traditional stuffed mushrooms, tiny cheese-filled tarts, shrimp, and crispy cheddar puffs. God, if I kept snacking this way I wouldn't be able to eat any dinner.

Oh yeah? This was the first time I'd enjoyed food in weeks—maybe months.

Rae picked up the thread of our earlier conversation, which I'd interrupted to go to the trough. "So you phoned the guy at Tufa Tower from the ranch and . . . ?"

"He—Amos Hinsdale—made an anonymous call to the sheriff's department. Asked that they send a car to make a welfare check at Rattlesnake Ranch. I walked out and he picked me up before the car arrived and an ambulance followed."

"You ream this Amos out about lending you a plane that nearly caused you to die?"

"I didn't have to; he felt terrible about putting me in so much danger. In fact, he drove me straight to a clinic in Bridgeport to have me checked out for injuries. Badly bruised ribs and sternum, was all, and he insisted on paying for everything, as well as telling the FAA that he was piloting the plane when it crashed. Now he's decided to scrap his other plane, which is even worse than the one I crashed."

"And Smith—what was he doing till the sheriff's people got there?"

"Still scrubbing. Lark said he'd damn near worn a hole in the rug."

"And then?"

"He went quietly. Looked puzzled when the paramedics lifted him up, then dropped his rag and . . . just went."

"It could've been an act, you know. He could be building an insanity defense."

"God, you've gotten cynical! It wasn't an act; I saw his eyes."

"So what tipped him over the edge? Did he come back to destroy the evidence?"

"Probably. But I think there was a more important reason: it was the only home he's ever cared about."

"Why do you suppose he went off and left the evidence in the first place?"

"After he killed Bud and disposed of his body, he had to get back to New York to try to hold his business together—time for the conglomerate's annual stockholders' meeting. But the board of directors scheduled a closed meeting and excluded him on a technicality.

"So then, I guess, to keep his mind off what was happening in New York, he flew his jet back to the ranch and stashed it in the hangar. He must've come in late Thursday night or early Friday morning, because Amos Hinsdale says he was at home asleep then and didn't hear the plane. On Friday at around noon Hanover called New York and was told his board had given him a vote of no confidence and ousted him. Then . . . I don't know. He must've just disintegrated."

"And now?"

I bit into the little cheese-filled tart. It was delicious.

"Mono County will file homicide charges—they have enough evidence for that—but the case'll never come to trial. Trevor Hanover and Davey Smith have ceased to exist. An empty shell will inhabit a facility for the criminally insane until it dries up and dies."

Rae once again looked skeptical. "These rich guys . . . I don't know."

"You're married to one."

"He's different. He has me to keep him honest."

I looked across the room. Adah and Craig had just arrived. "Excuse me," I said. "I need a few minutes alone with Adah."

Rae nodded and headed for the buffet.

Adah smiled at me as I approached, gave me a hug. When we separated, Craig had disappeared in Rae's wake.

"He's starving," she said. "As always." Then her expression sobered. "I guess you want my answer to your proposition."

"If you've decided."

"As far as I'm concerned, it's a done deal."

"Great!"

"An administrative position with your firm is perfect for me. No more getting called out in the middle of the night to look at decomposing bodies. No more SFPD politics. And best of all, I don't have to leave the city and move to Denver. My mom and dad, they're getting up there. Still feisty as hell, but . . ."

"Besides, this is home."

"Sure is. Born and raised on Red Hill." By Red Hill, she meant Bernal Heights, which used to be a hotbed of self-styled communists, socialists, and the occasional anarchist. Her Jewish mother and black father had been socialists with Marxist leanings, and now called themselves "wild-eyed liberals."

It was the perfect solution for me: I wouldn't have to sell the agency; it was a vital entity, the culmination of everything I'd hoped to accomplish in life—and then some. But I did want to cut out the administrative work and take on only cases that truly interested me, and Adah was the chief component in my scheme. Now that she'd accepted the position I'd offered her almost two weeks ago, I could move forward. And move forward without worrying about the rent increase from the Port Commission; Glenn Solomon's influence had staved that off for at least a year.

We shook on our deal, and she said, "Shouldn't we tell Patrick that I'll be usurping some of his duties?"

"I don't think he'll mind." I looked around the room, spotted Patrick, and motioned him over.

When he joined us, I told him I'd hired Adah as the agency's new executive administrator, meaning she'd handle approving reports and expenditures, plus interview new clients and assign them to the proper operatives. Patrick would continue to coordinate all investigations. Both would report directly to me. I would attend some staff meetings and, when I didn't, they would cochair them.

"Shar, that's good news!" he exclaimed. "I hate all the paperwork, and the staff meetings—I'm just not cut out for them. If you wouldn't mind"—he looked at Adah—"I'd prefer you chair them in Shar's absence."

"I can do that." She smiled at him. They'd work together just fine.

"So Adah's coming on board two weeks from Monday," I said to Ted as we were relaxing on the deck after the crowd had begun to thin.

"It's a damn good thing. We're swamped. Are you coming back in the meantime?"

"Monday. Hy and I are flying to the ranch tomorrow. We're having a delayed Thanksgiving with Sara, Ramon, and Amy tomorrow night. They're all pulling together, doing better, but today's got to be gloomy for them, and they'll need cheering up. And Saturday afternoon we have to greet the next member of our family. We're having a palomino delivered. To keep my horse, King, company."

"*Your* horse? You hate horses!"

"Let's say I hate horses as a breed, but love them on an individual basis."

"I don't believe this: you're backing off on the business, and you're in love with a horse?"

My cell rang. I checked to see who the caller was. Kristen Lark. I excused myself and went inside. There were still enough people there to make talking impossible, so I went down the hall to where the glass-block elevator—a classic from the thirties—stood, its doors open. Inside I sat down on the floor before I called Lark back.

"It's Sharon," I said.

"Happy Turkey Day."

"Thanks. Same to you. What's happening?"

"Nothing bad. Our perp is comfortably residing in the psych ward."

"The case will never to go trial."

"No. Save the county a lot of money. Philadelphia—where Davey Smith went to Wharton for his BA in finance—is looking at him concerning a series of rapes in the area when he was a student, and New York State is also interested. Recidivism of sex offenders . . ."

"Yeah. And how're you doing?"

". . . Better."

"Meaning?"

"All that drinking—which I'm sure you noticed? It was partly because of the pressure of the case, but mostly because the Rabbitt was being strange and distant, so I figured he was having an affair."

"And?"

"He wasn't. He'd been brooding and trying to decide how

to tell me he wants to leave the department and go to law school."

"How d'you feel about that?"

"Happy. He's got the GPA to get him into a lot of good schools on at least a partial scholarship. And I can get a job I'll enjoy almost anywhere."

"So this is a happy Thanksgiving for both of you."

"The best yet."

We chatted for a moment or two about her turkey that had turned out well and her pumpkin pie that had burned. Then we promised to keep in touch and broke the connection.

I sat there for a while, savoring the peace and happiness of one perfect holiday. The elevator doors closed, and the car began its slow downward descent. When they opened Hank Zahn, Anne-Marie Altman, and their daughter, Habiba Hamid, stepped in. They hadn't been able to make dinner because of a previous family obligation, but had promised to stop by later.

I looked at them and smiled. They were the perfect blended family: Hank, wire-haired and Jewish; Anne-Marie, blonde and WASPish; Habiba, with the beautiful dark-skinned features of her Arab forebears.

It was all about family, really—and I had such a huge one that seemed to be expanding all the time. A few years ago I'd embraced—albeit tentatively—both branches of my birth family. This fall I'd added the Perezes and, of all things, a horse.

But the family that was closest and dearest were all assembled in this building. I closed my eyes and sighed, grateful that I'd decided to come home to them.

Hank asked, "You all right, kiddo?"

"Better than I've been in a long time."

DISCARD